ROMANCING THE CROWN

The royal family of Montebello rejoices in the discovery of their newest member, yet a dark cloud hovers over the kingdom. Danger and desire clash once more as the hunt for the baby's kidnapper continues....

Meet the major players in this royal mystery:

Lieutenant Sam Coburn: The tough SEAL's friends always suspected a woman was behind his hardened heart. Now he's found the woman who stole it—and he's determined to get it back at all costs.

Lieutenant Kate Mulvaney: This cool officer has walled off her emotions for years—but it only takes one look at a certain SEAL to prove the wall is made of straw and the heat between her and Sam is an open flame....

Gretchen Hanson: This gullible midwife fell for her friend's dramatic promises of wealth and prestige. Now she refuses to take the fall for the crime all alone.

Ursula Chambers: She's given new meaning to the words *lie, cheat* and *steal*. Now it's time to pay the price...but this fugitive has one last trick up her sleeve.

Edwardo Scarpa: The palace guardsman's eye for a pretty lady has gotten him into hot water one too many times.

Dear Reader,

Things are cooling down outside—at least here in the Northeast—but inside this month's six Silhouette Intimate Moments titles the heat is still on high. After too long an absence, bestselling author Dallas Schulze is back to complete her beloved miniseries A FAMILY CIRCLE with *Lovers and Other Strangers*. Shannon Deveraux has come home to Serenity and lost her heart to travelin' man Reece Morgan.

Our ROMANCING THE CROWN continuity is almost over, so join award winner Ingrid Weaver in *Under the King's Command*. I think you'll find Navy SEAL hero Sam Coburn irresistible. Ever-exciting Lindsay McKenna concludes her cross-line miniseries, MORGAN'S MERCENARIES: ULTIMATE RESCUE, with *Protecting His Own*. You'll be breathless from the first page to the last. Linda Castillo's *A Cry in the Night* features another of her "High Country Heroes," while relative newcomer Catherine Mann presents the second of her WINGMEN WARRIORS, in *Taking Cover*. Finally, welcome historical author Debra Lee Brown to the line with *On Thin Ice*, a romantic adventure set against an Alaskan background.

Enjoy them all, and come back again next month, when the roller-coaster ride of love and excitement continues right here in Silhouette Intimate Moments, home of the best romance reading around.

Yours,

Leslie J. Wainger
Executive Senior Editor

Please address questions and book requests to:
Silhouette Reader Service
U.S.: 3010 Walden Ave., P.O. Box 1325, Buffalo, NY 14269
Canadian: P.O. Box 609, Fort Erie, Ont. L2A 5X3

Under the King's Command
INGRID WEAVER

Silhouette®

INTIMATE MOMENTS™

Published by Silhouette Books

America's Publisher of Contemporary Romance

Special thanks and acknowledgment are given
to Ingrid Weaver for her contribution
to the ROMANCING THE CROWN series.

 SILHOUETTE BOOKS

ISBN 0-373-27254-5

UNDER THE KING'S COMMAND

Visit Silhouette at www.eHarlequin.com

Printed in U.S.A.

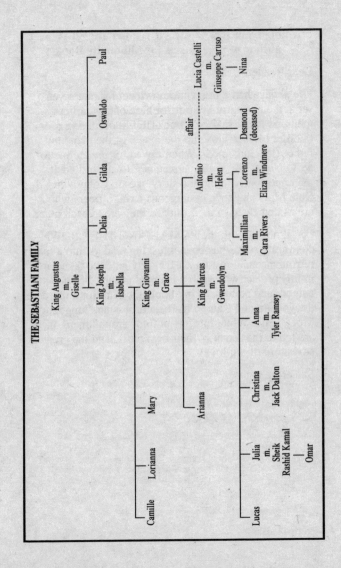

THE SEBASTIANI FAMILY

King Augustus
m.
Giselle

King Joseph
m.
Isabella

Camille | Lorianna | Mary | King Giovanni
m.
Grace

Delia | Gilda | Oswaldo | Paul

Arianna | King Marcus
m.
Gwendolyn

Antonio
m.
Helen

— affair — Lucia Castelli
m.
Giuseppe Caruso

Nina

Desmond
(deceased)

Maximillian
m.
Cara Rivers

Lorenzo
m.
Eliza Windmere

Lucas | Julia
m.
Sheik
Rashid Kamal

Christina
m.
Jack Dalton

Anna
m.
Tyler Ramsey

Omar

**A note from RITA® Award Winner Ingrid Weaver,
author of nine novels for Silhouette Books:**

Dear Reader,

I've always had a tremendous respect for people who serve their country in uniform. One of my earliest memories is of scaling a bookshelf in our living room in order to view close up the model of the plane my father flew in combat. When my editor invited me to write *Under the King's Command*, I was thrilled at the opportunity to tell the story of Sam Coburn and Kate Mulvaney, two courageous naval officers who are as dedicated to their duty as they are to each other.

For almost a year, the ROMANCING THE CROWN continuity series has been whisking readers into a realm of romance and mystery. I feel privileged to take part in this project with such a talented group of Silhouette authors and editors. In my book, the hunt for a murderer draws Sam and Kate to the beautiful island kingdom of Montebello. While intrigue unfolds around them, they are led to the secret in their own past…and the greatest adventure of all: love!

Sincerely yours,

Ingrid Weaver

Chapter 1

When Kate first heard the baby cry, she wanted to keep running. It was probably just a seagull in the harbor, nothing out of the ordinary. She had already passed the halfway point and was heading back. She needed a shower, she needed sleep.

But the gulls that wheeled and swooped over Montebello's capital of San Sebastian in the sunlight didn't usually fly at night. The cry couldn't have been from a bird. She slowed, turning her head to listen. All she heard was the slap of her running shoes on cobblestones and the rhythm of her breathing.

Who would take a child out for a stroll at this hour? The night wind was brisk for October in this part of the Mediterranean. Apart from a group of late theatergoers near the market square, Kate hadn't seen anyone for the past ten minutes.

It must have been her sleep-deprived mind imagining things, that's all. At the naval base, anyone not on watch would have the sense to be asleep, but Kate had come to rely on these late-night jogs. It was her time to herself, time to leave the day behind and focus on something blessedly basic, like putting one foot in front of the other.

Perhaps if she ran far enough, she'd be able to outrun not only the day but the past. And then maybe she wouldn't hear phantom babies crying when no one was around—

The cry came again. More distant than before, barely there, it echoed from the walls and skipped along the cobblestones like the shadow of a butterfly.

Despite the perspiration that sheened her skin, Kate felt the hair on her arms rise. There was no mistaking it that time. It had come from her left. For a split second, she wanted to turn right, to keep running to her base, to her bed, to exhaustion-induced oblivion.

Just as she'd been running for five years?

The split second passed. Since when had Lieutenant Kate Mulvaney chosen to take the easy road? She turned left.

The street narrowed, becoming an alley. Kate stumbled over a flowerpot that flanked a doorway, her shoulder scraping against crumbling brick. The walls that rose on either side of her were centuries old, their windows closed against the autumn night. The homey scents of olive oil and garlic still hung in the air here, remnants of someone's late supper, but no light showed from behind the shutters. By day, these historic alleys were magnets to tourists, but now the houses were simply homes.

Had she overreacted? Could the sound she heard have been that of a fussy baby behind one of those shuttered windows? Could some weary parent be pacing the floor, comforting the child and putting it back to bed with a kiss while Kate raced past like a fool?

No. An ordinary cry wouldn't have set Kate's hair on end. It wouldn't have stirred this instinctive uneasiness deep inside. She reached a crossroads and paused, holding her breath as she strained to listen. In the winding maze of the old quarter, sound traveled in deceptive patterns. The child could be a quarter mile away or it could be in the next alley.

There. Another cry. It seemed closer than before, but it was quickly muffled, as if someone were covering the baby's mouth.

Exhaling hard, Kate chose the middle street. She left the neighborhood of cobblestone alleys and entered a moonlit courtyard ringed by a hedge. There, at the opposite end, a figure moved furtively in the shadows. More cries wafted through the air, rapid and frantic enough to break a stone's heart.

"Hey," Kate called, breaking into a sprint. "Wait."

The figure appeared to be a female carrying a blanket-wrapped bundle the size of an infant in her arms. Instead of stopping, she scurried through a break in the hedge.

Kate followed, emerging on a sloping street that was illuminated by a line of wrought-iron street lamps. She blinked to adjust her eyes to the sudden brightness and spotted a sign for the King Augustus Hospital. The woman was on the opposite side, heading up the hill toward the hospital's back entrance.

Hesitating, Kate wondered if the woman might be taking her child for medical care. Was that the reason for her haste?

But instead of going through the hospital's doors, the woman stopped beside the low stone planter that jutted from the hospital wall and set her bundle on the flowers.

A gurgling wail came from the bundle.

The woman brushed off her palms. Her voice, dry and harsh, carried clearly on the breeze. "Go ahead and cry. Someone will hear you soon."

Kate scowled and jogged up the hill. "Excuse me, do you need some help?"

The woman snapped her head up and glanced over her shoulder. Instead of retrieving the baby, she took a step away.

Kate was close enough to see a tiny fist poke out of the bundle of blankets. It waved in the air, as if to punctuate its displeasure.

The woman's response to the infant's distress was to take another step away.

Kate's chest heaved, not only from the exertion of her run but from a growing sense of outrage. This woman acted as if she intended to leave the child where it was. "What are you doing?" Kate demanded. "You're not really planning on abandoning your baby there, are you?"

The woman glanced around, her gaze as furtive as her movements had been. In the bleak glare of the streetlights, her plain, pinched features and her mousy brown hair gave her the look of a rodent. "Keep out of this. It's none of your business."

"A child's welfare is everybody's business. If your baby is ill—"

"There's nothing wrong with the baby. He's fine. I just can't keep him anymore."

The resolution in the woman's tone deepened Kate's outrage. Nevertheless, she tried to reason with her again. "Ma'am, if you need help caring for your child, there are agencies that you can go to—"

"You know nothing about it. Get out of my way."

It took no more than a heartbeat for Kate to assess her options. As a U.S. naval officer and a foreigner in Montebello, she had no authority over this civilian. Yet turning away, continuing with her run, was out of the question. No matter how tired she was, no matter what flack she might take from her base commander for interfering, she had a clear duty that transcended the rule book and the need for sleep. Before the woman could take another step, Kate grasped her wrist. "Sorry, I can't let you leave."

"What do you think you're doing? Let go of me!" The woman yanked her wrist, a surprising amount of strength in her wiry frame, but she couldn't break Kate's hold. Muttering a curse, she aimed a kick at Kate's shin.

Kate neatly sidestepped the kick as her training took over. Without loosening her hold, she used the woman's momentum to spin her around, then twisted her arm behind her back. Exerting just enough pressure to hold her in place against the low stone wall without injuring her, Kate turned her head to look at the infant.

He had managed to kick off the blankets altogether and lay on his back with his feet and fists waving in the air. His cries had stopped, as if he preferred the cold embrace of the flower bed to being held in his mother's arms. His face was flushed from crying, and tiny shudders rippled over his body, but his blue eyes were bright with interest as he gazed around him at the crushed flowers.

How could anyone discard their child like this? Babies were so precious, their lives so fragile, what kind of monster would abandon, with such indifference, the life she had carried? Didn't she fear the nightmares that would follow? Didn't she realize how the cries would haunt her?

"Let go," the woman repeated. "Ow! You're breaking my arm!"

Kate wrenched her attention to her duty. Turning toward the hospital doors, she raised her voice to the level she'd learned to employ on the deck of a battleship and called for help.

After ten seconds the hospital door swung open and an elderly white-clad nurse peeked out. Her eyes widened when she saw Kate and the struggling woman.

Belatedly, Kate realized how the situation must look. Dressed in her sweat-damp T-shirt and running shorts, her face bare of makeup and her hair a windblown mess, she probably appeared like some kind of female mugger who was overpowering this hapless, mousy woman. Before the nurse could jump to the wrong conclusion about which one of them was calling for help, Kate spoke up. "I'm Lieutenant Kate Mulvaney, U.S. Navy," she said. "I'm making a citizen's arrest. I need you to call the police and tend to—"

"No! No police." The woman renewed her struggle to escape Kate's hold. "I didn't do anything!"

The nurse ducked inside before Kate could tell her to see to the baby. Lying in the planter the way he was, he wouldn't have been visible from the door. Now that he'd stopped crying, no one would notice he was there unless they were looking. If Kate hadn't witnessed what had happened, how long would the child have gone undiscovered?

She thought of what might have happened to the helpless infant and had to restrain herself from giving the woman's arm an extra twist.

A security guard emerged from the hospital. He was a large man with a generous belly that stretched his light gray uniform to the limit of its buttons. "What's going on here?" he asked.

Kate identified herself once again and guided her prisoner toward him. "This woman was abandoning her baby."

"Baby? What baby?"

As soon as the guard took the woman's arm, Kate released her and turned to the planter. "This baby," she said. Leaning over, she carefully picked up the child. "I'll bring him into emergency. I think a doctor should have a look at him…"

Kate's words trailed off. Too many sensations were hitting her at once. The warmth of the infant, the way he felt, so light, so vulnerable in her arms, the powdery baby smell that rose from his dark hair, all of it slid right past her defenses and stirred up the old yearning—

She should have kept on running. And she would, as soon as she had done her duty. She would hand the child to a doctor and stay until police arrived so she could answer their questions, but after that, there would be no reason to hang around any longer. The situation was unfortunate but under control. Whatever the woman's story, it wasn't Kate's concern.

But oh, how sweetly the baby nestled to her breast.

Damn.

"I didn't do anything wrong." The woman's voice was shrill as the guard ushered her through the hospital entrance. Several nurses had gathered in the corridor, evidently drawn by the commotion. The woman dragged her heels, appealing to her audience. "That's not even my baby. I've been taking care of him since his mother died. I was bringing him to his father, I swear, but I couldn't get into the palace and—"

"Lady, I don't know what you're talking about," the guard said.

"Did she say palace?" someone asked.

"I shouldn't be treated like this," the woman persisted. "I should get a reward. That's no ordinary baby. He's the son of Lucas Sebastiani. *Prince* Lucas Sebastiani. That baby is the royal heir!"

Sam took the corner on two wheels and floored the accelerator. The jeep leaped up the hill and skidded to a stop outside the hospital. Word must have already leaked out, judging by the crowd that was gathered near the doors. The security guards and Montebellan police quickly cleared a path when they recognized Sam's passengers.

"Thank you, Lieutenant Coburn." The deep voice came from the rear seat. "I like a man who can follow orders."

Sam had only begun his assignment in Montebello a few hours ago, so he was still unaccustomed to dealing with royalty. He was never sure whether to salute or bow. The moment he hopped to the ground, he turned to offer his hand. "I apologize if the ride was rougher than you're accustomed to, Your Highness."

King Marcus smiled and shook his head. "Believe me, I've had worse. You got us here faster than any of my drivers would have." He got out with an agility that belied his sixty-odd years and reached for the petite blond woman who was swinging her legs toward him. "Gwen, are you all right?"

"Heavens, yes. It was rather exciting, don't you think?" Blue eyes twinkling, Queen Gwendolyn smoothed her husband's white hair and placed her hands on his shoulders. She permitted him to lift her to the ground, then tucked her hand into the crook of his elbow. Despite their casual attire, the couple's bearing was unmistakably regal. "Lucas?" the queen asked. "Aren't you coming?"

Sam turned to look at the third member of the royal family who had accompanied him on the wild midnight ride. Lucas Sebastiani, Prince Lucas to the people of Montebello, hadn't exhibited the same excitement as his parents over the news of his possible child. He had been silent during the journey from the palace to the hospital, but Sam didn't mistake his stillness for indifference.

He'd seen this reaction before, when something was so important, the consequences so huge, a person couldn't dare to hope it was true. What was going on behind those tightly controlled, aristocratic features?

How would it feel for a man to suddenly discover he was a father?

Like all navy SEALs, Sam was accustomed to thinking on his feet, to adapting quickly to changes whenever he was on a mission, but this assignment was rapidly taking more twists than the cobblestone streets he'd just navigated. He was supposed to be advising the Montebellan police in their search for the woman who had murdered the king's nephew, Desmond Caruso. It wasn't a typical assignment for a SEAL who was trained in counterterrorism, but King Marcus had wanted someone with an objective viewpoint, someone with a reputation for success.

With little more than an artist's sketch of the murderer to go on, the search would be challenging, to say the least. But Sam thrived on challenges. He had been in a strategy session with the king when the call from the hospital had come in.

An abandoned baby? A possible royal heir? The news was a shock to everyone. And from the information the hospital staff had relayed, the woman who had attempted to abandon the child apparently had proof of its parentage. Moreover, she had some connection with the murderer Sam was seeking. With the swift decisiveness that was typical of his leadership, the king had terminated the meeting. Rather than taking the time to form a convoy of palace staff and bodyguards, he'd commandeered Sam and Sam's military jeep to take the fastest route to the hospital.

"Son?" Marcus laid his hand on Lucas's shoulder.

Lucas got out of the jeep, his movements stiff. He nodded to Sam to lead the way.

The hospital lobby was bustling with activity, yet silence spread as people recognized the royal family. A portly man in a gray security guard's uniform hurried forward, his face flushed. "Your Highnesses," he said, bowing to each of the royals in turn. "This is such an honor."

"Where's the child?" Lucas asked. His voice was hoarse, as tightly controlled as his features.

"The baby? He's in the emergency ward." The guard gestured toward a corridor on their right. "The doctors are checking him."

"If any harm has come to that baby—" Lucas paused, his jaw clenching.

"No, no, he seemed fine." The guard looked at Sam, his gaze flicking over his dress blue uniform. "Another American Navy officer found him. She has been seeing to his safety since we learned who the baby is."

"Where's the woman who tried to abandon the baby?" Sam asked.

"She says her name is Gretchen Hanson. We're holding her in the security office in the north wing."

"Good work," King Marcus said. "Lieutenant Coburn and I will want to question Ms. Hanson before you turn her over to the police, but first things first." He patted Queen Gwendolyn's hand and gave his son an encouraging nod. "Let's take a look at this baby."

Apart from the thick stone walls, vaulted ceilings and arching doorways that marked its centuries-old architecture, the King Augustus Hospital was a modern medical facility. The lingering scent of aged stone was overpowered by the smell of disinfectant. Sounds that could have been heard in any hospital—the squeak of crepe soles on tile, the beeping of a monitor, the metallic rattle of a gurney—echoed in the background as Sam and his group headed for the emergency ward.

It was easy to determine which examining room the child was in by the crowd of hospital staff gathered outside the door. The hush that had marked the royals' arrival in the hospital spread through the ward. Sam realized it wasn't awe, it was respectful affection. The Montebellan people genuinely cared about their monarch, and they all wanted to be part of the drama that was unfolding. As one, the crowd moved from the door.

In a circle of light, a trio of doctors was bending over an examining table. Sam focused on the tiny form at the top. The baby was lying on its back, gurgling softly as it clutched the end of a stethoscope.

"Oh, my Lord." Queen Gwendolyn drew in a sharp breath. "Marcus, look."

The king stared at the baby. In silence, he slipped his arm around his wife's shoulders.

"Look at his hair, look at his eyes," Gwendolyn went on. "And that chin. Do you see it?"

"Yes, Gwen," he said softly, pulling her close to his side. "I see."

Sam studied the child for a minute, then moved his gaze to the prince. What the queen had meant was clear. Lucas and the child shared the same dark brown hair, the same blue eyes, even the identical stubborn chin. The resemblance was so strong, it was unmistakable. A DNA test would undoubtedly have to be performed, considering the importance of proving the royal heir's identity, but to anyone with eyes, the paternity was obvious.

Like a man in a trance, Lucas moved forward. If he noticed that the child on the table was a younger version of himself, he gave no indication. He was holding onto the tight control he'd been exhibiting since they left the palace. "Is he all right? Is he healthy?"

One of the doctors stepped aside, allowing Lucas to reach the table. "Yes, Your Highness. We've done a thorough examination, and the infant appears to be in good health. His heart is strong, his lungs are clear and his reflexes are normal, although he's somewhat underweight for a child of three months."

It was clear to Sam that Lucas was no longer listening. The prince leaned over the table, his entire body brittle with tension as he regarded the baby.

The child stopped gurgling and met Lucas's gaze with a disconcerting solemnity. Then suddenly the baby smiled.

Lucas closed his eyes and tipped back his head, inhaling

unsteadily. He was silent for a moment, his shoulders shaking with emotions Sam couldn't begin to imagine. Finally, Lucas blinked and touched his fingertips to the baby's cheek. "Jess," he whispered. His eyes gleamed with tears. "You have Jessie's smile."

The doctor cleared his throat. "Apparently the child's name is Luke, Your Highness. We'd like to transfer him to pediatrics as soon as possible. We need to run some more tests and we'd like to get his weight up...."

"He has Jessie's smile," Lucas repeated, looking around as if the doctor hadn't spoken. An expression of wonder was dawning on his face. "Jessie's dimples. She always smiled like that. I thought I'd never see it again. I thought—" He clamped his jaw shut, his words choked off.

Sam didn't know all the details about the prince's story, but he did know the man was mourning the death of the woman he loved. And now Lucas saw his lover in his child.

Once more, Sam couldn't imagine the emotions Lucas must be going through. What was it like to love a woman that strongly? Love wasn't something Sam thought much about. With the demands of his career and the danger each mission entailed, he didn't have the opportunity or the inclination for serious relationships.

At least, that was the excuse he'd always given himself. Except for that one time five years ago...

Without warning, an image rose in his memory. Long auburn hair, green eyes, the sound of laughter, the feel of skin sliding over sun-warmed skin. The image was so vivid, he could swear he caught her scent.

Gardenias. Passionate and feminine.

And fleeting.

Sam rubbed his face, trying to concentrate on his duty.

"I want to thank you and the hospital staff for your diligence." King Marcus shook hands with each doctor. "My family and I are in your debt for your care of our newest member.''

Evidently the king didn't need to wait for the test results to confirm what he saw, either. He had publicly recognized the baby as a Sebastiani. Queen Gwendolyn was at Lucas's side, her elegant features lit in a grandmotherly smile as she cooed over her grandson.

''I'd also like to speak with the person who found him,'' the king said. ''I understand she was a Navy officer?''

''Yes, Your Highness.''

At the soft voice from the shadows in the corner of the room, Sam's mouth went dry. No, it wasn't possible. He had just been thinking of her, so he must be imagining her voice. How could she be here? Why now?

A woman moved into the pool of light, her jogging shoes padding quietly on the tile floor. A pair of running shorts bared her long legs. A black T-shirt molded her breasts, and a gold chain with a tiny charm circled her throat. Her auburn hair was a short-cropped mass of finger-combed tufts.

It hadn't been his imagination, Sam thought. Somehow, she really was here.

When had she cut her hair? When had she taken up jogging? Did she still cry over old movies? Did she ever think of him when she was alone at night and the sound of the waves were like sighs from the past?

Kate. *His* Kate. In the flesh, and close enough to smell.

And beautiful enough to make him want to forget the promise he'd made her five years ago.

Chapter 2

Kate couldn't meet Sam's gaze. Not yet. Not with this lump in her throat from the emotional scene she had just witnessed.

But oh, God, he was more handsome than ever. She'd studied him when he hadn't known she was in the room. There were sun streaks in his brown hair. There were new lines around his amber eyes. His cheeks were leaner, his shoulders broader. His entire bearing radiated the mature confidence of a man who knew what he wanted and had the strength to get it.

He had once wanted her.

That's over, Kate told herself. *Don't think about the past. Concentrate on your duty.*

Despite her lack of uniform, Kate drew herself to attention and snapped up her hand in a salute. "Lieutenant Kate Mulvaney, Your Highness."

As diplomatic as he was reputed to be, King Marcus ignored her dishevelled appearance and her lack of military attire as he returned her salute. "I gather you were jogging past and witnessed what happened?"

"Yes, sir. After I apprehended the suspect, I thought it best to guard the child until someone from the palace arrived. Admiral Howe, the base commander, agreed when I reported the situation to him. I'm at your service until you wish to relieve me."

"I appreciate your quick thinking, Lieutenant."

The baby was gurgling again, happy with the attention he was receiving from the queen and the prince. Montebellan royalty who just happened to be his grandmother and his father. Kate felt the gleeful sound grate across her nerves.

Standing guard over the baby had been difficult. Not because there had been any danger, but because she had wanted her involvement with all of this to be over an hour ago. Had she thought the baby stirred painful memories? That was nothing compared to what she'd felt when she'd seen Sam walk in the room.

Why couldn't she have kept on running?

"I was happy to help, sir," she replied.

"I hate to impose further, but I'd appreciate it if you could remain and answer a few questions for us." The king nodded toward Sam. "This is Lieutenant Sam Coburn."

Unable to postpone it any longer, Kate let her gaze meet Sam's.

Oh, God. Five years had passed, but some things hadn't changed. His golden brown gaze still had the power to make her knees weak.

She wanted to leap into his arms.

She wanted to curl into a ball and hide.

Duty, she reminded herself. *Do your duty, just as you've always done.*

"Yes," she said. She was proud of the way her voice

remained level though her pulse pounded in her ears. "Lieutenant Coburn and I have already met."

"Excellent." The king glanced at his son. Under the supervision of the doctors and the doting gaze of Queen Gwendolyn, Lucas was carefully lifting his child into his arms. A look of amazement softened his features.

Kate pressed her nails into her palms to keep herself steady. The emotions kept on coming. Seeing the prince cradle his infant so tenderly made her wonder what might have happened if Sam...

No. She wouldn't go down that road. She wouldn't let that thought form. She'd avoided it for five years. She could keep it at bay for another five minutes, couldn't she?

"Since you two are already acquainted," King Marcus continued, moving to join his family, "I'll let Lieutenant Coburn fill you in. Now, if you'll excuse me, I have a grandson to get to know."

And just like that, Kate found herself face-to-face with the one man she'd believed she'd never see again.

"Hello, Kate."

His voice strummed over her raw nerves in a melody too haunting to forget. She'd always loved his voice. It didn't belong here in the sterile efficiency of a hospital. It belonged on a moonlit beach, with the sound of the waves whispering over the sand and the rhythmic smack of naked skin on naked skin....

She tightened her fists, surprised her nails hadn't yet drawn blood. Her gaze returned to his. "Hello, Sam."

"You're looking well."

"You, too."

He smiled. "I guess it would be kinda too corny to say long time no see."

His smile deepened the new lines around his eyes and folded brackets beside his mouth and still made her stomach knot like that of a schoolgirl with her first crush.

Damn him, that hadn't changed, either. "The king said you would have some questions for me."

At her brisk tone, his smile dimmed. "That's right."

"All I did was recover the baby. I'm not sure I understand how that would involve a Navy SEAL."

Sam tilted his head toward the door. "I'll fill you in on the way to the security office."

She started to move forward when she saw him lift his hand. He was going to touch her. She felt his intent as plainly as if he had spoken aloud.

Sam had always been a toucher. In public it had been a palm on the small of her back, a brush of fingertips over her forearm or an easy drape of his arm over her shoulders. Casual, respectful touches that had kept her body humming with awareness.

And when they were no longer in public, he hadn't only made her body hum, he'd made it sing.

Kate stepped to the side to avoid his hand and strode out of the examining room. Sam might not have changed, but *she* had. She was older, wiser and in complete control of her life. She could do this. Yes, she could.

Sam fell into step beside her. "What would you like to know first?"

Where did you go after your letters stopped? Did you ever think of me? Did you ever wonder what would have happened if only circumstances had been different? The questions clamored in her heart, but she asked, "Why are you taking orders from the king of Montebello?"

"I'm working as an adviser. He requested our government to provide someone with my training to help coordinate the efforts of the police and our navy in the search for a murderer."

"The woman who killed his nephew, Desmond Caruso?"

"That's right. How did you know?"

"I saw the artist's sketch of the suspect in the paper today. It's logical that the king would ask for high-level help." She glanced at Sam. "And by someone with your training, you mean counterterrorism, I assume."

"Right again."

"Congratulations."

"Why?"

"If you're an expert in counterterrorism, then that must mean you're in SEAL Team Six. Just like you always said you wanted."

"There were plenty of things that I wanted, Kate."

She could tell by his tone that he wasn't referring to his career. But she wasn't going to talk about this now. It was over. The past was gone, gone, gone. "And you succeeded," she said, refusing to let the conversation get personal. "But how does all of this involve the prince's baby?"

"That's what I'm here to find out."

They reached a set of swinging doors. Sam stretched his arm past Kate's shoulder and pushed open the door before she could reach it. He didn't touch her, but she could feel the warmth of his arm as it passed near her head.

She tried to attribute the shudder to fatigue. "I still don't understand."

"I started this assignment today, so there are a lot of details that need filling in, but here's what I do know. Last year, Prince Lucas was in the States, flying over Colorado, when his plane went down. He was in bad shape for a while, wandered around not knowing who he was. That's when he met a woman named Jessica Chambers."

"Jessica. Jessie," Kate said, remembering the reverent way the prince had said the name. "That would be the baby's mother."

"Right. The prince had an affair with Jessica before his

duty brought him back to Montebello. Several months later, he found out she died in childbirth. Her, and the baby.''

"They thought the baby died, too?'' she asked.

"Yeah. What makes it worse is he hadn't realized she was carrying his child when he left. No wonder the poor guy is looking like he's been hit by a truck.''

Kate stumbled.

"Are you okay?'' Sam asked, catching her arm.

No, she was not okay. After five years of coping, it seemed as if every painful memory of her past was getting dredged up tonight. She wrenched free of Sam's touch, her heart pounding as if she were still running. "I'm fine.''

He tilted his head, his gaze more golden than brown as he studied her. "We could grab a coffee before we question the Hanson woman. From the looks of the family reunion back there, the king will probably be busy for a while.''

"No, I'm fine. I just want to get back to...'' She frowned, zeroing in on the pronoun he had used. "Before *we* question her?''

"Considering the way you were in at the start, I figured you'd want to see this through.'' He glanced pointedly at his hand and then at the place on her arm where he had touched her. When his eyes met hers once more, his gaze was direct and much too knowing. "You always did like to see neat, clean endings, didn't you?''

Whether it was an oversight by the renovators or had been left alone deliberately for the psychological effect, the room that served as the security office for the hospital looked as if it belonged in a previous century. One of the walls was bare stone, giving the chamber the chill of a dungeon.

"I want complete immunity. You promise me that, then I'll answer your questions.''

Sam propped a hip against the edge of the table and

shrugged. "Why would you want immunity if you've done nothing wrong, Miss Hanson?"

Gretchen Hanson tossed her mouse-colored hair out of her eyes with a flick of her head. She leaned back in her chair and attempted what she probably thought was a coy smile. "I already told you, I was trying to bring that child back to his father. I showed you baby Luke's birth certificate. That proves who he is. You saw the names."

The document had appeared genuine, Sam thought, and the date of birth was nine months after the prince had spent time at Jessica's ranch in Colorado. Each detail Hanson had revealed during her questioning so far had supported her story of the baby's identity, reinforcing what had been obvious to anyone seeing the prince and the baby together. "Considering the way you treated the child," Sam said, "you shouldn't be making any demands."

"What do you mean? I've been taking good care of that baby. I deserve a reward."

"That's an odd way to care for a child, Miss Hanson," Kate said. "Leaving him to fend for himself in the dirt of a flower bed on a cool October night." She paced across the small room and stopped at the opposite side of the table from Sam.

He tamped down the twinge of irritation he felt at Kate's movement. The room was small, but she had been careful to keep as much distance as possible between them since they'd arrived. She'd already made it clear that she didn't want him to touch her, no matter how casually—she had jerked away as if she'd been burned when he'd touched her arm in the corridor. And she seemed to have no problem staying away from him.

Didn't she remember being naked and screaming his name?

All right, this wasn't the time or the place to revisit the past. His irritation was unwarranted, nothing but a bruised male ego. It was sensible of her to treat him like a stranger. He was finding it difficult enough to concentrate with Kate in the room. If she were any closer, he wouldn't have a hope of doing his job.

Gretchen was continuing to protest her innocence. "I wasn't going to leave him there."

"Please, let's not waste any more time," Kate said, interrupting what was shaping up to be yet another whining plea. "We've gone over this before. I saw what you did and I heard what you said. You're in deep trouble, Miss Hanson."

Sam nodded. "Better listen to Lieutenant Mulvaney. Do you have any idea what the penalty for child abuse is in Montebello?"

Gretchen's gaze flicked back and forth between them, her bravado fading. "I'm an American citizen. I have rights."

"But you're in San Sebastian, the capital of Montebello. It's a very old, very traditional monarchy. And it's not just any child we're talking about, it's the royal heir." He lifted one hand toward the stone wall, deciding to use the setting to try a bluff. "I assume you've heard that there are dungeons under the palace?"

"What?"

"Those thick stone walls are centuries old and completely soundproof." Sam lowered his voice. "No one can hear what goes on inside, but there are stories...."

"You can't let them put me in a dungeon!"

"I'm trying my best to dissuade them, but unless you show some sign of cooperation, there's not much I can do."

"But I've been cooperating!"

"You told the hospital security guard you had information on the woman the police are seeking," Sam said. "If that's true, I can guarantee you won't be clamped in irons."

Gretchen's pasty complexion paled even further. "Irons?"

Sam saw Kate lift an eyebrow at him. She would know as well as he did that Montebellan justice was as modern as any system in the West. It was easy to guarantee that Gretchen wouldn't be mistreated because nobody was mistreated. Sam hoped Kate wouldn't blow his bluff.

"Better take Lieutenant Coburn's offer," Kate said. "It's not immunity, but it's the best we can do."

Obviously Kate understood what he was doing. And why shouldn't she? He'd always known she was an intelligent woman, he'd just never been overly concerned with her mind. He'd been occupied by…other things.

And he wanted to reach across the table and drag her to his side and make her remember every single one of them….

"I'm not the criminal here," Gretchen muttered, sinking down in her chair. "It's all Ursula's fault."

Sam rubbed his face. Yet again he tried to focus on his duty. "Go on."

"Ursula's the one who should be stuck in some dungeon, not me. She told me to bring the baby here. She was the one who made sure we had the birth certificate to prove who the kid is. We were supposed to get a reward from the royals. They were supposed to be so grateful that we'd been taking care of the royal heir that we'd be set for life. She had these big ideas, but she screwed it up."

"How did she do that?" Kate prodded.

"By getting her face all over the papers, that's how."

"What do you mean?"

"That sketch on the front page of the newspaper. The woman who's wanted for murder. It's Ursula. I just about fainted when I saw it. That must have been why she didn't show up to meet me. Didn't she think about how she was leaving me high and dry?"

"That was very inconsiderate of her," Kate said, not missing a beat. "But I don't understand how you came to be taking care of the prince's baby in the first place."

Gretchen exhaled impatiently. "I'm a midwife. I delivered it. That was Ursula's idea, too. She wouldn't help with that, either. It was her own sister, and I had to do everything."

"Her sister?" Kate asked.

"Yeah, the mother was Ursula's kid sister, Jessica. That's how come we got involved in the first place. The prince had knocked up Jessica and took off, so naturally she would ask her sister for help."

Sam sensed some pieces of the puzzle move into place. At the king's strategy session earlier that evening, Sam had learned that the prince felt the artist's sketch of the murderer, based on a description given by a young child witness and his father, looked familiar. That must have been why. Ursula's face would have borne some resemblance to Jessica's. Jessica Chambers. Ursula Chambers.

He nodded in satisfaction. Now he had a name to go with the artist's sketch that had been circulated to all the Montebellan news media. "Do you know where Ursula Chambers is now?" he asked.

"If I did, I sure wouldn't be here," Gretchen muttered. "I don't know why Ursula had to kill the king's nephew. Desmond was supposed to be helping us."

"Are you claiming that Desmond Caruso knew about the baby?" Sam asked. "He knew about the existence of the prince's son?"

"Oh, yeah. He knew. He was the one who paid the plane fare from Colorado to Montebello for me and baby Luke. He promised that Ursula and me would be made duchesses or countesses or something like that. The royals are filthy rich, you know. They were going to reward us."

Another piece clicked into place. So that was the victim's

connection with the murderer, Sam thought. He'd heard rumors of Caruso's less-than-exemplary character. The king's nephew had been an illegitimate branch of the royal family tree, and he had always resented the limitations of his birth despite the king's acceptance of him. It was definitely possible for the man to have been involved in a scheme to profit from the prince's child.

But why had Ursula killed him? Had he tried to double-cross her, to cut her out of the money she had been promised? Or had the motive been more personal?

"It was Ursula's idea to keep the prince's baby in the first place, but I had to do all the work," Gretchen said. "It wasn't easy, hiding out and taking care of the child."

"No, I imagine it wasn't," Kate said.

"I have my stupid brother to take care of, too, you know."

"You must be very busy."

"You bet I am. Gerald's too dim-witted to manage without me. Between him and the baby, I never had a minute to myself."

Sam doubted that. This woman was no self-sacrificing saint. With every word she uttered, she demonstrated her lack of compassion. "It was generous of you to take in the child after his mother died."

"Damn right. I've had that kid since the day he was born."

Sam frowned. "We were told Jessica Chambers died in childbirth, and that her baby died, too. What can you tell us about the birth?"

Gretchen's eyes narrowed, her face taking on a feral look. She glanced around as if searching for an escape route.

Sam leaned forward, acting on a hunch. "Miss Hanson, how did Jessica Chambers really die?"

"She was murdered," Gretchen burst out. "Ursula did

it. She killed her own sister just like she killed the king's nephew. I swear. She's the one you want. I didn't do anything wrong.''

It was an ungodly hour to be awake. No one but street cleaners and peasants was up before dawn. Instead of sneaking around these dreary old streets, she should have been safe and warm in some posh hotel room right now, dreaming of ways to spend her money.

Tucking a stray lock of her blond hair under her scarf, Ursula Chambers paused at the corner to check for police. Nothing was moving except a stray cat picking its way around some garbage cans. She hitched her carry-on bag over her shoulder, kicked the cat aside and hurried down the street.

She'd had high hopes when she'd arrived on this island. She'd had a surefire plan, too. Jessica had always had things easy—all their lives, she'd had the luck that should have been Ursula's. So it was only fair that Jessica's brat would be her big sister's ticket to easy street. Ursula had planned it all out carefully. She deserved success, but then everything had fallen apart.

She was surrounded by idiots, that was the problem. Idiots and double-crossers. Desmond had been almost as attractive as she was, and he'd been one of the best lovers she'd had, but he should have known better than to betray her with that little black-haired tart. She'd seen him kissing the girl, some princess or other, and yet when she'd confronted him later he'd tried to deny it.

It hadn't been Ursula's fault she'd had to kill him. He'd given her no choice. One minute Desmond was smiling through his lies, the next minute she found that statue in her hand and saw blood pooling around his head.

She'd wiped off her fingerprints and put the statue she'd hit him with on the shelf. She'd ditched the blood-spattered dress she'd been wearing. She'd slipped away from Desmond's cottage and made it off the palace grounds without anyone seeing her. She'd even gone back and burned the cottage to destroy any trace evidence.

She'd thought she was safe. Then some kid had screamed and pointed at her at the airport, and now everyone in the country could see her face when they turned on their TVs or opened their newspapers. It was a good thing she had noticed the police sketch on the front page of the *Montebello Messenger* before she'd tried to meet Gretchen.

She glanced at her reflection in a darkened shop window. The drawing had been surprisingly good for a police sketch, but considering the features the artist was working with, how could it not be? Ursula had always known she was blessed with a face that should have been on a Broadway poster or a movie screen. Along with her talent and her dynamite body, she'd been destined for stardom…if only her acting career hadn't been ruined by her manager.

But what more could she have expected from a man? All the men in her life had betrayed her in one way or another, hadn't they? The only smart thing to do was to use them before they could use her. And Ursula was smart. She was a survivor.

An aircraft took off in the distance, the throb of its engines magnified by the narrow streets. Ursula clutched her carry-on and looked up to follow its progress. The airport was still her best bet. Her credit cards were maxed out, but she had just enough cash left from the sale of her sister's heirloom ring to cover a one-way ticket to the States. As long as she made it through customs before that idiot Gretchen told someone her name, she'd be home by tomorrow.

Like any great actress, Ursula Chambers knew when it was time to make an exit.

Chapter 3

"Put this on so you won't be cold."

Kate shook her head quickly as she saw Sam reach for the buttons of his dress blue uniform jacket. "No, thanks. I'll be fine."

"The jeep doesn't have a top." He slipped the last button from its hole and shrugged off the jacket. "And you're only wearing your running clothes."

She told herself not to look. For the past five hours she'd been hearing variations on the same lecture in her head. But she was only human, so she couldn't prevent her gaze from wandering.

How could it be possible for his shoulders to be broader than she remembered, for his chest to be more solid? The white shirt he wore beneath the jacket was flattened to his body by the breeze, defining the masculine contours like a lingering caress.

She looked away. She was no longer his lover. She was his colleague, his equal in rank. "Keep it, Sam. You're only wearing a shirt yourself."

"Yeah, but haven't you heard? SEALs are tough."
Without waiting for permission, he settled the jacket around
her shoulders.

"Sam…"

He rounded the hood of the jeep and hopped into the
driver's seat. "Come on, Kate. I'll take you home."

There was no point arguing. Sam hadn't changed—he
still liked to get his way.

Which was one of the reasons she'd let him go.

She took the seat beside him and clutched the lapels of
the jacket together. Pleasant warmth flowed into her from
the heat of his body that was trapped in the garment. His
scent surrounded her, teasing her with awareness, daring
her to remember.

"How long have you been in Montebello, Kate?"

"Seven months tomorrow. And you?"

"Two days." He turned the jeep and headed down the
hill from the hospital.

"I didn't know you were being posted here."

"I wasn't. I had just finished an assignment in the Middle East and figured while I was in the neighborhood I
might as well spend my leave in Montebello. The leave got
canceled when I got the order to report to King Marcus."

"That's a shame. This is a wonderful place if you're here
on vacation. Tourism is one of Montebello's biggest
industries."

"Yeah. There are plenty of sights I never got around to
seeing, but duty called."

"It has a way of doing that."

"If I'd known you were here, I would have looked you
up. How have you been?"

They were picking up speed. Sam drove with the same
straightforward competence with which he did everything
else. Kate turned her face to the breeze so she wouldn't
keep inhaling his scent. "I've been fine, Sam. And you?"

"Busy."

"Judging from the service ribbons on this jacket, I'd have to agree."

"Like they say, I joined the Navy and saw the world."

"That's great. It's—" She almost said that it was what he'd wanted, but she remembered how he'd responded to that comment before. She had to keep things light, keep things friendly. The base was only a few more minutes away. Then this interminable evening would be over. "You said you always wanted to travel. And how's your mother?"

"She's doing well. She and Marvin moved to Arizona two years ago, and the climate's done wonders for her rheumatism."

"Is your stepfather still in the car business?"

"Uh-huh. He opened up a dealership in Flagstaff. Wanted to call it Marvelous Marvin's, but my mom couldn't stop laughing every time he said it so he settled for Oasis Autos."

She smiled. Sam had supported his widowed mother throughout his teenage years. He'd delayed joining the Navy until she was securely remarried. Noble, loyal Sam. He was a throwback to the days when men took care of their women no matter what.

Which was another reason she'd let him go.

"And your little brother?" she asked.

"Chuck's doing his master's degree at Stanford."

"Does he still want to be a paleontologist?"

"Uh-huh. At least now he's got an excuse to go on back-yard treasure hunts."

She heard the note of pride in Sam's voice, and her smile grew wistful. Sam had helped raise his younger brother, and he'd done a marvelous job. He would have made a wonderful father.

But he'd also deserved his shot at following his dreams.

She'd made the right decision.

Yes, she had.

"How are your parents doing, Kate?" he asked.

"They divorced four years ago."

"Oh. I'm sorry."

"Don't be. They're much happier now." And that was true. Some people simply weren't meant to be together.

Like her and Sam.

He remained silent as they approached an intersection. Instead of taking the road that would be the quickest route to the base, he turned toward the road that ran along the coast.

"It's shorter if you go the other way," Kate said, twisting to look over her shoulder.

"I know."

"But—"

"I wanted a chance to talk to you. Is the wind too cold?"

"No. With this jacket I'm fine, but—"

"It's a beautiful evening, isn't it, Kate?" he asked softly.

"Montebello averages three hundred days of sunshine a year, so the skies here are usually clear."

"Do you still like watching the pattern of waves in the moonlight?"

"I take the inland roads when I go jogging."

He slowed the jeep as he rounded a bend, his hand somehow brushing her thigh as he worked the gear shift. "Remember how we used to like listening to the whispers the waves made when they broke on the beach?"

Yes, she remembered all too well. She angled her knees toward the door, the skin on her thigh tingling. "The coastline along this stretch is mostly rock, but there are several popular beaches."

"Maybe you could show me sometime."

"Sam…"

"It still gets to me, you know."

"What does?"

"The sound of the water. It gets me right here," he said, taking one hand off the wheel to touch his chest. "Anywhere you go in the world, it's got a million different tunes that it plays. Sometimes it's restless, sometimes it's angry. A lot of times it's just plain lonely."

"I remember you always liked the sea."

"Good thing, considering my choice of profession, wouldn't you say?"

"Yes, it's fortunate."

"And only one of the things we have in common, Kate." He slowed further, finally pulling the jeep to a stop at the side of the road. He turned off the ignition and inhaled deeply. "I read somewhere that every drop of water on the planet has been through a cycle of life that takes it through practically every type of living thing before it returns to the ocean. But it still smells great, doesn't it?"

It wasn't only the sea that smelled great, she thought. Now that they were no longer moving, the hint of Sam's scent that rose from his jacket was stronger than ever.

The memories were battering at her mind, pushing to be released, but she held them back. She couldn't go through this again. Once was enough.

He turned toward her, draping his elbow over the back of his seat. "It's hard to believe it's been five years."

No, she thought. *Don't do this. Please. Let's keep talking about the climate or your family or our work.*

"I like your hair like that." He lifted his hand toward her ear.

She knew what was coming. He was going to smooth her hair behind her ear, just as he used to do when it had been long. She tipped her head to avoid his touch. "It's more practical to keep it short."

"Is that why you cut it?"

She gritted her teeth against an image from the past, yet

still she saw Sam smiling at her, his fists caught in her hair as he rubbed her curls in slow, sensual circles over her breasts. "Yes, it got in my way," she answered.

"Kate?"

"Mmm?"

"I've missed you."

And I've missed you, she thought.

But she didn't miss the pain. It was locked away with the memories. She couldn't release one without the other.

It had been the right choice. It had, damn it.

She kept her gaze on the horizon. "Like you said, Sam, it's been five years."

"Since we're both here now, maybe we could get together sometime. What do you think?"

She didn't reply. She could feel his gaze moving over her face. What did he see? What did he remember?

Sex. That's what he would remember. That's what it had been about, after all. Just sex.

Sure. Sex on the beach, with the waves lapping at their feet. Laughing, playful sex in the water with their skin slick and cool. And slow, thorough, toe-curling sex on the deck in the moonlight when they'd anchored their rented sailboat in that secluded bay and spent their last night together wrapped in a blanket and each other's arms....

Kate felt a flush work its way over her cheeks. She felt her pulse pound against the gold chain that circled her neck. She hoped the darkness would hide them both.

Sex had been all they'd wanted from each other. And they'd both been perfectly willing to supply it. They'd been young, they'd been unattached, they'd both been about to embark on their new lives in the Navy. So why shouldn't they have indulged in some good, healthy, uncomplicated lovemaking before they had parted ways?

No, not love. It had never been love.

And that was the final reason she had let him go.

"The past is over," she said. "We had an agreement. Let's leave it that way."

"Kate…"

"I was wrong, Sam. I believe I'm getting cold after all," she said. "Please, take me home."

Kate was running again, but in the panic of her dream, she didn't know where she was. The streets were a dark labyrinth of towering walls and dead ends. Her feet were heavy with nightmare paralysis. She had to find the baby. She had to reach it. She had to save it.

Pain doubled her over. It ground through her belly and shot down her thighs. She crossed her arms over her stomach, gasping for breath, and limped forward. She couldn't stop. She had to find it.

The streets grew narrower and transformed into corridors. The echo of her footsteps became the rattle of gurney wheels. The past tangled with the present as she was moving toward the emergency room.

"No. Wait." Kate mouthed the words, twisting on the mattress and clutching the sheets as if she could hold back the inevitable. She knew how this ended, but maybe if she tried harder, maybe if she held on longer she could make it end differently this time….

The pain was tearing a hole in her gut. Her strength was gone, but still she strained forward. The baby. It needed her. She had to try.

"It's too late. He's gone."

No. He couldn't be. She'd tried her best this time. Honestly, she had.

"I'm sorry." The doctor's voice was weary. "We did everything we could."

No. *No!* She wanted to scream, but the emptiness she felt in her body left no room for denial.

The baby was lost.

He'd never taken a breath. He'd never opened his eyes. He'd never once felt his mother's arms around him or nestled against her breast....

A telephone shrilled. Kate came awake with a start. Heart pounding, she tried to orient herself. She rubbed her cheeks and found them wet with tears.

This wasn't a hospital. This was her bed, in her bedroom. She was in Montebello, in the old hotel that had been converted to serve as the unmarried officers' quarters. It was over. Finished. Lost.

The phone rang again.

Kate rolled to her side and stumbled across the floor. Sunlight slanted through the window, casting an orange glow over the heavy wood furniture. Her hand shaking, she reached for the phone on her desk. "Mulvaney," she said.

"Lieutenant Mulvaney, this is Ensign Gordon. I'm Admiral Howe's assistant."

Kate wiped her arm across her eyes to dry her tears. "What can I do for you, Ensign Gordon?"

"You've been asked to report to Admiral Howe's office at oh-nine-hundred hours today."

She acknowledged the order and replaced the receiver mechanically, then dropped her head into her hands. *All right. Focus,* she told herself. *Concentrate on your duty, and this will go away. Just like it always does.*

But the dream still hovered, a gray shadow on the edge of her consciousness.

The nightmare had been worse this time. She didn't need a psychiatrist to figure out why. The reason was obvious. It was because she had seen Sam again. And because she had held that baby.

The thought she'd pushed back so desperately for almost twelve hours—that she'd run from for five years—finally broke free.

Damn it, it should have been *their* child, not the prince's, that she'd held in her arms. It should have been *Sam's* face, not Lucas's, that had lit with wonder as he'd gazed at his son.

But she'd never had the chance to hold their baby. The gentle butterfly motions she'd felt while she'd carried him were all she had to remember of the life she'd been entrusted with…and lost.

She pushed the heels of her hands against her eyes, trying to stop the tears from falling, trying to stem the tide of memories, but it was no use.

She had conceived that night on the boat. She hadn't planned it. Neither of them had. The responsibility of a family had been the last thing on their minds. They both had been due to ship out the next day and they hadn't wanted to waste one moment of their final night together.

They'd known from the start their affair would be brief. They'd each had dreams and obligations that would force them apart, so they had agreed to make a clean break. No regrets, no strings, no awkward clinging. The only promise they'd made had been to give each other an easy goodbye.

For the first few months, Sam hadn't tried to contact her. What was it he had said at the hospital yesterday? She had liked nice, neat endings? Well, that's what they'd promised and that's what they'd had.

When she'd missed her period, she'd told herself it was the excitement of her first posting. When the nausea had started, she'd thought it might be seasickness. Only when the signs had become too obvious to deny any longer had she finally taken a test.

Sam's first letter had arrived the day Kate had discovered she was pregnant. He had been about to leave for a training mission somewhere in the South Pacific. His life was taking the direction he had planned. She'd been able to sense his smile in the words he'd written.

She'd known he would have come back if she had told

him about the baby. That's just the kind of man he was. Noble, dependable, determined-to-get-his-way Sam. He would have insisted on doing the honorable thing and getting married.

But he'd just freed himself from the responsibility of raising his brother and supporting his mother. He'd been so eager to embark on his new life as a SEAL, how could she tie him down?

And how could she tie herself to a man who didn't love her? Sure, they'd been great together in bed—and anywhere else they could find to be alone—but a physical attraction was no basis for a long-term relationship. Getting married just for the sake of a baby would only lead to resentment and bitterness. That's what her parents had done. Kate had grown up vowing never to follow her mother's example, never to be dependent on any man. Especially one who didn't love her.

So Kate had never answered Sam's letter. She had returned unopened the ones that had followed. And after a while, the letters had stopped coming. He didn't try to contact her again.

He had kept his promise.

And so had Kate. She was still convinced she had made the right choice. She had fully intended to raise her child alone, even if it meant giving up her dream of advancing in her career.

But then fate had stepped in. She had lost the baby.

She sniffed hard and wiped her arm across her eyes, then dropped her hand to the chain around her neck. Her fingers rubbed the delicate charm that lay against her breastbone. She had made the motion so often the gold was becoming worn, yet the butterfly's wings still arched as if caught in mid-flutter.

She had bought the charm when she'd left the hospital after the miscarriage. It was her way of honoring the fragile life of the baby she had carried. She had worn it under her uniform, keeping the token as private as she had kept her grief.

Then she had chopped off her hair, sucked up the pain and focused on the career she'd always dreamed of.

Kate pushed herself to her feet. Focus. That's what she needed to do. Her duty had gotten her through the most painful episode of her life. It would do the same now.

The next time she went running, she would take a different route.

And considering the way she had rebuffed Sam's tentative overtures when he'd stopped at the coast the night before, chances were she wouldn't see Sam Coburn for another five years.

"The Montebellan police have the public airport locked down. Every passenger is going through a rigorous security check." Sam walked to the high-scale map of Montebello that hung from one wall of the base commander's office. He tapped his index finger against the location of the airport, then moved his hand toward the southeast shore of the island. "The private strip at the oil field is heavily guarded, as well."

Admiral Howe steepled his fingers and leaned back behind his desk. His bulldog features appeared to be set in a perpetual frown, even though he nodded in approval. "Good. Have you gathered any more information on the suspect?"

"Yes, sir. The FBI obtained Ursula Chambers's driver's license photograph from the Colorado DMV and faxed it to me thirty minutes ago."

"Got someone out of bed there, did you?"

Sam grimaced as he opened the file folder he had brought with him. There was a seven-hour time difference between Montebello and Virginia. The clerk he had reached at

Quantico hadn't been eager to chase down the Colorado people in what had been the middle of the night there.

That's when Sam had discovered one of the advantages of working for royalty. When the clerk had learned that Sam had the full weight of the king of Montebello behind him, the request had been filled within the hour.

"No problem, sir," Sam said, handing the admiral two items from the folder. "As you can see, the photograph closely matches the artist's sketch of the suspect."

Howe took the photo and the sketch from Sam and studied them briefly. "Yes, the features are very distinctive."

"The police are in the process of distributing copies of the photograph as well as the suspect's vital statistics to the security forces stationed at the airports."

Howe laid the papers on his desk. "Chambers is a striking woman. She should be easy to spot."

"Apparently she has had acting experience, so it's possible that she has disguised herself. But since she killed Caruso, who according to Gretchen Hanson was their main contact in Montebello, she probably doesn't have the resources or the connections here to obtain a false passport or other identification. Therefore it's highly unlikely that Chambers will be able to slip past the security that's in place at the airport in order to escape Montebello by air."

"Excellent."

"That leaves the water." Sam turned to the map. "We've alerted the cruise lines and other passenger ships. Police will be stationed at the ports, but we need to intensify the patrol of the coastline."

"King Marcus phoned me this morning to express his concern about that. Which is the main reason I've asked you here, Lieutenant Coburn. The king decided this mission requires a Navy officer who is more familiar with Montebello."

Sam moved in front of Howe's desk and clasped his

hands behind his back. As much as he would have liked to continue the leave that had been interrupted by the king's request for his assistance, he didn't want to be relieved of his duty before he'd accomplished what he'd set out to do. He didn't like leaving things unfinished. "This mission is still in the early stages, sir. Given the geography of Montebello, it was my understanding that the king was aware of the difficulties—"

"Relax, Lieutenant. King Marcus is pleased with your conduct so far. He still feels your training is a valuable asset in the search for the fugitive. In fact, he wants to give you some help."

"Admiral?"

Before Howe could explain, there was a sharp rap on the door. Ensign Gordon, the apple-cheeked young man who was Howe's aide, took a step into the room. "Lieutenant Mulvaney is here, sir."

Howe glanced at his watch. "Good. Right on time. Show her in."

Sam turned to face the door. Kate was here? Why now? That was the second time in less than a day he'd asked himself that question.

And for the second time in less than twenty-four hours, she took his breath away.

He had never seen her in her uniform. They had been on leave when they'd met, and they'd spent most of their time wearing as little as possible. It was difficult to reconcile the image in his memory to the tall, slim woman with lieutenant's bars on her sleeves. The dress blues complemented her coloring, making her eyes look greener and her hair appear a fiery shade of auburn. Her chin was up, her shoulders back, and she appeared to be the epitome of a confident, successful naval officer.

Yet when Sam looked at her, he saw the woman who

had once writhed in his arms. He felt Florida breezes and smelled gardenias.

She saluted Admiral Howe, giving him a crisp yet cordial greeting. She nodded politely to Sam, then gave the admiral her complete attention.

Once again, Sam felt a twinge of irritation. She was behaving appropriately for the circumstances, so he couldn't fault her for that. They were on duty. It wasn't the place for familiarity.

Yet they hadn't been on duty the night before when he'd driven her to the hotel where they had their quarters, and she'd treated him the same way. The memory of their affair might have haunted him for five years, but it didn't seem to have had any impact on Kate. She'd told him flat out last night that she wanted to leave the past in the past. And she'd returned the letters he'd sent years ago. When she'd said goodbye, she'd meant it.

Why couldn't he get that through his head? If her composure this morning was anything to go by, she had probably slept like a baby last night instead of being driven half nuts by dreams of hot sex.

To his disbelief, Sam felt his body stir. She'd always been able to do that to him. The mere thought of what it was like to hold her body against his could make him break into a sweat.

Deliberately, he moved his gaze away from Kate and concentrated on what the admiral was saying.

"Lieutenant Mulvaney, I'd like to compliment you personally on your handling of the situation at the King Augustus Hospital yesterday," Admiral Howe said. "King Marcus was very impressed with your conduct, both in apprehending Gretchen Hanson and in taking the initiative to ensure the welfare of the royal heir."

"Thank you, sir."

"I understand you assisted in the interrogation of Hanson afterward?"

"Yes, sir. That is correct."

"Excellent. Then we can get down to business. Lieutenant Mulvaney, you are hereby removed from your current duties."

Kate blinked. "Sir?"

"At King Marcus's command, you are to assist in the coordination of the Montebellan security forces and the United States Navy in the search for Ursula Chambers." The admiral leaned back in his chair, steepled his fingers and turned his gaze to Sam. "Lieutenant Coburn, meet your new partner."

Chapter 4

Wasn't there a saying about no good deed going unpunished? The king had probably thought he was doing Kate a favor. In return for the way she had rescued his grandchild from the hospital flower bed, he evidently had decided to put in a good word for her with the admiral and recommend her for a plum assignment. Right. Some favor.

Kate lengthened her stride as she crossed the base's central square in an effort to work off her frustration. Seagulls cried overhead, riding the wind that swept in from the pier. She firmed her jaw at the noise. It was as if the fates were conspiring against her, refusing to let her forget and get on with her life.

Seeing Sam and the baby, stirring up all those painful memories was bad enough, but she'd handled it, hadn't she? How was she going to cope with seeing him every day? Working with him? Breathing his scent, hearing his voice, seeing his smile?

Well, she wouldn't have to worry about his smile. So

far, he looked to be as pleased about their partnership as she was.

"I've been given a place to set up a command center in the north building. I'm meeting the superintendent of the Montebellan police there in twenty minutes." Sam touched her elbow as he changed direction. "Naturally I'll include you in the meeting now."

She couldn't help it, she flinched at his touch. "All right."

"Before he gets here, I need to ask you something."

"What?"

They had reached the building on the north side of the square. When the Montebellans had deeded this enclave to the U.S. Navy, they had stipulated that any structures had to reflect the character of the local architecture. Although this building housed an efficient complex of modern offices, the long windows, slate roof and iron-trimmed wooden entrance doors gave it the flavor of a Mediterranean villa.

Instead of going through those doors, Sam detoured to a corner that was shielded from sight by a large cedar tree. He stopped and turned to face her. "Are you going to have a problem working with me, Kate?"

Leave it to Sam to tackle the issue head-on. She kept her gaze on the top button of his khaki shirt. "No," she lied. "I'm grateful for the king's notice. This assignment is bound to look good on my record, so of course I don't object to it."

"That's not what I meant. Will it bother you to be my partner?"

"I wouldn't expect to be in charge, since you were the one who was called in for this project first." She paused. "Do you have a problem working with a partner?"

"No, I can use all the help I can get."

"Fine." She started to move past him, but he didn't budge.

"Kate, I'm not talking about our work, I'm talking about us."

"There's nothing to talk about."

"Given our past association, I thought you might feel awkward about taking this assignment."

Her gaze went from his shirt to his throat. And she thought about how that hollow at the base had tasted. She fought the urge to lick her lips. "Thank you for your concern, Sam, but as you said, our association was in the past. And I want to leave it there."

"Right. That's what you told me yesterday."

"I wouldn't let my personal business interfere with my duty."

"You never did."

"What does that mean?"

"Your career always came first."

That's because when she'd lost the baby, she had nothing else left. She frowned. No, that wasn't right. She had chosen this career. She loved it. She had put it first before she was pregnant, too. "I think we've covered this topic, Sam."

"Have we? As I recall, we didn't do all that much talking when we were together."

That was true. They'd had far more urgent things on their minds than conversation. She moved her gaze to his mouth, remembering how he'd used it on her neck...and her breasts...and her thighs....

Kate quickly looked away, focusing on the flag at the center of the square. "Maybe I should be asking you if you have a problem working with me, given our past association. You're the one who can't seem to let it go."

Can't let it go? She's right, Sam thought. He did have a problem. A major problem. It was distracting enough just thinking about her. How was he supposed to work with her? How could he keep himself from touching her, especially here in the sunshine with her hair gleaming like autumn and her pulse throbbing in the delicate vein at the side of her neck?

He'd been wrong before when he'd thought she looked composed. Now that they were in full daylight he could see she hadn't slept any better than he had last night. There were shadows under her eyes and signs of strain around her lips.

What was bothering her? It couldn't be the same thing that was bothering him, that was for sure. If she'd been dreaming of hot sex all night she wouldn't have brushed him off yesterday or continued to treat him like a casual acquaintance today. She had never been shy about her physical needs—their relationship had been as simple and basic as things could get between a man and a woman. He'd thought the memories they shared were good ones. And they had parted on friendly terms—he'd let her go as neatly as she'd wanted—so what was going on?

If this were five years ago, he would have cupped her cheek and drawn her head to rest against his shoulder. He would have stroked her back and pressed soft kisses to her hair and urged her to confide in him.

But he wasn't part of her life any longer. She didn't welcome either his touch or him. "Don't worry, Kate. You made yourself clear twice already, and the Navy has a strict policy regarding sexual harassment."

"Good." She moved toward the door.

"But if you ever change your mind," he added softly, "be sure to let me know."

A slight break in her stride was the only sign that she had heard him. "I think it would be best if we get on with our mission," she said briskly. "What have you done so far?"

As they climbed the stairs to the second story, Sam tamped down his frustration and told her what he had re-

lated to the admiral. They reached the office he'd been
assigned, and he stepped aside to let her enter first. He
couldn't help noticing that she was careful not brush against
him as she went by.

It was another jab to his already bruised ego. Had what
they'd shared meant so little to her? Had he deluded himself, distorted the memory of how good it had been? He
wanted to grab her arm, spin her around and haul her to
him so he could find out.

Instead, he closed the door behind them and watched her
walk around the room. He couldn't grab her. He couldn't
kiss her. He'd meant what he'd said about sexual harassment. It would be a serious charge, and he wasn't about to
risk his career to satisfy his urge for a woman.

No, not just *a* woman. Kate. His Kate. The lover who
had spoiled him for anyone else.

Aw, hell.

"Have you obtained charts of the coastline?" she asked.

He pushed away from the door and walked to the large
table he'd set up in the center of the room. "Right here."

She joined him, although she was careful to keep an
arm's length away. She braced her hands on the edge of
the table and leaned over to study one of the charts spread
out there. "I know this coast. Even though there are many
rocky stretches, there are innumerable places a small boat
can pick up a passenger."

"I take it you think she'll try to escape by small boat?"

"It's her best course of action. With the airports closed
to her and the cruise lines and ferries on alert, she won't
be able to escape the island by any form of public transportation. She'll likely try to obtain the use of a private
boat."

That was exactly the conclusion that he'd come to. Sam
moved closer to Kate's side and leaned over the chart with
her. He couldn't help inhaling her scent, and he was already

leaning nearer to get another whiff before he caught himself. Damn, how was he supposed to keep his mind on business if she smelled like that? He exhaled hard and traced a line on the paper with his index finger. "The nearest island to Montebello is Tamir. Although relations between the two countries have thawed recently, they don't have an extradition treaty. If Chambers makes it that far, it won't be difficult for her to disappear."

"A small private craft would be able to cover the distance to Tamir," Kate said. "Even a rowboat could make it as long as the weather conditions were favorable."

"You said you've been stationed here seven months. How many private boats do you figure there are on Montebello?"

Kate lifted her shoulders in a brief shrug. "This is an island. The sea is a major influence on Montebellan culture. There are fishing boats, sailboats and pleasure craft of all kinds. If you added them all up, the number would likely exceed the population itself."

"I suspected as much. That's going to make this challenging."

"From what you said, the Montebellan police will be able to cover the airports, but they don't have the resources to insure that Chambers doesn't escape by water." She continued to study the map. "Our navy has been doing coast-guard patrols as part of the lease agreement for this base, but with the number of ships in dry dock and the number on maneuvers, we're stretched too thin to step up the patrols to any significant extent."

"That's the problem I've been running into," Sam said. "The admiral authorized the use of any available naval resources to assist the Montebellans, but that only means telephones, radio equipment, this office and a handful of personnel who could be pulled from their regular duties. We couldn't justify diverting Navy vessels that are stationed in the Mediterranean into forming a blockade in order to look for one woman. That would be ludicrous, not to mention a threat to the stability of the area."

"So what's your plan?"

"Still working on it. For now, we're going to concentrate on checking any suspicious watercraft during the regular patrols of the coastline. The police helicopters will provide added surveillance."

"But that won't necessarily stop her from escaping. The craft she's on might not look suspicious. You would need to check out every single vessel to be certain, but considering the amount of daily boat traffic and the limited number of Navy vessels available, that would be impossible."

"Hey, I'm open to suggestions. Do you have a better idea?"

She didn't respond immediately. She studied the map for another minute, then straightened. "Sam, I don't believe we should rely on the regular coastal patrol."

He turned to face her, surprised by her comment. "Unless every soul in Montebello is a news junkie and is able to recognize Ursula Chambers from her photograph, and unless they're completely honest and willing to turn her in, we can't be certain she won't be able to find some private boat to hire."

"Of course, we can't rely on the general public to stop her from escaping. I meant that we shouldn't use a high-profile surveillance of the island."

"Why not?"

"There is already massive security in place at the airports, right?"

"Right," he confirmed. "Chambers won't get off Montebello that way."

"So if her only alternative is leaving by boat, a high-profile search using naval ships and police helicopters might force her underground."

"Ah, I see your point."

Kate nodded. "She's already a suspect in two murders, so she has nothing to lose by killing again. For the sake of public safety, I'm positive the king would want her captured as soon as possible."

"You're right. He does. That's why he's pulling every diplomatic string he's got to get help."

"Which should make our job easier. We're going to need to pull a lot of strings to organize what I have in mind."

He crossed his arms and looked at her expectantly. "Which is?"

She lifted her chin. "I think we should use the fleet of Montebello."

Did she know how appealing her neck looked when she angled her chin that way? She used to like the way he would run his tongue along her jaw. And he liked that low purr she made when he would suck on her earlobe....

"Sam?"

He jerked his attention to what she had said. "What fleet? The Montebellans have no fleet."

"They have fishing boats and pleasure craft."

"Kate…"

"Think about it, Sam. The waters around this island are usually busy with small craft, so those boats wouldn't arouse suspicion as they cruise the coastline. They would serve to draw Chambers out. They're maneuverable, and if coordinated properly they could systematically cover a large area."

"If coordinated properly?"

"We could man the boats with all available Montebellan police and Navy personnel, who would remain in constant radio communication."

He stared at her as he rapidly assessed her suggestion. SEALs were trained to make use of anything available when they were on a mission. But civilian vessels? In a naval operation? It was unconventional, but it just might work. "I see where you're heading, Kate. If we chart a course for each vessel so that it covers one section of a grid near the coastline—"

"With naval vessels positioned offshore as backup for the small boats—"

"And spotter aircraft on standby," he added.

"By tomorrow we could draw a surveillance net around the island that a rubber raft couldn't slip through."

"All right. Sounds good. Let's set this up."

She lifted her eyebrows. "Just like that? You're willing to go with my idea?"

"Yes."

"Oh."

"You sound surprised."

"Well, yes."

"Why?"

"I was under the impression that you liked getting your way."

"Sure I do. In this case, I want to complete my mission by catching a murderer, and if your idea gets me there, I'll use it."

"I see."

"Kate, just because I was more interested in your body than in your mind doesn't mean I thought you didn't have one."

She took a step back, her cheeks flushing red. "Sam, we agreed—"

He muttered an oath and held up his hands. "Sorry."

"No problem." She cleared her throat and turned to the table. "We'd better get started."

Ursula hated the water. She'd never learned to swim. The only reason she owned a bikini was that she looked so scrumptious in one.

She lifted her arm to hold her hat against the breeze and inhaled deeply. ''I just love sailing,'' she said. ''It's so exciting, don't you think?''

The boy nodded quickly, his gaze riveted to her cleavage. His frame hadn't yet fleshed out, and he looked all coltish arms and legs in his swimsuit, but the gleam in his eye was all man.

Ursula twitched her shoulders so her breasts jiggled, hiding a smirk when she saw the boy's eyes widen. Teenagers were so easy to manipulate. This one appeared to be sixteen, maybe seventeen, and like all adolescent males, he could be led around by his sex drive.

He swallowed hard, his Adam's apple bobbing like a cork. ''I have a sailboat.''

Of course, she knew he had a boat. She'd noticed him drag up some little thing with a rainbow-striped sail on the sand ten minutes ago. It was the only reason she was giving him this free show. She needed that boat now that she'd had to abandon her plan to leave Montebello by plane.

The past twenty-four hours had been simply dreadful. When she'd reached the airport yesterday, she'd found it crawling with security. She'd been smart enough to work her way past them, but when she'd seen the cop behind the ticket counter, checking everyone's ID, she'd known it was no use. She wouldn't be getting on a plane anytime soon.

There weren't many choices open to her. Either she continued to hole up in the hotel room she could no longer afford until the heat at the airport died down, or she had to leave this godforsaken island by water. And she hated the water.

She should have known better than to team up with Gretchen Hanson. Sure, they'd been childhood chums in Shady Rock, Colorado, but Gretchen had always reminded Ursula of a rat. The woman must have spilled everything the instant she'd been caught. Now the police knew Ursula's name, and the photo from her driver's licence was on wanted posters all over the country.

It was dangerous to be seen in public—with a face and body as outstanding as hers, she naturally drew attention. Yet she could have saved herself the trouble of donning the sunglasses and concealing her hair under her hat when she'd decided to troll the beach for prospects this morning. This kid hadn't looked at her face yet.

"A sailboat. How marvellous." She paused and tipped down her sunglasses, giving him a slow, suggestive perusal. "And I'll just bet you've got a big one."

"B-big?"

"I like them long and sleek. Is yours?"

"My…"

"Your boat, honey. Is it big?"

"She's a twenty-three-foot catboat."

"Ooh, sounds yummy. Are you…experienced?"

"Uh…"

She adjusted her hat and leaned toward him. "I meant at sailing."

"Yeah. I've been sailing for years."

"I can see that," she murmured, drawing her fingertips along his scrawny forearm. "You have such lovely muscles here."

His jaw went slack. "Uh."

She sighed, giving her breasts an extra heave. "I wish I knew someone who could take me."

"T-take you?"

"For a sailboat ride."

"I could take you out."

"You? What a great idea. I hadn't thought of that."

"We could go now."

"Mmm. Evening would be so much nicer. The moonlight, the darkness." She traced his wiry little biceps with a fingernail. "It's so romantic."

His Adam's apple threatened to bob out of his throat. "I, uh..."

"How far have you gone?"

"What?"

"Have you ever gone all the way?"

He shifted from one foot to the other, his body twitching with discomfort. "Sure. Lots of times."

"Wow." She rested her fingertips on his chest and leaned closer still. "All the way to Tamir? You must be a really good sailor."

"Tamir?"

Ursula hid her impatience. The hormones that were raging through the kid's system were starting to shut down his brain. That's what she was counting on, but not before she got what she wanted out of him. "You know. Tamir. The island that's nearest to Montebello."

"Uh, my mom won't let me go that far."

She flicked her little finger teasingly against his nipple. "Do you always do what your mommy says?"

His breathing was getting shallow. "The currents are t-tricky. Sometimes the swells can reach ten meters, and my cat's not—"

"I would be very, very grateful to get a ride to Tamir." She rubbed her knee lightly between his thighs. "*Very* grateful."

"I, uh." He inhaled quickly, beads of sweat popping out on his upper lip. "Oh, geez."

"Would you like a sample of my—" she dropped her hand to the front of his swim trunks "—gratitude?"

He trembled and pushed himself against her hand. His eyes were glazed. "Oh, geez. Oh, geez."

"We could meet here at sunset." She glanced up and down the beach. This cove was practically deserted, except for some kids tossing a Frisbee and a handful of sunbathers. And speaking of a handful, this boy felt about ready to burst. He'd probably never been this close to a real woman, let alone felt one touch him. How tiresome. She squeezed lightly and withdrew her hand. "It can be our secret, hmm?"

He fumbled for her wrist. "Sure. Whatever you say. Just do that again."

It was easy to twist out of his grasp since his palms were so sweaty. Unconcerned with the state she was leaving him in, Ursula turned away, wiping her hand on her thigh. "Later, honey. When we're on the way to Tamir."

Chapter 5

It was hard to believe that such a change could take place in twenty-four hours, but the quiet office Sam had led Kate to the day before was now a hive of activity.

Because of the special nature of their assignment, they had been able to bypass the Navy's usual requisition procedures and had commandeered equipment from every available source. Telephones and a fax machine had been hooked up, along with a row of computers. A printer chugged away in one corner, spewing out maps of the surveillance grid and the course each boat would take. Uniformed men and women, some from the navy, some from the Montebellan police, moved purposefully at their tasks.

The unconventional fleet was already taking shape. In order to keep the operation from the public, only members of the Montebellan police had been asked for the use of their private vessels. The response from the police had been overwhelming. Offers of everything from cruisers to runabouts to sailboats had been coming in all day. As of twenty minutes ago, the number of boats that had been volunteered would be sufficient to cover the grid.

There had been no shortage of volunteers from the Navy and the police to help crew the boats. Cruising the picturesque coast of Montebello in search of a lone woman—and being the acting captain of one's own vessel, no matter how small—was one assignment that had them lining up at the door.

Communication specialists from both the police and the Navy had set up the radio links, assigning a separate frequency for the boats in each grid and for the nearest Coast Guard or Navy vessel that was cruising offshore. All the frequencies would be monitored at the command post so that reinforcements could be dispatched at any sign of trouble.

Unless they ran into a major snafu, the first shift should be in place within the hour. They just had to hope that Chambers hadn't already managed to find a boat.

Kate was still surprised that Sam had gone along with her suggestion without protest. In her experience, men usually preferred to put their own stamp on an idea before acting on it. She'd run into this time and again during her rise through the ranks and had learned to handle it with calm, steady logic.

Yet Sam had listened to each of her points and accepted her conclusion without argument. Of all the men she knew, he was one of the most stubborn about getting his way, yet he'd given her credit for having a brain.

Just because I was more interested in your body than in your mind doesn't mean I thought you didn't have one.

She should have taken offense at his comment the day before, but in all honesty she couldn't. After all, she knew perfectly well their relationship had been purely about sex. They'd been clear about that from the start. Five years ago, she'd been more interested in his body than in his mind, too.

Kate glanced over the top of the clipboard she held. Sam was leaning over the shoulder of a young petty officer who was typing furiously at a computer keyboard. The pose flexed Sam's arms against the short sleeves of his khaki shirt and tightened his pants in a way that outlined his taut buttocks.

He was six feet two of lean, well-muscled Navy SEAL. Broad shoulders, tapered waist and a set of buns that would get the notice of any woman who had a pulse.

She shouldn't be looking, but simply looking wasn't going to reawaken the pain, was it? The attraction was there, it would always be there, but she wasn't going to let it screw up her life again. They had reached an understanding yesterday, and they'd managed to function well together for a full day. The emotions that had been stirred up by the incident at the hospital were once more firmly under control. Yes, they were. She could handle this.

"Lieutenant, I have the meteorological data you requested."

Kate quickly yanked her gaze away from Sam's rear end and focused on the young blond woman in front of her. She glanced at the insignia on her police uniform as she searched for a name. "Thank you, Sergeant Winters."

"Here's a copy of the printout," the sergeant said, handing Kate a thick stack of papers. "We'll be getting hourly satellite updates on the major weather systems affecting the region."

"Good work. What about forecasting?"

"I've networked my computer with the research station. We'll have the latest forecasts the moment they're available."

Kate stacked the printout on top of her clipboard. "Excellent."

"Would you like me to coordinate the data with Petty Officer Thurlow?"

"Who?"

"He's setting up the program for current patterns." The sergeant nodded toward the young man at the computer keyboard, but her gaze was on Sam. To be more exact, it was on Sam's butt.

Kate wasn't proud of the feeling that went through her. She had no claim on Sam—she'd been crystal clear to both of them on that issue—so she had no right to be annoyed at the woman's interest. Furthermore, she had just been enjoying the view herself. It would be hypocritical to disapprove when another woman did the same.

Sam clapped the petty officer on the shoulder and straightened, arching his back in a brief stretch that rippled the muscles in his arms.

Kate's pulse thudded hard. Enjoying the view was an understatement. He wouldn't be aware of the display he was putting on. He had always been comfortable with his body and was completely unselfconscious about using it. It went along with his penchant for touching. He was a physical man, so he naturally drew the interest of women, even one who vowed never to let a man get under her skin like that again.

If you ever change your mind, be sure to let me know.

"Lieutenant?" the sergeant asked.

"Yes, that would be helpful," Kate answered belatedly.

She turned her attention to the papers she'd been given. She could handle this, she repeated to herself. No matter how difficult it was to concentrate, the situation was only temporary. As soon as Chambers was captured, this mission would be over and Sam would be on his way to his next one. Just like last time.

No, it wasn't going to be like last time, not by a long shot. They were colleagues, that's all. She wasn't going to get drawn into a physical relationship with Sam Coburn again. She lifted her hand, her fingers touching the small bulge where her necklace rested beneath her uniform. When they parted this time, her life wasn't going to take any painful twists. She was going to insure they had an easy goodbye.

The Montebellan policeman who was manning the tip line that had been set up for the public pulled off his head-set and swiveled in his chair. "Lieutenant Coburn?" he called. "We have a development."

Sam strode across the room. Kate hesitated only briefly, then set down her clipboard and followed him.

"A woman just called," the policeman said. "I thought you would want to listen to this."

Sam glanced at Kate, then waved away the telephone headset. "Put it on the speaker, Sergeant Chelios, so we can all listen," he said.

Chelios nodded and punched a button on his console. "Go ahead, ma'am. Please repeat what you just told me."

"Hello? Yes, my name is Sophia Genero. I'm worried about my son."

"I'm Lieutenant Sam Coburn, United States Navy," Sam said. "What seems to be the trouble, Mrs. Genero?"

"Armando's only sixteen. He's usually a responsible boy, but he didn't come home for dinner tonight and I just know something is wrong."

Sam glanced at the policeman who had taken the call. "Ma'am, this is a special police tip line. It sounds as if you should be talking directly to someone at—"

"No, you don't understand. He'd been out sailing this morning, and his friends told me they saw him, uh, flirting with a strange woman on the beach around noon."

"Flirting?"

"He's only sixteen," she repeated. "He's a wonderful boy but not the kind a grown woman would be interested

in. It didn't sound right. He went back out in his boat after
that, and no one has seen him since.''

"Your son has a boat?" Sam asked. "What kind? How
large?"

"It's a catboat. Only twenty-three feet." The woman's
voice hitched. "We gave it to him for his birthday last
month. He knows we don't want him going far offshore
with it."

Sam looked at Kate. She could see by the hard set of his
jaw that he didn't think this was a case of an overprotective
mother worrying about a wayward teenager. "Mrs. Genero," he asked carefully. "Do you have a description of
the woman your son was last seen with?"

There was a muffled sob. "That's why I called this number. From what Armando's friends said, she sounds as if
she could be that woman on the news. The one who's
wanted for murder."

The police helicopter swooped low over the headland.
Shadows from the setting sun stretched across the sand and
into the surf like camouflage stripes, making it difficult to
focus on the change from light to dark. Sam kept the binoculars pressed to his eyes as he peered through the
window.

The surveillance net wasn't yet fully in place. Most boats
had made it to their assigned grids, but there were still
holes. Nevertheless, he believed Kate's idea for a low-key
blockade by civilian vessels was already proving to be a
good one. Otherwise, Chambers might not have dared to
come out of hiding so soon.

"We're coming up to the beach now, sir." The pilot's
voice came through Sam's headset. "This was the spot
where the boy was last seen, right?"

"Yes," Sam said into his mike. "Can you drop your
speed so we can get a better look?"

As the helicopter slowed, Sam continued his scrutiny of the area. There was a man tossing a stick for a dog, an elderly couple strolling along the tide line and a few cars parked in the lot on top of the bluff. The police were on their way and would arrive within minutes to do a ground search. This helicopter was the first on the scene.

"Do you see anything, Sam?" Kate asked, her voice crackling in his headphones.

"Not yet." Sam didn't lower his binoculars as he replied to Kate's question. He knew she was peering through a pair of her own as the pilot headed along the coast. "What about you?"

"Two fishing vessels, a moored sloop but nothing matching the description of the boy's boat. This could be a wild-goose chase."

"That's a possibility, but we can't afford to dismiss it."

"I agree. The boy's mother sounded distressed."

"I don't blame her. Her kid was last seen playing touchy-feely with a woman in a bikini. Given the lure of sex, a kid that age would be willing to do just about anything."

There was a silence. Sam could have kicked himself for bringing up the topic.

What he'd said was true, though. Men of all ages tended to put their common sense on hold when it came to sex. He was no different. It didn't matter how many times he reminded himself of Kate's disinterest, he still responded to her.

Well, if she didn't want his interest, she should stop wearing that gardenia perfume, he thought irritably. And stop sitting so close.

He frowned. He knew he was being unreasonable. Neither of them had any choice in the seating arrangements in this helicopter. If they had, Kate would probably have opted for a perch on the landing strut. He instructed the pilot to fly a pattern of parallel sweeps that would take them progressively farther from the shore.

As the helicopter started its fourth sweep, Kate spoke. "I see something that looks like debris in the water about a hundred yards to starboard."

The pilot brought the helicopter around in a stomach-wrenching one-hundred-eighty degree turn.

Sam felt Kate's warmth as she leaned toward him to look past his shoulder. "Over there. Do you see the colors?"

Something red glinted on the crest of a swell. Sam adjusted the focus on his binoculars. Red, yellow and blue stripes flowed in a listless swirl on the surface of the water. "Looks like a sail. Fits the description of the one on the kid's boat."

The pilot brought them closer. The rotor's backwash pushed the water into a circle of fuzzy waves.

A long white object glistened in the spray.

"Could be a hull," Sam said.

The object bobbed in the turbulence from the helicopter, revealing a long, thin keel.

"That's a hull, all right," Kate said. "It must be the Genero boy's boat."

"Any sign of Chambers or the boy?"

"Not here."

Sam instructed the pilot to radio their coordinates to search and rescue for assistance as they began a slow, methodical examination of the area.

"If Chambers was aboard that boat," Sam muttered, "our mission could be over. She might not have survived her escape attempt."

"Let's hope she didn't take the life of an innocent boy with her," Kate said.

"Yeah. From what we've learned about her, I doubt if she'd have cared."

''We've got to find him,'' Kate said, startling Sam by slipping her hand onto his knee. ''We can't let him die.''

He lowered his binoculars to look at her. ''We'll do our best, Kate.''

She was leaning toward the window, her frame stiff with tension. She didn't take her gaze from the sea. ''Armando's mother said he's only sixteen. Imagine what she must be going through. He's barely started to live.''

She probably didn't realize that she was touching him, Sam thought. She was so intent on scanning the waves, she wasn't aware of what she'd done.

But Sam was. From his knee to his groin, he was extremely aware.

This was the first hint of passion Kate had shown. Okay, it was because of her duty, not him, but at least it was something. She'd always been a passionate woman. It was good to know his memory hadn't misled him about that much.

He lifted his hand to give hers a reassuring squeeze. Before he could complete the motion, he reconsidered.

If he touched her, she would doubtless snatch her hand away. She would draw herself up in that cool way she had and make some comment about not letting personal feelings interfere with their duty. Sure, she was the one who had touched him this time, but she hadn't meant to. His hand hovered above hers for a long moment before he closed his fist on empty air and turned to the window.

Five minutes later and four hundred yards farther out, they spotted the boy. His arm was hooked over a piece of what must have been the mast. He didn't acknowledge the arrival of the helicopter. His face was drained of color, his eyes closed. He appeared to be unconscious.

''Bring us down as low as you can,'' Sam instructed the pilot.

"Sir, the swells are too high to risk going lower. Search and rescue has our coordinates and will arrive—"

"Too damn late," Sam said. "The kid's going to slip under with the next wave." He took off his headset and got out of his seat.

Kate twisted to face him, shouting over the noise of the engine. "Sam, what are you going to do?"

"Give Armando some company." He kicked off his shoes and moved to the door. "It's no fun to swim alone."

"Sam, this helicopter doesn't have a winch. There's no way we can get you back on board."

"No problem. The kid and I will hitch a ride with the rescue launch."

"Sam, no!"

Without further discussion, Sam opened the door in the side of the helicopter, lowered himself to the landing strut, then jumped.

Full darkness had fallen twenty minutes ago, but the pier was alive with more than its usual activity. Several cars with the black and gold markings of the Montebellan police were parked next to a waiting ambulance. A small crowd milled around the vehicles. As the helicopter approached, a dark-haired woman in civilian clothes pulled away from the crowd and hurried toward it.

The moment the helicopter settled onto the tarmac, Kate gathered Sam's shoes and pushed open the door. Ducking under the rotor downdraft, she went to meet the woman. Kate guessed her identity as soon as she saw the anxious expression on her face. "Mrs. Genero?" she called.

"Yes, yes. Where is he?" She made as if to go past Kate. "Is he here?"

Kate put her fingers on Mrs. Genero's arm to stop her. "Your son is being brought back on a search and rescue craft. It should arrive in a few minutes."

The woman spun to face Kate. "How is he? Is he all right? They told me he was found alive, but—" Her chin trembled. She waved her hand, unable to speak.

Kate hooked her arm and drew her away from the noise of the helicopter. "He was unconscious when we found him. The paramedics are giving him the best care available, Mrs. Genero. Young people are very resilient, so—"

"Oh, God," she said. "This is my fault."

"Ma'am, it appeared to have been an accident. The boat capsized."

"No, it's my fault," the distraught woman repeated. "I shouldn't have let him have that boat. I should have known better."

The boy's mother was blaming herself for what happened, Kate realized. Guilt seemed to go along with motherhood, didn't it? Whatever happened to a child, even an unborn child, a mother would forever be haunted by feelings that she should have known better or tried harder, or that if she only had another chance things would have turned out differently….

Kate forced herself to focus. She was doing that a lot lately. "Mrs. Genero, do you remember the Navy officer who spoke with you on the phone earlier?"

"Who?"

"Lieutenant Coburn. He and I are coordinating the naval search for Ursula Chambers. He was in the helicopter with me when we found your son."

Mrs. Genero looked around. "Yes?"

"I thought you might like to know that Lieutenant Coburn is a Navy SEAL. He jumped into the water from the helicopter in order to see to your son's welfare until the paramedics could reach him."

The woman spun to Kate and clutched her hand. "A SEAL? Like in the movies? And he saved Armando?"

Kate nodded, pleased to see that Mrs. Genero was taking

comfort from her words. The boy had been on the verge of slipping under, so Sam very likely had saved him from drowning. The search and rescue launch had arrived less than fifteen minutes later, but it had been an agonizing wait. All Kate had been able to do was watch helplessly from above as Sam had clamped one arm around the boy, anchored his other arm around the broken mast and let the waves toss them about in the gathering dusk.

There had been no guarantee that the rescue boat would get there as quickly as they'd hoped. Furthermore, a sudden gust of wind could have buffeted the helicopter and knocked its searchlight off Sam and the boy, leaving them to drift off alone into the darkness. They could have been run over by another boat, or they could have encountered sharks. Anything could have happened, and in her anxiety, Kate thought of every nerve-racking possibility, no matter how far-fetched.

Sam had risked his life to save the life of a strange boy. It had been a heroic act, but he hadn't hesitated. He'd even made light of what he had been about to do. Considering the dangerous missions he must have been on during his years with the SEALs, he probably hadn't blinked an eye at the risk he was taking.

What he had done today proved he hadn't changed. He was still the same impulsive, adventure-loving man who had left her five years ago. Witnessing his heroism should have reminded Kate of the reasons she needed to keep away from him.

But it hadn't worked that way. Seeing him drifting on the swells, so near and yet so far, opened a crack in the wall of duty she'd struggled to keep between them. She'd wanted to stand in the doorway of the helicopter and scream at him for taking the chance he had. And at the same time, she'd wanted to weep over the wonderful, selfless gesture he'd made.

God, she was a mess.

"I can see the lights from the rescue boat now, Mrs. Genero," she said, pointing to the left of the pier. "If you'd like I could take you—"

There was no point completing the sentence. The boy's mother was already racing to the edge of the pier.

Armando was conscious and was talking with two policemen as he was wheeled on a stretcher toward the ambulance. His mother stayed by his side, grasping his hand and stroking his hair. The tears on her cheeks glistened in the flashing lights.

Sam was one of the last people off the launch. He had draped a gray blanket over his shoulders, his hair was wet and his feet were bare, but otherwise he seemed no worse for wear. He spoke with the policemen who had questioned Armando, then scanned the crowd. As soon as he caught sight of Kate he started toward her.

She wanted to hold him. There was no logic to the reaction. It came straight from her heart. Her arms felt so empty, it was almost a physical pain.

She hadn't realized she was running until she saw the surprise on his face.

She slowed before she reached him, stopping a yard away. Oh, God. Now what? "Are you all right?"

"I'm fine."

"You're sure? You hit the water hard, and the surface temperature that far from shore would have been in the fifties."

"Kate—"

"Shouldn't you be getting checked over by a doctor?"

"What for? I just took a little dip, that's all." He looked at her carefully. "Why? Are you worried about me, Kate?"

"I…" Oh, God. It was no use pretending to herself that she didn't care. Even now that she'd stopped herself from barreling into his arms, she still wanted to kiss him. Right here, right now. Despite the people who milled around the pier, despite everything she'd told him and herself, she wanted to grab his wet shirt in both hands, haul him toward her and press her lips to his.

Damn it, she should have run the other way. "I just don't want you coming down with pneumonia on me," she said. "We're partners, and we have a lot to do."

Sam rubbed his hair with a corner of the blanket, trying to stem his disappointment at her reply. What had he expected? When he'd seen her race across the pier to him, for a crazy moment he'd hoped she would fling herself into his arms.

Yeah, right.

"I noticed the Genero boy was conscious," she said. "How is he doing?"

"He'll be okay. He got hit on the head by the boom when the cat went over, so he's going to have a headache for a few days, but otherwise he should recover."

"That's a relief."

"Yeah." Sam watched the ambulance pull away. "He was lucky."

"Thanks to what you did," Kate said.

He returned his gaze to hers. Was that concern he saw in her eyes? Worry? Or his own wishful thinking? "It was no big deal. Haven't you heard? SEALs are—"

"Tough," she finished for him. "You mentioned that before."

"So I did."

She continued to regard him with an expression he couldn't identify, then held out the shoes she'd been carrying. "How tough are your feet?"

He smiled crookedly. "No match for the pavement. Thanks, Kate." He slipped his bare feet into his shoes, rolled the wet blanket into a bundle and started forward. "Come on. I'm going to get rid of these wet clothes."

She didn't move. "I think you can manage that on your own."

He had a sudden memory flash of a hot night, with Kate peeling his damp shirt off his body one inch at a time, her lips brushing each inch of skin she uncovered....

She'd been good at undressing him. She'd been good at everything.

He glanced over his shoulder to where she was still standing. She was also good at her job, he reminded himself. "I thought you'd be interested to hear what I learned from Armando Genero. Seeing as we're partners and have a lot to do," he added, giving her own words back to her.

She strode after him, falling into step as he resumed his progress down the pier. "What did you find out?"

"First of all, it's certain that the woman Armando met on the beach was Ursula Chambers. The police who met the launch showed him her photograph, and he positively identified it."

"So his mother was right."

"Ursula wanted him to take her to Tamir."

"That's just what we figured."

"Uh-huh. She practically seduced the poor kid to get him to agree. Promised him more of the same in payment."

"She would be short of cash by now, and her credit cards are at their limits, so that would be her only, uh, asset left to bargain with."

"Well, she used her assets effectively. Armando had agreed to meet her at sunset."

"Was she on the boat when it capsized?"

"No. Armando was the only one on board."

"Had he already taken Ursula to Tamir?"

"He hadn't had the chance. He had spent the day cleaning up the cat's cabin and finagling a way to buy some wine in preparation for what he'd thought would be a hot date. He was in a hurry to meet her and admitted he wasn't paying attention to the sailing conditions when he ran into trouble.''

"Where was he supposed to meet her?"

"At the same beach where they met this morning."

"We have to alert the police," Kate said immediately. "They need to search the area."

"It's already being done. I radioed the information from the rescue launch."

"Oh. Good."

"I doubt Chambers would have hung around waiting if the kid was late."

"Probably not," she said. "At least we know she's still on the island."

"Yeah. Our mission isn't over yet." He looked at Kate. "And neither is our partnership. Sure you don't want to help me with my buttons?"

"Sam…"

He held up his hands. "Just checking."

Chapter 6

Kate lowered her binoculars and turned her face to the sun, inhaling the scent of the ocean as she braced herself against the breeze. It had been too long since she'd sailed. Odd, when she thought about it, that someone who was in the Navy would think she didn't spend enough time on the water. Still, there was nothing like the crack of canvas and the hissing slap of waves on the hull to remind her why she loved the sea.

"Can you take the wheel for a minute?" Sam asked. "It's my turn to check in."

She let her binoculars dangle from the strap around her neck, grasped the top of the cabin house to steady herself and made her way to the cockpit. This sloop had been volunteered for the mission by a retired Montebellan police captain. It was a nimble boat, responding superbly to each adjustment in their course as they navigated along the coast. Although it was equipped with an auxiliary motor, both she and Sam preferred to use the power of the wind.

Of course, they both knew this wasn't a pleasure trip.

The surveillance net had been in place for almost a week now. Ursula Chambers hadn't yet been spotted despite the close scrutiny the undercover "fleet" had provided. When Sam had suggested that they direct from the front rather than from behind a desk today, Kate had been quick to agree.

Professionally, it was a good idea, but as far as her peace of mind was concerned, it was bad. She had found it difficult enough to ignore Sam when they'd been working together at the base. Hadn't she realized how much worse it would be when they were alone on a sailboat? Didn't she realize that sailing with Sam would evoke memories of their time together five years ago, when they'd been on another boat, another sea?

Or was that one of the reasons Sam had suggested this?

Those were questions that were better left unanswered, she decided. She took the wheel from Sam, her gaze following him as he went below.

Like the rest of the personnel who manned the fleet, neither of them was in uniform today. Sam wore a faded T-shirt with a beer logo and a pair of well-worn jeans. To a casual observer he would look like an ordinary man out for a sail.

No, not an ordinary man. Not with those broad shoulders and rangy muscles. Not with that air of determination around him. To Kate he looked good enough to make her palms sweat.

She curled her fingers more tightly around the smooth wooden spokes of the wheel and concentrated on keeping the boat on course.

They were following the eastern shoreline, skirting the edges of several established surveillance grids to verify the effectiveness of the search pattern. So far, they had been spotted by undercover police and Navy personnel at least two times in each grid. From the communications they'd heard on the radio frequency assigned to each area, they had been visually checked out and their progress tracked all morning. It was encouraging. Chambers was bound to make another attempt to leave the island soon, and this time they would be ready.

Sam was carrying two mugs when he emerged from the cabin. "Here," he said, holding one out to her. "I thought you might like some coffee."

"Thanks." She took a mug and eyed it cautiously. Sam liked his coffee strong enough for a spoon to stand up in. It had been an ongoing joke between them five years ago. He'd claimed he'd needed the caffeine boost to keep up with her, but they'd both known he hadn't needed any chemical help. In fact, he used to demonstrate his stamina delightfully each morning within minutes of awakening....

No, this excursion probably hadn't been a good idea at all. She took a tentative sip. To her surprise, the coffee was smooth and perfectly brewed. He had even remembered to add a teaspoon of sugar, just the way she liked it. She lifted her eyebrows. "This is good."

A corner of his mouth curled in a lopsided smile. "Didn't think I knew how, did you?"

"Well, I remember you prefer it stronger. I wasn't expecting you to, uh…"

"Compromise?"

"I didn't say that."

"But you seem surprised each time I do something reasonable." He tilted his head and regarded her closely. "Why is that, Kate?"

What could she say? That she believed he was too stubborn to change, too strong-willed to bend to someone else's point of view?

Well, she wasn't wrong. He was still the same man he'd been five years ago. The differences she was noticing lately were minor details. They couldn't mean anything.

"Did you hear any news when you checked in?" she asked.

"Mmm?"

"On the radio. I couldn't quite make out what was being said. Any developments?"

His smile faded. He shook his head. "Not really. Someone in sector three is keeping track of a slow-moving trawler, but other than that there's nothing."

"Chambers can't stay hidden forever. It's only a matter of time before she tries to escape the island again."

"Yeah." He looked at his mug for a moment, then drained it in two gulps. "I don't like waiting."

All right, that much hadn't changed. When Sam had wanted something, he'd always gone after it in a straight-ahead take-charge fashion. Sometimes he'd have her half naked before she could blink. Once they had been about to leave the motel room for dinner when he'd reached out to tuck a stray lock of hair behind her ear. His hand had lingered on her neck, then dropped to her shoulder and eased the strap of her sundress down her arm. The next thing she knew the dress had pooled at her feet and his shirt front was rubbing across her bare breasts.

They had ordered Chinese take-out later. Much later.

She sipped her coffee, hoping he didn't ask why her hand was shaking. "What was your last assignment like?" she asked quickly.

"A lot dryer than this."

"What do you mean?"

"My team was doing advance reconnaissance. We spent three days in a desert hide."

"A hide?"

"A camouflaged hole in the dirt. Had to wait then, too."

"Were you successful?"

"Yes and no."

"How's that?"

"Well, we confirmed the supply route for the terrorist group we were sent to locate."

"That's good."

"Sure, but we also stumbled onto a village of goat herders."

"Goat herders?"

"Or, to put it more accurately, they stumbled onto us. An old woman chasing after a goat walked right over the hide. She spotted the hole where we'd extended the radio antenna and ended up eye to eye with me." He set down his empty mug and rubbed the back of his neck. "I knew she would raise the alarm if she got back to the village, but if she didn't go back, someone else would come looking for her."

"What did you do?"

"What else? We had to cut our losses and get out."

"Was it difficult?"

He looked at her. "Wouldn't have been, if the terrorists hadn't chosen that minute to come to escort their shipment of weapons."

"What happened?"

"We radioed for the chopper. Made it to the rendezvous with everyone still upright and a whopping twenty-five rounds of ammunition left among us, so it could have been worse."

"At least you weren't hurt."

He remained silent.

She frowned. "You weren't hurt, were you?"

"The bullet passed through."

Her mug dropped to the deck, coffee splashing over her shoes. "What!"

He paused, watching her carefully. "Now I know better than to think you might be worried about me, right, Kate?"

"How bad was it?" she demanded. "Was that why you were supposed to be on leave?"

"I never pay attention to doctors."

He hadn't really answered her question, she realized. "Sam!"

"It was just a flesh wound." He twisted to one side to pull up the edge of his T-shirt. "See for yourself."

She didn't even think about the impropriety of Sam pulling up his shirt, so intent was she on examining his injury. She focused on the skin on his side. There was a small puckered scab below one rib and a long, shallow red mark angling toward his armpit. The first was an entrance wound, the second was the gash where the bullet had torn its way out. "Oh, my God."

"It's almost healed, Kate."

"You never should have jumped into the water last week to help the Genero boy. You could have torn this open."

"I wasn't going to let the kid drown just because of this."

She touched her fingertips to his side. "Another few inches to the left and it would have hit your heart."

"Hey, another few to the right and it would have missed."

"How can you make light of it?"

"It's really no big deal." He paused. "But if you like, you can kiss it and make it better."

Her fingers trembled at his teasing words. She was standing so close. She had already breached the distance between them by touching him. It would be so easy to go further. All she had to do was lean down and she could press her lips to his taut, tanned skin. Rub her cheek across the washboard ridges of his abdomen. Savor the fresh tang of his scent the way she used to when they were lovers...

Slowly she raised her gaze to his. She recognized the expression in his eyes. It had nothing to do with duty. He looked at her mouth, a brief glance that she felt as clearly as a physical touch.

He'd been doing that more and more lately. A lingering look. A flip comment. Small, unmistakable signals to remind her that he was still interested.

She should tell him to stop, but they had worked together

well for a week. Technically he was keeping his distance. He wasn't harassing her. How could she voice an objection without coming across as uptight and paranoid?

At least, that was the excuse she gave herself.

Let me know if you change your mind....

The words he'd uttered more than a week ago echoed teasingly. For a breathless instant she swayed toward him. Her fingers splayed over his side, soaking up his warmth, tingling at the strength that pulsed under her hand.

The radio in the cabin crackled, snapping her to her senses. She snatched her hand away and bent to retrieve her mug. "We'd better get back to work."

The black car glided smoothly through the palace gates. At the end of a curving cobblestone drive, the sun-bleached stone of the main structure rose from the surrounding greenery. The car eased to a stop in front of a gracefully arching marble portico. Instantly a young man in the black, white and gold royal livery appeared to open the door.

Kate and Sam were ushered past a pair of guards who flanked the palace entrance. She tried not to gawk as she walked inside, but it was impossible to remain unmoved by the splendor around her. Sam had been here before when he'd initially been assigned to this mission, but this was her first time inside the palace. The entrance foyer took her breath away, its marble floor reflecting stately pillars that stretched two stories to the roof. Sunlight streamed in from a hexagonal dome of glass in the center, illuminating the huge room with warm shafts of gold.

"Gets to you, doesn't it?" Sam asked. "All this wealth and power?"

She nodded. "It's beautiful, but it's a little intimidating."

"It's meant to be. The Sebastianis know what they're doing," he said wryly. "Ruling Montebello has been the family business for centuries."

"Some family business."

Sam lowered his voice. "You're not looking forward to this, are you?"

"Not really." Kate smoothed her skirt and checked that her cuffs were straight. "It would be different if we had some progress to report."

"Yeah. King Marcus seems like a reasonable man, though. He probably didn't order us here to chew us out."

"He has no reason to. We've done our best with what we have."

"That's right. But if they try to take us to the basement, I'm outta here."

"The basement?"

He winked. "The dungeons, remember?"

She gave him a nervous smile. She knew he was trying to ease her tension and she was grateful for his effort. "Very funny."

"Lieutenant Mulvaney, Lieutenant Coburn, if you would follow me, please? The king will see you in the solarium."

The speaker was a short man in his early sixties. His gray hair and salt and pepper mustache were neatly trimmed, his expression the blank politeness of someone who had spent his life as a servant. He led them past the grand staircase that rose majestically from the foyer. They progressed through a corridor, their footsteps echoing between rows of gilt-framed oil paintings of Sebastiani ancestors.

Eventually, the marble floor gave way to carpet and the splendor became less formal. It appeared to Kate as if they were leaving the public area of the palace and moving toward what must be the royal family's private quarters.

She couldn't understand why they were being shown here. If the king wanted a progress report, shouldn't they have been meeting in a more official setting?

Their escort halted in front of a set of ornately carved

arched wooden doors. Voices drifted faintly from the other side, along with the fretful cries of…a baby.

Kate looked around quickly. No. There must be some mistake. This butler had brought them to the wrong room and—

The doors parted to reveal a blaze of sunshine. The far walls of the room were all windows. Long, lush cream-colored couches and chairs were arranged to take advantage of the view of the garden and the ocean beyond. It was a beautiful, airy room, as splendid as any of the others she'd glimpsed on their route through the palace, but this one was obviously designed for living.

Several people were gathered, including King Marcus and Queen Gwendolyn. No one had noticed Kate and Sam's arrival. Everyone's attention was focused on Prince Lucas as he awkwardly tried to comfort the baby who fussed in his arms.

Unconsciously, Kate lifted her hand to the place where her butterfly charm rested under her uniform. She would have preferred being reprimanded for her lack of progress. She didn't want to be here to witness this. It had nothing to do with her duty.

"Poor bastard," Sam muttered, dipping his head close to Kate's. "He still looks like he's been hit by a truck."

She and Sam were standing just inside the doors, but even from this distance Kate could see what Sam meant. Lucas's chiseled, aristocratic features were as tense as they had been a week ago when she'd seen him in the hospital. His dark hair lay in crooked furrows, as if he'd been raking it with his fingers. Although his shoes were polished and his pants were neatly pressed, his tailored shirt was misbuttoned.

"Fatherhood is going to take some adjustment for him," she said, keeping her voice low so they wouldn't be overheard. Still, considering the noise the baby was making, nothing short of a shout would be noticed. "Until this last year, when his plane crash and the business with Jessica happened, he was reputed to be a real playboy.''

''He must have enjoyed his freedom.''

''A lot of men do.'' She shifted her scrutiny to Sam, unable to stop the past from tangling with the present. ''That's probably why he left, so he could live the life he'd planned.'' *Like you,* she added silently.

''Why would you assume that?'' Sam asked. ''I heard he had to leave. There were duties he had to attend to. He tried to contact Jessica but she wasn't at the ranch where they'd met. By the time he sent someone to look for her, it was too late.''

''If he really cared, why didn't he try to find her sooner?'' she challenged. ''If he had, it might not have been too late.''

''I wonder why Jessica didn't contact him when she discovered she was pregnant in the first place,'' Sam said. ''She should have. He had a right to know.''

''I disagree. He left her to deal with the situation on her own. Why should she tell him?''

''He still had a right to know he was going to become a father. If he'd known—''

''What? He would have gone back for her sooner? He would have ignored his duties just because of the baby?''

''Well, yes.''

Kate stretched to look Sam in the eye, her words a harsh whisper. ''No relationship should be based only on a child. Jessica must have realized she would be better off without a man who didn't love her. She could raise the child alone and give him enough love for two parents instead of making everyone miserable by forcing an instant family on a man who hadn't planned to settle down. She made the right choice, I'm sure of it.''

Sam glanced across the room, then looked at Kate carefully. ''Jessica is dead, Kate. We'll never know the real story of what went on between her and Lucas. Why are we even having this discussion?''

She forced herself to take a deep, calming breath. She couldn't tell him the truth. She couldn't let him know they had been discussing their own past.

There were too many unresolved issues between her and Sam that would have to stay unresolved. That was the only way they would be able to continue their mission...and it was the only way she knew how to cope. ''Sorry,'' she said. ''You're right. The prince's personal life isn't our concern. I have no right whatsoever to judge him.''

Sam brushed his knuckle over her cheek. ''I can see you're upset about this, Kate.''

She wanted to close her eyes and lean into his caress. But that was crazy. It was because of him she was upset in the first place. ''It's a tragic situation, that's all.'' She moved her head back. ''I...got carried away.''

''You were always a passionate woman.'' He dropped his hand to his side. ''Your emotions run deep. That's one of the things I—''

''Lieutenant Coburn, Lieutenant Mulvaney,'' King Marcus called above the baby's cries as he walked across the room. ''Sorry to keep you waiting. I hadn't realized you'd arrived.''

Kate took another calming breath, trying to bring her emotions under control. What had Sam been about to say? Part of her wanted to know, and part of her was grateful for the interruption.

''We've been having a little celebration here,'' the king said. ''Considering the role you two played in my grandson's discovery, I thought you might like to be included. Baby Luke was released from the hospital yesterday. He's been given a clean bill of health.''

''That's great,'' Sam said.

King Marcus chuckled and glanced over his shoulder. ''We don't need a specialist to tell us there's nothing wrong with his lungs.''

Queen Gwendolyn reached out to take the baby from her
son's arms. "He probably has a sore tummy from eating
too fast," she said. "You were the same way." She transferred the baby to her shoulder and placed her fingertips
over his back. "You need to rub right here. That helps all
the little air bubbles find their way upward."

Lucas put a new set of furrows in his hair with his fingers. "I'm interviewing several nurses later today. I'll make
sure Luke has the best."

"I'm sure you will, dear. Just remember, babies don't
break."

"Oh, he's just the cutest thing, isn't he?" A petite young
woman squeezed past Lucas to stand at the queen's side.
Her dark eyes danced as she reached out to tickle the baby's
chin. "Despite the fact that he looks just like my big
brother."

"The resemblance still amazes me, Anna," Queen
Gwendolyn said. "Except for his sweet little smile, he's
the image of Lucas."

The baby lifted up his head, looked around and let out
a loud, gurgling burp. His cries ceased immediately.

There was a chorus of laughter and calls of, "Well
done." Anna took her nephew from her mother and cud-
dled him with delight. She gave a warm smile to a tall,
auburn-haired man who leaned against the back of a couch.
"Are you ready for one of these, Tyler?"

He grinned. "Ready as you are, darling."

There was another round of chuckles. It was apparent
from the gentle swell of Anna's stomach that soon there
would be another royal baby. Lucas backed away from the
group, his smile tinged with sadness. He caught sight of
Sam and Kate with his father and moved to join them.

"Lieutenant Mulvaney," he said, holding out his hand.
"I'm sorry I didn't get a chance to thank you a week ago.
I'm in your debt for your care of my son."

Kate was surprised by the strength of his grip as she took

his hand. For a royal playboy, he was in excellent shape. "I was only doing my duty, Your Highness. I was merely in the right place at the right time. I'm glad that your son is healthy."

"Yes, his weight is almost up to normal, and he has a good appetite." Lucas glanced over his shoulder at the baby. "He's doing well, all things considered."

"That's wonderful."

"I only wish—" Lucas clenched his jaw on the rest of his words, leaving the statement unfinished. When he turned to face Sam and Kate once more, all traces of his smile were gone. "My brother-in-law, Tyler Ramsey, is advising the police in the land search for Ursula Chambers and has kept us informed of their efforts. How is the search of the coast progressing?"

Sam spoke, giving both the king and the prince an update on the measures that were in place to insure the fugitive didn't escape Montebello by water. Kate added a few details, wishing she could give them better news. When they were finished, there was a brief silence.

To her relief, the king appeared satisfied with their efforts, giving them a few words of encouragement before going back to his family.

Lucas remained where he was. He turned the full force of his piercing blue gaze first on Kate, then Sam. When he spoke, his voice echoed with the authority inherited through generations of royalty. "I want you to find her."

"We'll do our best, Your Highness," Sam began.

"She killed my cousin," Lucas said. "And she killed the mother of my child. She wanted to use my son as a pawn in her twisted scheme to get rich. If not for Ursula Chambers, I could have seen the woman I loved hold the life we created."

There was no mistaking the look of regret on the prince's face. As Kate listened to the poignant sounds of the royal family getting to know baby Luke, she saw Lucas's eyes grow misty.

Whatever problems there might have been between Lucas and Jessica, whatever had kept them apart, Kate shouldn't project her experience on them. Theirs was a different story from hers and Sam's. And Lucas was obviously suffering.

"Find Chambers," Lucas said. "Whatever it takes, whatever you need to do, I want you to get her."

Sam dipped his chin once in acknowledgment. "Understood."

"I can't bring Jessie back," Lucas said. "But the least I can do is give her justice."

Ursula sipped her soda, keeping her gaze on the big wrought-iron gates on the other side of the piazza. They swung open as a black car came through. A red-haired woman and a broad-shouldered, good-looking man were inside, some kind of Navy officers judging by their uniforms. Ursula felt a stab of envy. It should have been her in that chauffeured car. Instead of hanging around this tourist-infested sidewalk café, spying on the palace gates, she should have been riding through them in style like those Navy people.

She batted impatiently at a bee that veered toward her soda. This was getting intolerable. An entire week had passed, and still the security at the airport and the ferries was as tight as ever. Didn't these Montebellans have anything better to do? Why were they persecuting her?

That was the story of her life, though, wasn't it? She never got a break. She'd had to fight for everything she had, only to have success snatched away through no fault of hers.

If that stupid kid had shown up with his boat when he was supposed to, she would have been free and clear by now. But no, he'd had to wreck his boat, the idiot. It was a good thing she'd been watching from the bluff and had seen the thing tip over or she might have wasted all night waiting for him.

A stocky, bearded figure moved through the gates. Ursula scrutinized him until the man was close enough to be seen clearly. As soon as she recognized the dark hair and fleshy features, she hitched her purse over her shoulder and wove her way through the tables to the cobblestone square. It was about time. She'd been nursing that soda for an hour waiting for him to finish his shift or watch or whatever it is that palace guards called their work schedule.

"Edwardo," she called.

Edwardo Scarpa lifted his head and looked around.

"Over here." Ursula paused near the entrance of a shadowed alley and beckoned him toward her with a flick of her fingers.

He smoothed his hair, curling his lips into a smile as he moved closer. "Well, hello, lovely lady. What can I do for you?"

He didn't recognize her, Ursula realized. It had been a smart move to trim her trademark blond hair to chin length and dye it black. The hat and sunglasses were serving her well, too, especially with men who didn't notice anything above her cleavage. And there had never been anything subtle about Edwardo. He'd been easy to manipulate before when she'd needed him. A bit of money, a bit of feminine coaxing and the man had been eager to accommodate her. She took off her sunglasses and tucked them into her shoulder bag. "Edwardo, it's me."

He lost his smile, his jaw going slack. "You! What are you doing here?"

"Waiting for you, lover." She smiled and stepped closer, sliding her palm up his chest. "Aren't you happy to see me?"

He grasped her wrist and dragged her deeper into the alley until they were concealed from the square by the dangling ladder of a fire escape. He gave a quick look around before he spoke. "Don't you know that everyone's looking for you?"

Did he take her for an idiot? Why else would she be disguised? She pushed her lips into a pout. "It's just a big misunderstanding."

"You're wanted for murder. I heard the whole royal family wants your head."

She placed her hand above her breasts, spreading her fingers in a way that would draw attention to her curves. "I know. It's horrible. That's why I have to get home. You can help me, can't you?"

"What? Help you?"

"I need to get out of Montebello. I'm sure that an important man like you could find me a boat."

"No way. I'm not risking—"

"Please, Edwardo." She slid her fingers up his chest again. This time she grasped his shirt to make sure he couldn't get rid of her so easily. "We have something very special between us. I've always felt it, haven't you?"

He glanced over his shoulder, obviously nervous.

Ursula dropped her other hand to his belt, slipping her fingers into the waistband of his pants. Without money to bribe him, she had only one option. "Let's go somewhere private where we can be more...comfortable, hmm?"

For a moment he wavered, his eyes losing their focus. But then he frowned and shook his head. "I can't help you, Ursula. If anyone found out, I'd lose my job, maybe go to prison."

"Nothing will happen to you. All I'm asking is that you find me a boat." She wiggled her fingers. "I'll make you glad you did."

Roughly he yanked away from her touch. "No. I'm sorry. I can't help you."

"You did before."

"That was different."

"You helped me get into the palace. You were risking your job then, too." She narrowed her eyes. "You know, if anyone found out about the bribe I gave you, that could get you in a lot of trouble."

"You wouldn't tell anyone. You're wanted for murder. I know you killed the king's nephew. You saw him that day."

"And who was it that let me into Desmond's quarters, Edwardo?"

"I didn't know you were going to kill him."

"It doesn't matter what you thought. If I get arrested for murder, you'll be arrested as my accomplice."

"You wouldn't—"

"If I go down, you go down, Mr. Palace Guard Scarpa." She watched the realization of his predicament spread across his face. Good. She wouldn't have to seduce him, after all. Blackmailing him into helping her was better. Actually, it was even more exciting to exert control over a man this way. She preened, enjoying the sensation of power. "So tell me, Edwardo." She smiled and took his arm. "How soon will you get me that boat?"

Chapter 7

"Two fishing boats and a seventy-foot yacht," Sam said as he climbed to the sloop's deck from the cabin. "Sector C is getting busy."

"Do we have enough personnel to track them?" Kate asked.

"Yeah, no problem. We've got four vessels in the area. They'll keep us posted."

She hovered beside the wheel, her hand lifting to the gold chain she wore around her neck. "With so much activity in that sector, we should send a spotter plane for backup."

"Already done."

"Sam, do you think this is working?"

"What? You mean the search?"

"Yes. Maybe we would have been better off trying to put together a conventional patrol. It's been nine days now."

He noted the way she rubbed a fingertip over the tiny charm that hung from the chain. Even if he hadn't heard the tension in her voice, the gesture would have given it away. She often fiddled with her necklace when she was agitated. "We already ruled that out," he said. "We didn't have access to enough Navy vessels to provide the coverage we need, and we didn't want to scare Chambers into going underground. Give it a chance, Kate. Our strategy is sound."

"Sure, but—"

"But our visit to the palace made the mission more personal, right?"

"Yes, it did. I wish we'd met the king in his offices instead of being part of that family celebration."

"They're nice people for a bunch of blue bloods. I think it was beneficial to be reminded of why we're doing this."

She dropped her hand and sighed. "I know what you mean. I can't forget the expression on Lucas's face."

Neither could Sam. Even though Lucas was rich beyond most people's dreams and was destined to rule this prosperous, picturesque island, anyone could see the man wasn't happy.

That was the problem with love, Sam thought. When you gave your heart to a woman, you were left completely vulnerable.

He took the wheel from Kate and watched as she made her way toward the bow. She moved lithely, her body shifting effortlessly to compensate for the roll of the deck. It was a warm day, so she had dressed in loose, pleated shorts and a modestly cut tank top. Sam knew her garb was in keeping with their guise of vacationing tourists, that this was all in the line of duty, but he was having a hard time keeping his gaze off her legs.

She'd always had fabulous legs, long, tanned and firm, but it seemed as if they were more appealing than ever. Maybe it was because of all the running she did. Or maybe it was because he was slowly going crazy being able to look but not touch.

He wished he could still be annoyed, but the annoyance he'd felt a week ago at the indifference she displayed toward him had faded. The bruise to his ego had healed even faster than the bullet wound in his side. Too bad. That made the situation all the more difficult.

It didn't seem to matter what she said or how many times she took refuge behind her duty, the old connection was there. And despite her resistance and the demands of their mission, that connection was strengthening with every day they spent together.

She could go ahead and change her hair and change her attitude, but she was still *his* Kate.

"Over there," she called, pointing toward the port side. "There's something dark near the shore."

Sam took his binoculars out of the locker beside the wheel and focused on the area she had indicated. "I see it."

"Was there anything reported in this sector today?"

"A white cruiser moving southeast of our position."

"Then that couldn't be it." She ducked under the boom and climbed to the cabin roof to get a better vantage point. "I can't tell whether it's a boat. If it is, it's a small one."

"Perfect for getting in close enough to pick up a passenger."

"We'd better take a look." Kate leaped down to the foredeck and was already moving to trim the spinnaker when Sam spun the wheel. The sloop responded quickly, the bow slicing through the waves as it swung toward shore.

The coastline along this part of the island consisted of tumbled rocks at the base of towering cliffs. If a boat could navigate through the rocks, there were innumerable small coves where it could stay concealed.

They lost sight of the object briefly as they tacked against the wind. Sam kept them on a course that would bring them past a low peninsula where waves crashed against jagged rocks. He was counting on the height of the cliffs to block the wind and provide calmer water closer to shore.

He was right. The moment they cleared the peninsula, the wind dropped and the waves calmed to lazy swells.

"Can you see it yet?" Sam called.

Kate scanned the shore through her binoculars. "Yes. It's not a boat, it's some kind of dark area in the cliff."

"Dark area?"

"I think it's a cave, Sam. Right at the waterline."

"A cave? How big?"

"Large enough to hide a small boat."

"Radio in our position. We'll take the dinghy and check it out."

Ten minutes later, they had anchored the sloop in the cove and lowered the small wooden dinghy that served as the sloop's lifeboat. Sam handed Kate the sidearm he'd requisitioned, then took up the oars and stroked toward shore.

She regarded the weapon with raised eyebrows. "You're trusting me with your gun?"

"Why shouldn't I? You know how to use one, don't you?"

"Of course."

"My hands are full," he said, nodding toward where he gripped the oars. "If we run into trouble, I wouldn't be able to react as fast as you could."

"Thanks for the vote of confidence."

She was doing it again, he thought. She kept acting surprised when he didn't behave like some macho chauvinist. Did she really have such a low opinion of him? Or had something happened during the last five years to her to make her suspicious of men in general?

Kate was a complex woman. He hadn't really thought that much about it when they'd been lovers. They'd both been content to keep things simple. Maybe it was just as well he had to keep his hands off her while they were on this mission. He was getting to know her in a whole different way....

Who was he kidding? If he had the chance he would drop these oars and haul her into his arms right now. He'd reacquaint himself with every inch of those long, gorgeous legs she'd been flashing all day. He'd kiss her until she forgot the years that had passed.

As if her thoughts paralleled his, her expression softened. She leaned closer, parting her lips as she sighed in pleasure. "Oh, Sam."

He had already dropped the oars and was reaching forward before he realized she wasn't looking at him when she spoke. She was looking over his shoulder.

He twisted on the seat to look behind him.

They had reached the entrance of the cave. It arched overhead, high enough that he wouldn't be able to touch the roof if he stood and stretched out his arm. Carved by the sea out of the same pale rock as the cliff, its walls sloped gracefully to rounded pebbles at the waterline. Sunlight reflected from the water and from the sand beneath, illuminating the entire chamber with an otherworldly blue-green glow.

"It's beautiful," Kate murmured.

"Yes." He faced her in time to watch a smile spread across her face. "Beautiful."

"It's a wonder the place isn't marked on the tourist maps."

"I'm glad it isn't."

"I know what you mean. I'd hate to see it developed."

Sam pulled lightly at the oars, guiding them through the opening. As they left the sunlight the air grew hushed, closing around them in a cool embrace. Water dripped from the oar blades, echoing hollowly from stone that had been smoothed by eons of tides.

Kate craned her neck, looking around in silence for a while as they drifted over the mirror-smooth water. "It's as grand as the royal palace, but in a different way."

"It's hard to believe that the destructive forces of the sea could create something as peaceful as this. It's like a natural cathedral."

"What a perfect way to describe it. It's one of those places that makes a person want to whisper." She set the gun on the seat beside her. "I don't think I'll be needing this."

"A few centuries ago you would have. I bet this was a favorite place for pirates to hide out."

Her laughter tinkled through the cavern. "Pirates? Oh, Sam, you would have liked that, wouldn't you?"

He stowed the oars, propping his forearms on his knees as he leaned toward her. He knew they should be getting back to the boat now that they could see the cave was empty, but it had been too long since he'd heard her laugh. Another few minutes wouldn't hurt. "How's that?"

"I can picture you now, a sword in one hand, a spyglass in the other as you sail the seven seas to hunt down some notorious pirate captain."

"What makes you think I would have been one of the good guys?"

"Oh, come on. You always believed in doing the right thing. That's just the way you are. Noble, responsible Sam."

"Sounds boring."

"I doubt if you could describe your life as a SEAL as boring. I remember how eager you sounded to go on your first training mission to the South Pacific." She smiled. "Was it as much an adventure as you'd hoped?"

"Not really. Aside from paddling around a mosquito-filled swamp with my team..." He paused, struck by what she had said. "You know about my first mission. So that means you must have read my letter, after all."

Her smile faded. She shifted her gaze to the patch of sunlight at the entrance to the cavern. "We should be getting back to the boat."

"How come you didn't reply?"

"Sam..."

"And you sent the other letters back. Why, Kate?"

"It's what we agreed."

He should let this go just as he'd let it go for a week, he told himself. Accept the way things were now and get on with their duty. Why keep clinging to the past when she'd made it crystal clear the past was over?

But that was just it. The past *wasn't* over, no matter how much she tried to pretend differently. He couldn't keep burying this under duty—he'd tried that for a week, and it wasn't working.

Sam caught Kate's hands, enfolding them firmly in his. "Was it that bad, Kate?"

"What?"

"Is my memory of what we shared that wrong? Am I the only one who felt we had something special?"

She tried to pull away but he held on, twining his fingers with hers. "Don't," she said. "There's no point—"

"I need to know, Kate. Am I the only one whose heart speeds up when our eyes meet? Don't you ever dream of moonlight swims and making love on the warm sand?"

"Please, Sam. I don't want to—"

"Don't want to what? Remember?"

Sudden heat came to her eyes. Her features tightened. "Yes. That's right. I don't want to remember."

He brought her hands to his lips. Holding her gaze, he

pressed a slow kiss to each of her knuckles in turn. "It wasn't bad, Kate," he murmured. "It was magic."

Her lips trembled. "Sam…"

"I remember the night we met. You were wearing a blouse with no sleeves that was the color of your eyes. Your skirt was covered with flowers that reminded me of laughter. But do you know what really caught my eye?"

She shook her head.

"Your feet."

"My…feet?"

"They were bare."

"That's because I was walking on the beach."

"And when I saw the way you curled your toes to feel the sand I said to myself, 'This is a passionate woman.'" He rested his chin on their joined fingers and smiled. "It didn't take long for you to prove me right. Remember the first time we kissed?"

She remained silent, her gaze on his lips.

"We'd heard the saxophone music from the beach and followed it to that club. All I could think about while we danced around the floor was that I wanted to know how your smile tasted. I didn't even realize the music had ended." He chuckled softly. "We might still be standing there if you hadn't grabbed my cheeks and kissed me yourself."

Kate stared at his mouth, trying to shut out the memories, but they came anyway. She remembered every detail of that night. She had never done anything as bold before, but there had been something so seductive about the throaty wail of the saxophone and the feel of Sam's body moving in rhythm with hers that she hadn't been able to resist lifting up on her toes and guiding his head to hers.

They had met mere hours before, but they had kissed as if they'd known each other all their lives. The power of it had blown them both away. They hadn't even thought that what they were doing was fast or reckless. They hadn't been able to stop.

He was right. It had been magic.

But it was over.

Gone.

As dead as their baby.

She shuddered as the good memory was swept aside by the bad. She yanked her hands from his before the inevitable wave of pain could follow.

The small dinghy rocked from her sudden movement. Off balance, Kate threw her arms out to stop herself from tumbling backward.

Sam reached for her, catching her before she could fall overboard. But as his large hands closed over her shoulders, his thumb hooked the delicate gold chain that circled her neck.

Kate felt a sharp pinch a split second before she heard the snap. Over the sound of the water lapping against the rocking boat, she heard a tiny splash. She tried to twist around.

"Steady, there," Sam said, shifting his grip to her forearms.

Kate shook off his hold and grasped the gunwale to peer over the side. "Oh, God."

In the blue-green illumination from the reflected sunlight that filtered through the water, she thought she saw a glint of gold. She lunged forward, thrusting her arm underwater as far as she could, but she was unable to catch the necklace before it sank out of reach.

Strong arms wrapped around her waist. A moment later, she was jerked against Sam's chest. "Take it easy, Kate. You don't need to jump overboard to get away from me."

"What?"

"If I'm that far out of line, just tell me and—"

"No, Sam. You don't understand." She tipped her head

to look at him. "I lost my necklace. It must have broken when you caught me."

His eyebrows angled together. He looked at her neck. "Do you mean that gold chain with the little butterfly you always wear?"

"Yes, I..." She was shaken to hear him describe it so casually. "I didn't realize you'd noticed it."

"I notice everything about you." He touched his fingertips to the side of her throat. "I can see the line the chain left on your skin. Damn, I'm sorry, Kate."

To her disbelief, she felt tears come to her eyes. "It's not your fault. It was a fine chain. It would have broken easily."

"I'll replace it when we get to San Sebastian. There's a jeweler's shop near the palace that's supposed to be very good."

She shook her head. How could she explain that it was irreplaceable? What would he do if she told him why that necklace was so important to her?

"If they don't have a butterfly that you like, I'll have them make one, okay?" He skimmed his fingers from her throat to her cheek. "Let me make up for this. Please."

Make up for it? she thought wildly. How could he possibly make up for the child she'd lost? "Forget it, Sam. It's gone." *Like our past,* she thought. *Like our baby.*

He brushed his fingertip under her eye, catching a tear. "I'm sorry, Kate. It must have meant a lot to you."

Yes, the necklace had meant a lot. It had given her a way to focus her grief. It had also been a reminder of how destructive love could be.

But it hadn't been love. No, what had gone on between her and Sam had been sex, that's all.

But he was touching her so tenderly, and he was ready to comfort her for something he didn't even understand. Could she have been wrong not to give him a chance?

No. She'd been through this before. She wasn't going to get drawn into anything with him again. She pulled away and returned to her seat in the stern. "We'd better get back."

Sam didn't pick up the oars. Instead, he toed off his shoes, then reached for the hem of his T-shirt and tugged it off.

"What are you doing?" she asked.

"Going on a treasure hunt." Dressed only in his cutoff jeans, he braced his hands on the seat behind him and swung his legs over the gunwale. "Lean back so we don't flip."

Automatically she moved to balance the dinghy. "Sam, you can't really mean to dive for it, can you? You'll never find anything as small as the necklace in this light. I can't even see the bottom."

"It's worth a try." He touched his fingers to his forehead in a parting salute. "Don't go anywhere, okay?"

"Sam!"

With a movement that was too fast to follow, he twisted his hips, arched his body and neatly slid feetfirst into the water.

"Sam, you idiot!" she cried. She fought to steady the boat, then leaned over the side as far as she dared.

The surface roiled where he had entered the water. By the time the ripples cleared, she could see that he had turned himself around and was kicking his way downward.

Kate wiped her eyes and blinked hard, straining to keep him in focus. Ripples of reflected sunlight moved over his body, becoming fainter and fainter until finally he blended into the darkness around him and disappeared.

"Sam, you idiot," she repeated, this time in a whisper. What kind of man would jump overboard in a cave merely to retrieve a necklace? They were on a mission, for God's sake. He shouldn't be wasting his time with something personal like this. It was reckless and irresponsible.

It was also an incredibly sweet thing to do.

Sam? Sweet? He'd laugh if she told him that. He was a rough, tough Navy SEAL. He shrugged off bullet wounds. He craved excitement and adventure and freedom. He—

He'd been underwater too long, she thought, peering into the depths. She scanned the surface around her for bubbles, but there was nothing, no sign of any movement.

This was the kind of work he was trained for, she reassured herself. He had to know what he was doing. This dive wasn't really dangerous. She shouldn't be feeling so very...alone.

She glanced around the cavern. Without Sam's presence, the grandeur of the place seemed to dim. It was like that with many of the things they'd experienced together. After the night they met, she'd never been able to listen to saxophone music without thinking about him and the dance they'd shared. And that first kiss.

Unbidden, the memory returned. She braced herself for the pain that would follow, but this time it didn't come. She remembered the pleasure. And the power that had sparked between them. He hadn't been sweet then. He'd been hot, hard and sexy enough to steal her breath.

There was a splash behind her. She pivoted quickly and saw Sam's head break the surface ten yards away. She grasped the oars and propelled the dinghy toward him.

He treaded water, tipping back his head as he inhaled in deep gulps. "Sorry. Couldn't spot it."

"It doesn't matter, Sam," she said.

"There are some weird currents near the bottom. It must have drifted on the way down." He turned to get his bearings, then took a deep breath, swept his arms to the side and jackknifed under the water.

"Sam!"

Of course, he didn't pay any attention to her protest. That's the way he was, stubborn and determined to get his way.

Only, in this case, she couldn't find anything wrong with that. Maybe those weren't such bad qualities in a man. Maybe things could have worked out if she'd given him a chance....

Oh, God, no. She couldn't think like that. It was only because of this mission. They'd been together for practically all their waking hours. It was only natural that the old feelings would begin to reawaken. As soon as the mission was over, they would go their separate ways, and everything would get back to normal. Yes, it would.

He surfaced and dove twice more, each time working closer to the mouth of the cave. Kate followed him with the rowboat until, finally, he came up right beside her.

"Sam, that's enough," she said immediately before he could go under again. "Get in the boat."

He shook his head quickly to flick the water from his hair, then grinned and tossed something shiny toward her.

Kate caught it in the air. It wasn't her necklace. It was a flat disk, about two inches in diameter, and it was shaped like a... "This looks like a coin!"

"Yeah. I told you there must have been pirates here."

"Oh, my God." She rubbed the coin on her shirt and studied it more closely. "This is gold."

"It's gold, all right. That's why it isn't corroded."

"It almost looks like..." She shook her head. "I've only seen pictures of them, but it couldn't be a Spanish doubloon. Not here."

"Why not? Doubloons were common currency in the seventeenth century, and this area was always a major trade route."

"But the chances of you finding this—"

"Were slim but not impossible," he said. "Like I told

you, there are some weird currents near the bottom. They could have shifted the sand enough to expose the coin today and then bury it again tomorrow.''

''I suppose so.''

''There's probably more down there. I could go take another look and—''

''Don't you dare do another dive.''

He kicked his feet lazily to keep himself upright in the water. His gaze gleamed like the gold in her palm. ''Why not?''

Because you worried me, she thought. *Because I want you with me…even though I don't want you with me.* ''Because our mission doesn't include a salvage operation,'' she replied. ''We can tell the people at the Royal Montebellan Museum about this find. They'll take it from there.''

''Where's your sense of adventure?''

''You're the one who always has to go after the next adventure, not me,'' she said, her tone harsher than she had intended.

His smile disappeared. ''I'm sorry about upsetting you earlier, Kate.''

''It's all right. Let's just forget it, okay?''

''No, we can't forget it. That's the whole point. We've been trying to pretend that our past didn't happen, and it's not working.''

He was right, she thought. It wasn't working. But that only meant they had to try harder. ''We're on a mission, and you're in the water. I don't think this is the time or place for a discussion, Sam.''

''Then what is?''

''Would you just get in the dinghy now, Lieutenant Coburn?''

He watched her in silence for a moment before he clamped his hands over the gunwale. ''Better lean back.''

Just as she'd done when he went in, Kate leaned over

the opposite side to help balance his weight. He kicked hard to heave his upper body out of the water, then hooked one knee over the side of the boat and rolled smoothly inside.

The dinghy was designed to accommodate two people easily, but it suddenly seemed too small. Kate returned to her seat in the stern and tried to do what she'd done for a week. She tried to ignore the six feet two of ruggedly handsome male in front of her.

But as Sam had said moments ago, it wasn't working.

"Kate…"

She held up a palm. "Please, Sam. We've said more than enough. Let's just get back to the boat."

This time he didn't argue. He slicked the water from his chest and arms with his palms, completely unselfconscious about being half-naked. Without another word he took the oars, spun the dinghy around to point out of the cavern and rowed across the cove to their anchored sloop.

The moment they had secured the lifeboat over the stern and stowed their gear, Kate headed for the cabin. But before she could reach the cockpit Sam stopped her with a firm hand on her arm. "Wait," he said.

"I need to get on the radio and check in," she said almost desperately. She had to establish distance between them. She had to focus on her duty to keep the memories—and the doubts—at bay. They had to get back to the base before they dug up more things better left buried.

"This will only take a minute." Sam transferred his grip to her shoulders and gently turned her to face away from him. There was the click of an opening stud and the rasp of a zipper.

"Sam! What are you doing?"

"Trying to get my hand into my pocket." He grunted. "This wet denim is like glue. Couldn't get my hand inside unless I opened my fly, and I didn't want to try this on the dinghy or you might have tried to jump overboard again."

She felt her breath stop. He was already half-naked. Now he was unfastening the only garment he wore. And he was standing right behind her, close enough for her to sense every whisper of motion. She closed her eyes, but she could all too easily picture how the sun would be gleaming off his moist skin, how each ridged muscle would tighten with his movements, how pale and slim her hand would look as she caressed his body…

No. It was over. Gone. She could control this. She had to.

"Got it. Hang on a minute." The zipper rasped closed. A moment later he turned her around to face him and held out his hand.

A fine gold chain was draped between his fingers. A gold butterfly glinted in the center of his palm.

Kate's heart was pounding so hard it took her a moment to realize what he was showing her. When she did, she felt a surge of warmth that had nothing to do with sexual awareness. "Oh, Sam." She reached out to touch her fingertip to one of the butterfly wings. "You found it, after all."

"Yeah. I'm sorry about the broken chain, but I think it can be fixed."

She couldn't move, caught by the image of his large, strong hand holding her delicate necklace. Her throat grew tight with a sudden lump of emotion. This was too much. The man who had created a baby with her, a precious and fleeting life, now held the symbol of it.

He ducked his head to catch her gaze. "I thought you'd be happy."

She didn't know what she was. Right now, she was too mixed up to analyze it. She clasped her hand over his and lifted her face. "Thank you, Sam."

"You're welcome, Kate."

And then, as naturally as drawing her next breath, she stretched up and kissed him.

Chapter 8

It was like coming home. Something familiar, something treasured but left behind. Something she hadn't known was precious until it was gone.

Only Kate had never really had a home. There had been a neat split-level house in the Miami suburbs that her mother had kept spotless and tastefully decorated. Her father had worked himself into a heart attack to avoid spending time in it. A home should have been warm and welcoming, but that house wasn't. It had been brittle, the atmosphere charged with the tension of impending arguments. Eventually the arguments had ceased altogether, not because things got better but because her parents had simply given up and stopped talking.

Kate had grown up with one ambition—to leave. She wanted to leave that house and that life as far behind as she could. And so the Navy had become her family. Each time she packed her bags to move to another base, she left that soulless split-level further behind and proved she would never be trapped in a marriage like her parents.

No, she'd never really known a home.

Then why did Sam's kiss make her think of one?

She pulled back her head to look at him.

He smiled slowly, his eyes sparkling in a way that was achingly familiar. Treasured. Left behind.

Kate trembled. Now was the time to stop. She could claim the kiss was just from gratitude. It wasn't too late. She could pretend—

"Again," Sam said.

"What?"

"You did it again." He slipped his free hand into her hair, combing it from her temple with his fingers. "One of these days, Kate, I'm going to be the one to kiss you first."

"But—"

"Shh." He cupped the back of her head to hold her steady as he lowered his mouth to hers.

Duty, reason, memory, everything logical and reasonable was screaming alarms in her head, but she didn't want to listen. She closed her eyes and met him halfway.

The only music was the soft beat of the waves against the hull and the whistle of the breeze in the rigging, but Kate could have sworn she heard a saxophone.

The magic hadn't dimmed. It was as potent now as it had been before.

That was why Kate had struggled so hard against it.

And that was why she found it impossible to resist.

His lips slid across hers in a caress as soft as a sigh. He didn't hurry, yet he didn't give her a chance to retreat. It was an exploration and a reminder, coaxing her to respond.

She did. Heaven help her, she did. She parted her lips, inviting him to deepen the kiss. He tasted of salt from the sea and a dark, heavy thirst that wouldn't be quenched by a kiss. Kate felt his hand tighten in her hair as his tongue stroked hers, and she swayed against him, pressing her body full-length to his.

His skin was damp and his cutoffs still dripping wet. Kate could feel the water soak into her tank top and shorts, but she didn't care. After a week of watching him, she was finally touching. And she couldn't get enough.

How could she have forgotten how well they fit together? His angles to her curves, his strength to her softness was so…right, it was as if she belonged here.

The necklace slipped from between their hands and fell to the deck unnoticed. Kate slid her arms around Sam, cupping her palms to the curve of his shoulder blades and splaying her fingers as if she could absorb him.

How could she have forgotten how good he felt beneath her hands? His skin was sleek and hot, stretched tight over muscle that had been hardened by years of dangerous missions. He craved adventure, he thrived on freedom, but that didn't seem to matter to her now. Not when he was in her arms at last.

He moved his mouth to her neck. She felt his breath puff warmly over her skin as he said her name. She tipped up her chin, savoring the sensation.

"Kate," he repeated, his voice rough. "My Kate."

Another alarm sounded somewhere in her brain, but she was beyond listening. His lips brushed her throat, and tingles raced through to her toes. She felt as if she were awakening after a long sleep, her heart pumping, her blood flowing the way it was meant to. It couldn't be wrong.

She curled her fingers, pressing her nails to his skin, hanging on as her head whirled. He dipped the tip of his tongue into the hollow at the base of her throat. A sound rose between them, a soft moan of longing. She hadn't realized it was her until she felt an answering rumble vibrate from Sam's chest.

He lifted his head. His eyes met hers without wavering. "I've missed you," he said simply. "So much."

It still wasn't too late to stop, she thought dimly. He

wasn't pushing her. And he would never force her. That's just the kind of man he was. Straightforward and honest. Responsible. Stubborn.

Tender. Sweet.

She parted her lips, but the lie wouldn't come. "I've missed you, too, Sam."

The corners of his eyes crinkled with the beginning of a smile. But then he dropped his gaze, and his smile froze. "You're wet."

"I'll dry off. It's warm and…" Her words trailed off as she followed his gaze. Water had seeped into her cotton tank top. The once modest garment clung to her breasts, clearly outlining her erect nipples.

She watched him bring his hand between their bodies, and her knees went weak. He spread his fingers, holding his palm a whisper away from one straining peak.

No, don't, she thought. *If you touch me now we won't be able to go back.*

A tremor shook his fingers. His chest vibrated with another rumbling moan.

She looked up and found his gaze on her face. His smile was gone. His eyes glowed with an intensity that gave her no chance to hide. Even in the sunshine that poured on the deck she felt the heat from his hand. She couldn't breathe as every nerve strained toward him, yearning for the moment when he would close the gap.

Yes, oh, yes, she cried silently. *Please, Sam, if you don't touch me now…*

He closed his hand over her breast.

Kate was unable to stop her soft gasp of pleasure. It had been so long. She had forgotten how good this felt.

No, she hadn't forgotten, she had chosen not to remember.

He rubbed his palm across her nipple. The soft friction of the wet shirt over her sensitive flesh made it swell more.

She locked her hands behind his neck, arching her back and shamelessly lifting herself more fully into his caress.

He cupped her breast boldly, lifting, squeezing, driving her mad. With a groan, he curled himself over her body and fitted his mouth to hers.

There was nothing coaxing about this kiss. He took her lips with swift certainty. His tongue plunged inside, demanding a response. She gave it, matching him stroke for stroke. Needs that she'd believed had died were blossoming. She wasn't merely awakening, she was coming alive.

It was wonderful. Glorious. She couldn't think why she had fought it so long. Then she stopped thinking altogether and raked her fingers over his naked back.

Sam shifted, bracing his legs apart and wrapping his arms around her waist as he drew her more firmly against him. The position brought their hips together. Beneath the cool, wet denim he was hot and hard.

Kate hooked her foot behind his leg to improve the fit.

She didn't know how they ended up on the deck. One moment they were standing, the next they were on their sides, their legs entwined, their feet halfway down the companionway, their hands everywhere they could reach. She pushed Sam to his back and climbed on top of him, pressing kisses to his chest. She paused only long enough to help him yank her tank top over her head and get rid of her bra before she fell on him greedily.

He tasted the same, she discovered, running her tongue down the center of his six-pack abs. The years had honed his body to perfection. He had a few new scars, a small ridge of white skin to the left of his navel and a long curving one beneath his right ribs. She kissed them both, then did the same for the recent bullet wound in his side.

With a sound she could only describe as a growl he grasped her shoulders and reversed their positions, straddling her hips as he came down on top of her. He went straight for the zipper of her shorts, cursing colorfully when the zipper stuck halfway down.

Breathless, she pushed his hands aside and unfastened it herself.

He cursed again.

Kate glanced up.

Sam wasn't looking at her. He was looking behind him toward the cabin.

"Lieutenant Coburn, Lieutenant Mulvaney, do you read me?"

The voice was faint, barely audible over the sound of the breeze and the gentle lap of the waves. It came from the radio.

Sam sat back on his heels, and warm, damp denim brushed her thighs. He rubbed his face hard.

Kate drew in a breath, trying to clear the haze from her vision.

"Lieutenant Coburn, Lieutenant Mulvaney, please report." It was the policeman who was overseeing the communications at the command post. Sergeant Chelios. And judging by his anxious tone, it wasn't the first time he'd tried to contact them.

Sam dipped his head and met her gaze. "Kate…"

She swallowed hard. "We have to answer."

"I know." He made no move to get off her. "Are you all right?"

No, she was not all right. She ached. She throbbed. Her body was clamoring to complete what they'd started.

What they'd started…

Suddenly everything came into focus. Clear, brutal focus.

What *had* they started?

"Oh, my God," she muttered.

Sam brushed his knuckles along her cheek. "Don't, Kate."

"We almost…we could have…" She couldn't seem to catch her breath. "Oh, God."

"Don't regret this, Kate. It was bound to happen."

No.

"We'll finish this later." He leaned over and gave her a swift kiss, then rose to his feet and disappeared down the companionway. A moment later his voice came from the cabin. "This is Lieutenant Coburn. Over."

Numbly, Kate sat up and looked for her top. It had ended up hooked over a cleat. Her bra dangled from the ship's wheel. She gathered her clothing and scanned the cove. Fortunately, no one was in sight, but she hadn't thought of that, had she? She hadn't thought about anything other than satisfying the need Sam had stirred.

She put on her bra, but her hands were shaking too hard to fasten it. Stupid. Pathetic. How could she have lost control so totally, so fast? She bit her lip and concentrated, willing her fingers to function.

She was an officer in the United States Navy. She was a mature, rational woman. And now she was incapable of guiding a hook through an eye.

Exhaling hard, she finally managed to fasten her bra. She yanked on her top. It was still wet, clinging to her breasts in the same way that had started all of this.

No, what had happened here had started before today. Before last week.

We'll finish this later.

She combed her fingers through her hair. Her short hair. She'd cut it to get rid of the memories. And to punish herself. She should have remembered that. Instead, she'd remembered how good Sam could make her feel.

Something glinted near her feet. She looked down. It was her necklace.

With a sob she fell to her knees. She scooped up the

chain and the worn gold butterfly, enclosing them in her fist protectively.

Sam's hand settled on her shoulder. "Kate?"

She jerked away from his touch and glared at him.

His feet were bare. The stud at his waistband was still unsnapped. He hadn't put on his shirt. His damp hair stood up in finger-combed tufts, and his eyes still gleamed with awareness.

God help her, she wanted to kiss him again.

Kate felt a twinge of panic. They had almost had sex in broad daylight while on duty. And if that wasn't stupid enough, the sex would have been unprotected. She hadn't given any thought to birth control. What was wrong with her? Was she trying to destroy her career and her life? Did she *want* history to repeat itself?

She rolled to her feet, tightening her fist until the gold butterfly pricked her palm. "What's going on? Why was Sergeant Chelios trying to contact us?"

Sam looked at Kate as she faced him. Her chin was up. So was the wall she'd done her best to raise between them. But her lips were swollen and her cheeks were flushed. Her top was damp and crooked, and she'd forgotten to zip her shorts.

For the first time in his life, Sam didn't want to do his duty. He didn't want to be responsible. He didn't want to think about his career or his rank or the struggle it had taken to get this far. He wanted to tumble Kate down to the deck and feel her nails in his back and her legs around his waist and—

"Sam, is there a problem?"

Damn right, there was a problem. "The cabin cruiser they've been tracking is moving erratically along this stretch of the coast. We've been asked to take a look."

"I'll raise the anchor," she said, starting past him.

He snagged her elbow. "Kate, we have to talk."

"Not now."

"For God's sake, Kate. We almost made love. You can't pretend nothing happened."

"We almost had sex," she said, spitting out the words as if she were reading an indictment. "But we didn't. Let's move on."

He stared at her, trying to understand how she could turn it on and off so easily. Had he deceived himself? Was he the only one whose world had just been shaken?

No. He knew what he'd felt. He hadn't done this alone. She'd been a willing participant. Hell, she'd been the one to kiss him first.

"What is the cruiser's position?" she asked. "It may be better to use the auxiliary motor in order to get directly to it if it's upwind."

He released her arm. She was right. This wasn't the time to talk.

They raised anchor and headed for the last reported position of the cruiser. The wind was with them, so they made better time with the sails than they would have with the auxiliary motor. A powerboat with a twin-engine diesel would have been easier to handle than this sloop, but half the vessels that had been volunteered for this mission were wind-powered, and Sam hadn't considered giving himself any special privileges over the people under his command. A good leader didn't expect his men to do anything he wouldn't do himself.

And to be honest, he'd wanted to see Kate smile. He knew how much she loved sailing. He'd hoped getting out on the water would help dispel the shadows that always seemed to be present in her eyes.

She was still the same woman inside—the embrace they'd just shared had proved that to him beyond a doubt. Yet the Kate he'd known wouldn't have turned on him after they'd been interrupted. She would have been as eager as he was to find the opportunity to pick up where they'd left off.

What had happened to her? What had made her so cautious? A lot could take place in five years. Had some other man hurt her? Is that why she tried so hard to tamp down her real nature?

Sam tightened his hands on the wheel at the thought of some other man mistreating his Kate. The idea of some other man even touching her was enough to make him want to punch something.

"There she is," Kate called. "To starboard."

Sam nudged the wheel to adjust their course. Within minutes, they were close enough to the cruiser to see that it wasn't under power. No one was on deck. It drifted like a large white rubber toy, tossed by the vagaries of the wind and waves.

Kate studied the boat through her binoculars, then slipped past him to radio an update to the command post. By the time she emerged from the cabin, Sam could hear the chug of an engine growing louder from the northwest.

"That would be Petty Officer Thurlow," Kate said, nodding toward the squat, dark blue vessel that was approaching. "The fishing boat he's been assigned to has been keeping track of this cruiser. I've directed the nearest spotter aircraft to swing past, as well."

"She looks abandoned," Sam said.

"Yes. That gives us a good excuse to hail her without compromising our cover."

Sam nodded, bringing the sloop as close as he dared in the heaving swells. He cupped his hands around his mouth. "Ahoy on the cruiser!"

Minutes went past but there was no reply.

Thurlow's fishing boat was closing now. It slowed as it reached two hundred yards. A speck appeared on the horizon, growing fast. The spotter plane would be here in minutes.

Kate sounded the sloop's horn. "Ahoy on the cruiser," she shouted. "Do you need assistance?"

The seemingly abandoned boat wobbled, as if weight had suddenly shifted near the waterline.

Sam took his gun from the locker where he'd stored it and slipped it into his waistband at the small of his back. "Kate, be careful," he said.

She looked at him. It was the first time she'd met his gaze since they'd left the cove. Her demeanor was once again all business...except for the flush in her cheeks. "You, too, Sam."

Before he could say anything more, she sounded the horn again.

A pale face appeared in the window of the cruiser. Sam had a glimpse of tousled hair and widened eyes before the face dropped out of view.

He moved his hand over the butt of his gun, prepared to use the weapon at the first hint of trouble.

A few seconds later a young man and short, plump woman stumbled from the cabin. The man wore nothing but a pair of boxer shorts, and the woman was wrapped in a flowered sheet. They gaped across the water at Sam and Kate, looked around at the idling fishing boat, then turned as one and stared openmouthed at the aircraft that was passing overhead.

For a long, drawn-out moment no one moved. Finally, Kate made her way closer to the bow and called to the couple from there. "We saw you were adrift. We wondered if you needed help."

The couple exchanged a look. Then the man hitched up his shorts and shook his head. He cupped his hands around his mouth and called, "No, thanks, we don't need assistance. I think I'm getting the hang of it now."

The woman turned scarlet and smacked her fist into his chest. Her companion just grinned and pulled her into his arms.

Whoever that woman was, she wasn't Ursula Chambers, Sam saw immediately. And it didn't take a rocket scientist to figure out why that cruiser had been moving erratically.

Evidently, Thurlow and the crew of the fishing boat had figured it out, too. Over the open radio link Sam heard rapid conversation, followed by hoots of laughter.

"We're on our honeymoon," the man called, although further explanation wasn't really necessary. "We were, uh, busy and didn't realize you were hailing us."

"No problem," Sam said. "Carry on."

"I intend to. As soon as possible." Sappy grin still firmly in place, the man went up to the bridge while the woman ducked into the cabin. The cruiser's engines started up with a throaty rumble. A few minutes later, the cruiser was skimming over the waves toward Montebello.

Sam waved to the crew of the fishing boat as they resumed their charted course. He didn't share their laughter. If not for the interruption of the radio, he and Kate could have been as oblivious to the world around them as that pair of honeymooners.

He turned his gaze to Kate. She was still standing at the bow, her body rigid, her fingers white where she gripped the railing. She wasn't laughing, either. She looked at him, her chin angling upward in a mannerism he wasn't sure he liked anymore.

The hell of it was, she was right. They shouldn't have kissed. What if he hadn't heard the radio? What if this call hadn't been a false alarm and Chambers had escaped because he and Kate were too busy making love, or having sex, or whatever she wanted to call it? How would they be able to explain that to the admiral who had entrusted them with this assignment, and to the king whose nephew had been murdered, and to the grieving prince who was depending on them to capture his lover's killer?

Sam ground his teeth. All right, fine. They were still on a mission, but as far as he was concerned, the mission parameters had just changed. He'd keep his hands off Kate while they were on duty, but that didn't extend to their off-duty hours.

There was no going back now for either of them. He wouldn't let her.

Chapter 9

One foot in front of the other. Breathe in, breathe out. Simple, basic, mindless motion. Kate listened to the slap of her running shoes on cobblestone and the rhythmic rush of her pulse and waited for the calm that usually came over her by this point in her run.

It didn't happen. Despite working twelve hours straight at the command post today and pushing her body near its limit tonight, she couldn't empty her mind. She couldn't leave this tension behind. All she could think of was the taste of Sam's kiss yesterday, the feel of the deck beneath her back and his weight on top of her.

Once again, the past tangled with the present. She remembered their last night on the sailboat they had rented. They'd used the foredeck then. There had been more room. They'd propped their backs against the cabin house and watched the stars come out. Then Sam had taken her clothes off one item at a time and shown her new stars, whole constellations that weren't in the sky.

That had been magic, too.

She pushed her pace up a notch.

"Hi. Mind if I keep you company?"

She snapped her head toward the voice. A male figure jogged toward her from the darkened alley she had just passed. For a large man he moved silently, his tread as easy as a loping predator's, leashed power in every line of his body.

She would have known who it was even if she hadn't recognized his voice. Only one man she knew had a body that could move like that.

Damn him, damn him. The silent curse matched the beat of her footsteps. This had been her last refuge, her escape, her time to herself. Now he'd intruded on this, as well. "What are you doing here, Sam?" she demanded.

He caught up to her and adjusted his pace to hers. "Enjoying the evening."

"Sam…"

"This breeze is a nice change from the heat we had today. I've heard it's been unseasonably warm for October lately. Have you noticed that?"

"Yes, it's been warmer than usual."

"We're bound to get a weather change soon. Might as well enjoy it while we can."

How could he be making small talk when her painstakingly constructed world was teetering around her? "Sam, did you deliberately follow me?"

"Absolutely. How else would I have found you?"

His ready answer struck her speechless for a moment. She hadn't expected such a blatant admission.

"Why didn't you want to go out with our fleet today?" he asked.

"I had other things to catch up on at the command post."

"You missed the meeting with the police chief."

"I was busy. I thought you could handle that by yourself."

"Uh-huh. I looked for you when I got back to the base, but you'd already left. We're partners, Kate. You can't keep avoiding me."

She hated it when he was right. "Has there been a development?"

"Not with Chambers, no, but I thought you'd like to know I took the coin I found yesterday to the Montebellan Museum."

"Oh. What did they say?"

"It's a Spanish doubloon, just like you thought."

"Is anyone from the museum going to investigate the cave?"

"I gave the location to the antiquities coordinator. He said old coins have been turning up around the coast for years, so finding one wasn't that unusual, but he'll pass the information on to the university anyway. They'll probably send some graduate students out to investigate."

"Sometimes it's better to let the past stay buried," she muttered.

"Ah, but sometimes with a little persistence one finds a lost treasure. You're in great shape, you know. When did you take up jogging?"

When? As soon as her body had recovered sufficiently from her miscarriage, that's when. "A while ago."

"It shows. Your legs are fantastic." He turned and ran backward in front of her as he looked at her appreciatively. "But you already know I'm a leg man."

"Sam, I think we should change the subject."

He fell in by her side as the street curved up a tree-lined hill. "Why? I like the subject of your legs. But if you like, we can talk about those dimples you have right below the small of your back above the place where—"

"Sam, stop it."

"Why?"

"I thought we agreed that we wouldn't..." She paused. "We agreed to leave the past alone."

"That agreement expired the second you kissed me, and you know it."

"Then we'll make a new agreement."

"Okay. We won't kiss while we're on duty."

"Sam—"

"That will be oh-seven-hundred tomorrow. By my reckoning that leaves us almost ten hours to find an opportunity to kiss again."

"This is ridiculous. I'm not going to schedule anything like that."

"You're right. It's better to be spontaneous." He grabbed her hand, using her momentum to whirl her into his arms. With three strides he left the road and backed them both into the shadow of a tree.

"Sam!"

He smothered her protest with a swift, hard kiss.

She flattened her palms on his chest, intending to push him away. But then his mouth softened, moving with gentle, teasing nips that made her lift her face to follow him.

He smiled against her lips and pressed closer until her back came up against the tree.

Oh, damn him, damn him. This time the curse kept pace with the pulse she felt pounding in her ears. How could he do this so effortlessly? One touch, one kiss, and her resolve simply crumbled. She turned her head and gulped for air, trying to clear her mind.

He ran his thumb along her lower lip. "I said I wanted to kiss you first, remember?"

She also remembered how she'd told herself to stop...and she vividly remembered what had happened when they hadn't. She clasped the tree trunk behind her and used it to lever herself out of his embrace. "I have no intention of picking up where we left off yesterday, Sam."

"That's okay. I'll enjoy starting from the beginning."

She shook her head and turned toward the street. She had put half a block between them before she heard the light pad of his footsteps behind her. He moved to her side and matched his stride to hers, seemingly content to continue the run in silence.

But he didn't have to say anything to make her aware of him. She heard his breathing. She inhaled his scent. She could still taste his kiss on her lips. She even imagined she could feel the warmth that was coming off his body.

They left the cobblestone streets behind as they reached the road that led to the naval base. Although traffic was sparse at this hour, they kept to the side of the pavement. They were less than a mile from the base when Sam finally spoke again. "Do you remember that restaurant we used to go to in the Keys?" he asked. "The one with the fishing net that was hung from the ceiling?"

Yes, she remembered. They'd liked to eat at one particular table in the corner because it had been private, but the net had drooped low over that spot. Sam had tangled with it on more than one occasion, usually because he wasn't paying attention to his surroundings—he was too focused on getting them to someplace even more private.

"I kept whacking my head into the edge of the net every time I stood up, remember?"

"Vaguely. What about it?"

"I found a restaurant west of the base that does seafood almost as good."

"The Flying Jib?"

"That's right. Do you know it?"

"I've heard of it. It's very popular."

"But you haven't been there?"

"No, I—" She stopped herself from explaining. As a

rule, she kept herself too busy to socialize much. Oh, she had made plenty of friends at the various postings she'd had, but lately most of her off-duty hours seemed to be taken up with solitary runs or studying naval regulations.

Why was that? She used to enjoy going out and having fun whenever she could. It had been another way to escape that soulless house in the suburbs. All that had changed after her miscarriage. At first she'd been too depressed to think about fun. Then she'd turned all her energy toward her career. And there was nothing wrong with that. She'd achieved the independent, successful life she'd wanted.

That is, it was what she'd wanted until last week when she'd held that infant and she'd seen Sam's face again. It was all she'd thought she'd needed until she'd felt herself come alive with Sam's kiss.

Damn him.

"Would you like to have dinner with me there tomorrow?"

"That wouldn't be a good idea, Sam."

"We'll be off-duty. You need to eat sometime."

"Thanks, but I'll pass."

"What are you running from, Kate?"

"I don't know what you're talking about."

"It must be something big to have made you want to bury the woman I remember."

"I'm not running from anything, Sam. I'm jogging. It's a form of exercise. Many people do it."

"Sure, but you run as if you're trying to get away from something," he persisted. "What is it? What happened, Kate?"

He was too perceptive. Yes, she ran to escape. She ran from her past, her memories and her guilt. But Sam kept stirring them up, making her think about them when she'd done just fine for five years by keeping them buried. She quickened her pace, hoping the increased demand for oxygen would make it too difficult for him to talk.

He stayed by her side effortlessly. "See? You're doing it now."

She didn't reply because he was right.

"Was it a man, Kate? Did he hurt you? Is that why you try to bottle up your passion?"

The irony of Sam asking her questions like these might have made her laugh if she'd had the breath left for it.

"Because I know you're still the same inside," he continued. "I felt it when we kissed on the boat."

"That was a mistake."

"No, it wasn't, although I admit the timing could have been better. That's why we need to talk."

"You pick the worst times to have these conversations, Sam."

"Then have dinner with me tomorrow. Talk to me then."

"No, thanks."

"Lunch?"

"No."

"Breakfast?"

"Sam..."

A horn blared behind them. Kate automatically moved closer to the side of the road. A military jeep drove past, but instead of continuing toward the base, it screeched to a stop a dozen yards ahead of them. A large man jumped out and began to approach.

Kate had already slowed her pace when Sam extended his arm in front of her, blocking her path. He spoke low and fast, all traces of warmth gone from his voice. "Stay behind me until we see what's going on."

She leaned over and braced her hands on her knees, breathing deeply a few times to catch her breath. "Sam, I can take care of myself."

"Humor me, okay?"

The man was larger than Sam, possessing the solid build of a linebacker, yet despite his size he moved with the cat-footed grace of a martial arts expert. Kate straightened and watched him warily, but the closer he came, the more Sam relaxed.

The stranger passed beneath the pool of light from a streetlight, revealing a thick thatch of red hair. "Hey, there," he called. "Maybe you could help me out. I'm looking for a buddy of mine. Heard I could find him around here."

Sam crossed his arms and waited, an odd expression on his face.

"You'll recognize him if you see him," the man continued. He didn't stop until he was standing toe to toe with Sam. "Real ugly character. Puny, too. Owes me money."

"I take offense at that, Reilly," Sam said.

"Oh, yeah? Which part?"

"I paid you back that fifty I borrowed a month ago."

The tall man laughed and gave Sam a slap on the back that would have knocked a smaller man down. "How's it going, Coburn? Still breathing through that bullet hole in your side?"

Sam broke into a smile and clasped the man's shoulder while he shook his hand. "Nope. Using my gills instead." Sam stepped aside and turned to Kate. "Kate, meet Joe Reilly."

Reilly swept into a graceful bow, then took Kate's hand and carried it to his lips. "Pleased to meet you, Kate. Leave it to Coburn to find the prettiest girl on the island to chase. If it was me, I wouldn't be chasing you down a road, though. I'd be chasing you around a—"

"Shut up, Reilly," Sam said.

He grinned and gave Kate a wink. "Come with me, dar-lin', and I'll guarantee you won't be wanting to use those running shoes."

"Chief Petty Officer Reilly, this is *Lieutenant* Kate Mulvaney," Sam said.

"Whoops." Reilly dropped Kate's hand and straightened immediately. Although his demeanor was instantly respectful, his eyes still twinkled with mischief. "Sorry, ma'am."

Kate shook her head. "Don't worry about it, Reilly."

"It's just that when I saw you with Cass I never—"

"Cass?" Kate asked.

"Sure. Casanova Coburn." He cocked his head toward Sam. "That's what we call him."

"We've got to keep moving before we cool down," Sam said, taking Kate's elbow. "We don't want to be stiff in the morning."

She shook off his grip. "Casanova? Why do you call him that, Reilly?"

"Well, it wasn't me who gave him the nickname, it was the other guys on the team."

"He's talking about my SEAL team," Sam said. "Who are all supposed to be on leave, the last I heard. Weren't you in Greece, Reilly?"

"Everyone's leaves got canceled, Coburn. We're assembling here. I thought you knew."

Sam frowned. "This is the first I heard. What's going on?"

"We're using Montebello as a jumping-off point for the operation. The rest of the team should be here within four hours. I'll be briefing them then."

"*You'll* be briefing them?"

He lifted his hands, palms up. "Sorry, Coburn. While you're on this special assignment for King Marcus, looks like I'm in charge."

Kate watched the emotions flicker across Sam's face. She saw a flash of anger in his gaze, followed by regret. A moment later, his expression had smoothed into the businesslike competence he had displayed every day during their mission.

She was sure he would rather be leaving with his team. Wherever they were heading, whatever they had been ordered to do, it would probably be more exciting than this waiting and watching he was doing in Montebello.

Well, as soon as this mission was over, he'd be joining his team on the next one. He'd leave her behind and he'd resume whatever lifestyle had earned him the nickname Casanova.

Fine. Another easy, no-strings goodbye. And all this... disturbance he was bringing into her life would be gone. That's what she wanted, wasn't it?

Well, wasn't it?

Sam stared at his untouched beer and rolled the base of the glass along the bar, making a ring on the varnished wood. Most of the customers in the Flying Jib were Navy personnel. He'd recognized many faces on his way in and had given everyone a friendly greeting, but he wasn't feeling particularly friendly right now.

"You could always request to be reassigned." Reilly slurped at his cola, the strongest drink he ever allowed himself so close to a mission. "Unless that bullet wound is giving you trouble."

"It's pretty well healed."

"Good. Admiral Howe's going to be at the briefing. If we said you were vital to the mission's success, he could make the red tape disappear."

Sam made another ring with his glass and turned his head toward Reilly. "My mission here isn't over."

"Sure, but we could use your input on this operation. From what you've told me, you've got everything set up here. It'll run without you, won't it?"

Would it? Perhaps. The surveillance grid was firmly established, and it had proven to work well on several occasions. The cooperation between the Montebellan police and the U.S. Navy was going better than anyone could have hoped. Sam's leadership wasn't absolutely necessary to the success of the mission. Kate was fully qualified to handle it on her own from here.

Kate. He'd wanted to bring her, not Reilly, to this restaurant. He had been certain she was softening toward him. With a little more time, he'd have her back in his arms for sure. The longer the hunt for Chambers dragged on, the better his chances....

No, that was wrong. He wanted Chambers apprehended as soon as possible.

"We're doing an extraction," Reilly said, lowering his voice. "One of our reconnaissance aircraft went down in the Gulf. We've picked up the pilot's signal. He's in unfriendly territory."

"How long has he been down?"

Reilly checked his watch. "Six hours, forty-five minutes."

"What kind of shape is he in?"

"No way of knowing. But his signal has been stationary for the past three hours."

"Stationary?"

"He's not on the bottom, he's inland. Two klicks from the shore."

Sam listened as Reilly shared the sparse information he had. He discussed some options, made a few suggestions and nodded agreement as his friend told him his plans. The operation was going to be risky. It would require every man giving his all. It was exactly the kind of challenge Sam thrived on.

He felt a familiar prick of adrenaline. What he wouldn't give to be going on this mission with his men...

But there would be other missions. It wouldn't kill him

to miss one. What he was doing here was important, too. It wasn't as urgent as rescuing a downed pilot, but there were people who were depending on him to see that justice was done.

And he couldn't leave Kate yet. Yes, he would leave eventually, but they had unfinished business between them.

No, not business. What they had was pure pleasure.

"We'll be leaving right after the briefing," Reilly said. "Are you with us?"

Sam deliberately drained half his beer. "Not this time, Joe. I'm going to see what I've started here through to the end."

"Right. No problem." He stood and gestured toward Sam's glass. "Can I buy you another before I go?"

"Not a chance. You'll lie and say I owe you money."

Reilly laughed. "That's true. How about sitting in on the briefing with me anyway? Let the rest of the team see that you're still alive."

Sam put his glass on the bar and stood up. "Sure, why not?"

"Lieutenant Coburn?"

He turned toward the voice. A young blond woman was standing near his shoulder, a half-empty wineglass in her hand and a wide smile on her face. She looked different without her uniform, so it took him a moment to connect the face with a name. "Hello, Sergeant Winters."

She tilted her head, giving him a slow perusal. "We're off-duty. Don't you think you could call me Shannon?"

"And I'm Joe," Reilly said. "But you can call me whatever you like."

"Sergeant Winters is with the Montebellan police, Reilly," Sam said. "She's part of the team who is working at the base."

Reilly smiled. "You can play on *my* team anytime, darlin'."

The blond policewoman spared Reilly only a brief glance before she turned her attention to Sam. She dipped the tip of her little finger in her wine, then lifted it to her mouth while she watched him. "Mind if I join you?"

Sam was certain the wineglass she held was far from the first she'd emptied this evening. He gave her a polite smile and took a step to follow Reilly. "I'm sorry, Sergeant Winters, but I need to get back to the base. I'll see you tomorrow."

She lifted one shoulder in an uncoordinated shrug. "Okay. Can't blame a girl for trying," she muttered, moving off.

Reilly gave Sam an elbow in the ribs as they reached the parking lot. "Yup, that's our good old Cass, all right. Wouldn't know an opportunity if it wiggled in front of his face."

"Shut up, Reilly," Sam said mildly, heading for the jeep Reilly had borrowed.

"You're so ugly, I don't know how you do it. What do women see in you, anyway? Do you think it's the challenge? This blond cop, that tall chick you were running with who had legs that went on forever—"

"Her name is Lieutenant Mulvaney, mister. She's not just some chick, so give her some respect."

Reilly lost his smile. "Hey, take it easy."

"Kate and I work together."

"Right. You mentioned that." Reilly climbed behind the wheel and slipped the key in the ignition, then paused. He watched Sam settle into the passenger seat. "It just hit me. Your friend with the legs is named Kate."

"Right."

"She wouldn't happen to be *your* Kate, would she?"

"What do you mean?"

"Kate. The woman you told me about. The one you

spent that leave with in Florida and haven't been able to forget. The one who got away. *That* Kate.''

Sam hesitated. ''Yes, she's that Kate.''

Reilly gave a long, slow whistle and started the engine. ''Oh, man, I had no idea. Sorry if I came on too strong to her back there on the road.''

''She ignored you. Most women do.''

''Damn, she's as much of a knockout as I imagined. No wonder you wanted to stay put.''

''I'm in Montebello under the king's command. Kate just happened to be here, too. It was a coincidence.''

''And I thought it was your bullet wound that was making you look this way.''

''What way?''

''Like you've been hit by a truck.''

The comparison made Sam uneasy. That's how he'd described Prince Lucas on more than one occasion. But the prince looked that way because he was in love.

Sam knew what was between him and Kate was far simpler than that. He wasn't in love. There was no room for love in the career he'd chosen. Love meant marriage and family. Responsibility, commitment and roots.

He'd left that behind when he'd joined the Navy. Oh, sure, he loved his family, but he'd shouldered the responsibility for them from the time he was a teenager. Love meant giving up a part of yourself, giving up your freedom.

Above all, love meant vulnerability. He'd seen how devastated his mother had been after his father had died. And there was no mistaking the prince's grief over losing Jessica. Sam wanted no part of that.

No, he wasn't in love with Kate. She had it right. What was between them was sex. Great sex. Any red-blooded male who'd had a taste of what they'd shared would want more. That's the reason she had haunted him for five years. That's why he couldn't leave her alone now.

when this mission was over, they would... What? Go their separate ways again? He wouldn't feel her lithe body next to his or inhale the scent of gardenias for another five years. Is that what he wanted?

Sam was silent as they drove to the base, his gaze on the darkness beyond the headlights. He'd been too focused on chasing Kate and on wondering what she was running from.

One of these days he was going to have to consider what he was running toward.

Chapter 10

Ursula crossed the room to the plain wooden table where she'd left her handbag, her shoes stirring up puffs of dust as she went. Coughing, she took a nail file from her bag and went to work on the rough edge of her thumbnail. Somebody really should clean the place. This so-called hillside cottage was a hovel. She deserved better than this, but Edwardo Scarpa swore it was the best he could find for her.

She put away her nail file and inspected the dirt on her pumps with dismay. She'd already had to get rid of one pair of shoes because of the blood that had seeped into them when she'd had to kill Desmond. She'd had to get rid of the dress she'd worn that day, too. It had been one of her favorites, but the bloodstains had ruined it.

If things had gone as she'd planned, she would have been shopping for designer gowns by now. She'd be rubbing elbows with royalty at the palace instead of hiding in this miserable excuse for a shack.

She moved to the room's only window, checking her reflection in the darkened glass. Why did these things happen to her? She was beautiful and sexy. She was smart. That should have guaranteed her what she wanted. It should have been enough for Desmond. Yet again she wondered why he had spoiled all the plans they'd had by messing around with that little brunette princess.

Men. They were all the same. Not an ounce of loyalty in the lot of them. She'd thought she'd picked a winner this time. Desmond had been so suave and sophisticated, he'd been nothing like the jerk in New York who had mismanaged her acting career, yet he'd betrayed her, too.

Still, being betrayed by men had started long before Ursula had hooked up with Desmond. It had started with her father. He'd never given her a chance once his darling Jessica had come along. He'd made no secret about loving Jessica best. She could still hear his grating, sanctimonious voice. "Ursula, if you concentrated on your schoolwork instead of carousing with those boyfriends, you'd get straight As like Jessica." And, "Please don't swear like that, Ursula, you're setting a bad example for your little sister." And, "If you don't start demonstrating some responsibility and pulling your weight around this ranch the way Jessica does I'll have to cut off your allowance."

It wasn't fair. Little Miss Goody Two-shoes hadn't had to work for anything. And as a final betrayal, their father had even willed the ranch to Jessica when he'd died. It should have gone to Ursula. She was the oldest. She needed the money its sale would have brought. Yet again, Jessica had stood in the way of what Ursula deserved.

And now Jessica was dead. Her body was in the grave where Gretchen's stupid brother, Gerald, had buried her. Jessica's death had been a necessary part of the plan. How else would Ursula have been able to use the prince's baby to ensure her own future?

For a split second, Ursula thought she saw Jessica's face superimpose itself over her reflection. Soft blue eyes stared into hers with unfathomable sadness.

Ursula gasped and took a step back from the window. Her eyes were so much like her baby sister's, it had momentarily startled her. And just for an instant, she felt a stab of something sharp, something uncomfortably close to guilt.

She remembered how Jessica had been toward the end, swollen and awkward with the last stage of her pregnancy. Jessica hadn't been the favored sister then. She'd been helpless and vulnerable, devastated because her Prince Charming had deserted her. She'd been completely dependent on her older sister. For the first time in their lives, Ursula had been the one on top, the one with the power.

She spun away, clasping her hands over the back of a rickety wooden chair. What was done was done. She wasn't going to feel guilty about it. Why should she? Jessica had stolen their father's love on the day she was born. For twenty-nine years she had robbed Ursula of the life she should have had. Jessica's death had evened the score.

So Ursula should have been happy. The hard little core of discontent that gnawed away inside her should have dissolved. Why hadn't it?

Why? Because her plan hadn't worked, that's why. Everything would have been different if Desmond hadn't made her kill him, if Gretchen hadn't told the cops Ursula's name, and if that loser Scarpa had done what he'd promised and had found her a boat by now. She was surrounded by idiots. It wasn't her fault.

A mouse scurried across the floor. Ursula lifted the chair and smashed it toward the mouse, but she wasn't fast enough. The rodent raced away unhurt.

Ursula stared after it, her chest heaving. Suddenly, her frustration boiled over. With a cry of rage she brought the chair down again and again, striking at the dust-covered floor until the wood splintered in her hands.

A dog barked in the distance. The door to the shack swung open, and Edwardo Scarpa slipped inside. ''Hey, what's going on?'' he demanded, closing the door behind him and throwing the bolt. "I could hear the noise from the street.''

Ursula flung the remnants of the chair at him. "And who's fault is that, you fool? There are mice in here. Vermin!''

Scarpa jerked aside to avoid being struck by the pieces of wood, then hurried to the window and pulled down the shade. "You have to be more careful or someone's going to notice you.''

"Then you should have found me someplace more decent to stay.'' She breathed deeply a few times, waiting for the rage to subside. When she had regained control, she smoothed her hair and straightened her blouse, then regarded Scarpa with narrowed eyes.

He wore a ridiculous black hat pulled low over his forehead and his collar turned up to his chin. During the past few days his caution about being caught with her was turning to paranoia. For a palace guard who always talked like a big shot, he was surprisingly spineless. It made him easier to manipulate with her threats, but it was proving to be a disadvantage. "Have you obtained a boat yet?'' she asked.

"I'm working on it.''

"What does that mean? Either you have one or you don't.''

"It's been more difficult than I thought it would be. I figured my cousin would lend me his fishing boat, but he says he lent it to someone else for the week.''

"Not only can't you get a boat, you can't even come up with a good excuse.''

"It's the truth. My cousin's a policeman, he wouldn't lie.''

"Right. And neither would a palace guard, eh?''

Scarpa didn't appear to notice her sarcasm. "Tonight I went to check out the marinas to see if I could rent something,'' he said. ''But there were people hanging around there. I'm sure they were cops.''

''You've got cops on the brain. How do you know who they were? Did you see their badges?''

''No. They weren't in uniform, but they had this look about them, and they seemed to be watching me.''

''Most of the Montebellan police are watching the airport. Any idiot can see that. That's where they're concentrating their manpower because that's where they're expecting me to go. Which is why I intend to outsmart them and leave by boat.'' She flicked a contemptuous gaze at his hat, his sorry attempt to conceal his features. ''Besides, if they were at the marina, they would have arrested you for fashion crime.''

He snatched off his hat and ran his stubby fingers through his hair. ''We shouldn't risk the trip to Tamir tonight, anyway. I heard there's a storm predicted for tomorrow. We'll have to wait until it blows over.''

''Another excuse. I don't accept it. Go talk to your cousin again.''

''I told you, his boat's been loaned for the week. You'll just have to be patient and stay here for a few more days until—''

''Patient?'' Ursula went to the table and picked up her bag. ''I've waited all my life for a break. I don't want to be patient.''

''What are you going to do?''

She dug through her bag and whipped out a silk scarf. She put it loosely over her hair, wrapping the ends around her neck European-fashion, then took out her sunglasses. ''You're going to go back to have another chat with your cousin, of course. And this time, you'll take me along.''

Scarpa wrung his hands. ''It won't do any good.''

''Leave it to me, Edwardo. I'll get him to change his mind.'' She took out her compact, touched up her lipstick and kicked aside the broken chair as she walked to the door.

Men. Apart from their usefulness in bed, they weren't good for anything. If she wanted something done right, she'd have to do it herself. Mmm. Come to think of it, even in bed it was usually better when she did it herself.

Sam eased the balcony door closed behind him and paused for a full minute to listen for any sign that his presence had been detected. Nothing stirred in the shadows. No sound disturbed the silence other than the whisper of the ceiling fan. Dawn was thirty minutes away. He waited until his eyes had adjusted to the dim light, then cautiously moved forward.

The layout of the suite was similar to the one he'd been assigned—an oblong sitting room with a door that led to a small bedroom and attached bathroom. Like the other rooms in this former hotel, it was decorated with a Mediterranean flair, heavy furniture, plenty of dark wood embellished with carvings and gilt-framed oil paintings on the papered walls.

Sam did a thorough survey of what was visible. Other than the books that covered the desk and the briefcase that rested on the floor, there were no traces that someone had lived here for seven months. No snapshots or little mementos cluttered the surfaces. There weren't any homey touches like flowers or potted plants—it was clear the resident was merely passing through. He had a moment of doubt whether or not he had the right room, but then he spotted a pair of discarded running shoes near the door that he recognized as Kate's.

He slipped the straps of his backpack off his shoulders and moved silently to the bedroom doorway. Kate slept on the left side of the double bed, her knees curled and one arm dangling over the side of the mattress. One pillow was on the floor, and the sheet was wrapped around her legs. The pale nightgown she wore was twisted in taut folds across her breasts. By the looks of things she'd had a restless night.

He hoped she'd been dreaming of him.

An aircraft rumbled overhead, rattling the windowpanes. Sam reflexively glanced at the window. He knew the plane that carried his team had left hours ago, yet he still felt a dull pang at the thought of being left behind. All the more reason to finish this mission—and everything connected with it—so he could get on with his life.

He'd done a lot of thinking since he'd left Reilly and his team after the briefing. He'd lain awake for hours, twisting the sheets almost as badly as Kate had. Twenty minutes ago, he'd come to a realization. Which was why he'd just broken into a fellow officer's quarters and was standing at the foot of her bed while he held a backpack laden with breakfast.

Kate stirred as the noise from the plane faded. Her forehead creased as she pulled her knees more closely to her chest and drew in her arm, yet she didn't awaken.

Sam hooked a small table with his foot and slowly dragged it from its place near the wall to a position next to the bed, keeping one eye on Kate all the while. She had always been a heavy sleeper. He'd enjoyed waking her up. She used to greet him with a smile and open arms as she welcomed him into her body.

But he wasn't here for that, he reminded himself. Sure, he'd taken to carrying condoms in his pocket again like he used to do, but he wasn't here to seduce her. At least, not right away. Not unless it was at her urging. The primary reason for this unconventional visit was to get a chance to talk, and this was one way they could be guaranteed some uninterrupted privacy.

He switched on the bedside lamp, opened his backpack and began to withdraw the items he'd brought. Paper rustled softly as he unwrapped two pastries. He arranged them on a plate, then opened a flask and poured the contents into two mugs. The aroma of warm cinnamon and sweetened coffee drifted through the room, and Kate stirred again, making a low sound in her throat.

Sam smiled and squatted beside the bed to bring his face level with hers. "Good morning, Kate," he whispered.

She frowned, her lips moving in what looked like a silent denial.

"Hey, sleepyhead."

Her eyelids flickered. She groaned, wrapping her arms around her knees as she curled into a ball.

Sam's smile faded. He put his hand gently on her shoulder and found her cotton nightgown damp to the touch. "Kate?"

Her body jerked, and a sound like a sob escaped her parted lips.

It was obvious to Sam that she was dreaming. And from the looks of her, it wasn't about anything pleasant. His hand firmed on her shoulder. "Kate, wake up."

"No." Her voice was hoarse, a rasping exhalation. Her breathing grew shallow and rapid. "No!"

"Kate, it's only a dream. You're all right."

She flung out her arm, her fingers stretching as if she were trying to reach for something. "No—no—"

Sam caught her hand. "It's okay, Kate. Wake up."

Her fingers stiffened. Her body jerked as her chest heaved with another sob.

Sam wanted to lie down beside her and shelter her from whatever nightmare was tormenting her, but he didn't want to risk frightening her and making it worse. He rubbed his thumb lightly over the back of her knuckles and leaned closer. "Kate, it's me. Sam. I'm right here."

Her eyes flew open. She looked around blankly.

"That's it, Kate," he said softly. "Let me see those baby greens."

Her gaze swept over his face. Sobbing, she propelled herself into his chest.

Sam caught her easily, wrapping his arms around her to hold her on his lap as he sat on the floor. "Hey, there. It's okay. You're fine."

Her hair rubbed his chin as she burrowed into his embrace. Her body was still tightly curled, her shoulders shaking with silent sobs.

Sam wasn't accustomed to feeling helpless, but that's how he felt now. He wanted to comfort her, drive the nightmare away and turn her into the teasing, carefree Kate he used to know.

He shifted her on his lap, twisting on the floor to prop his back against the side of the bed. He brushed a kiss over her forehead, then stroked her hair from her cheek. His fingertips came away wet.

Something knotted in Sam's chest. Kate was crying. Except for the times they'd watched old movies, he'd never seen her cry. He passed his thumb under her eyes, wiping away her tears. "Want to tell me about it?"

She turned her face against his neck.

"I want to help, Kate. What can I do?"

Her lips moved at the base of his throat. The tip of her tongue tickled his skin.

"Kate, I know you're upset. Maybe—"

She grasped his chin in her hand and yanked his face down to hers.

Sam could feel her lips tremble as she kissed him. She was experiencing the aftereffects of her nightmare, he told himself. She was vulnerable and still half-asleep, so she probably didn't realize what she was doing.

Her kiss firmed as she brought both hands to his head, tangling her fingers in his hair. She drew his lower lip into her mouth and stroked it boldly with her tongue.

He shuddered as a shaft of pleasure shot through him. It sure felt as if she knew what she was doing. He dropped his hand to her thigh and dragged her nightgown upward until he encountered bare skin. He groaned, digging his fingers into the curve of her hip.

Her hands fell to his shoulders, then slid to his back as she twisted her upper body and pressed her breasts into his chest.

The shift in weight sent them over on their sides. Their feet struck one leg of the table where Sam had laid out their breakfast. Coffee splashed in a warm, aromatic arc.

Kate stilled. A moment later she gasped and pulled back her head, breaking the kiss.

Sam paid no attention. He kissed her throat, then slid down her body, licking the dark spots where the coffee had spattered her nightgown.

She started to wriggle away. "Sam?"

He slid farther down, hooked one arm behind her knees and licked a droplet from her thigh.

Kate made a strangled noise.

He rolled her to her back and was rubbing his forehead along her inner thigh in search of more spots to taste when he felt a hard smack on his shoulder.

He looked up.

Kate was staring at him, her eyes wide. "What..." She took an unsteady breath. "How..."

He'd been right the first time. She hadn't known what she was doing. He sighed and sat on his heels. "Good morning, Kate."

Kate rubbed her eyes, hoping for a wild moment that Sam might be part of her dream, but when she looked again, he was still there. He was dressed in black pants and a black T-shirt. The clothes clung to his body, outlining tensed muscles, making him look hard and dangerous. But his hair was standing up in endearing little tufts, and his lips were moist from the kiss they'd shared. And the desire to fling herself into his arms was the most dangerous thing of all.

"You had a nightmare," he said when she didn't respond. "I was trying to help."

Yes, she knew she'd had a nightmare. It was the same one she'd had for five years. She'd lost her baby yet again.

Except this time, it had been different. Sam had been there to comfort her. He'd held her. He'd pushed the pain away. Their passion had sent the dream in another direction altogether. And just as when they'd kissed on the boat, she'd felt herself come alive…

"What was it about?" he asked.

She had another wild moment. For the only time since she'd held his first letter to her in one hand and her pregnancy test results in the other, she wanted to tell him everything. The whole painful truth. She wanted to share this burden she'd been carrying alone for so long.

What would he do? How would he react? Would he comfort her the way he'd just done? Would he understand and sympathize, help her to find closure?

Tell him, tell him.

The urge was so sudden and so strong, her lips parted and the words were already rising in her throat when she thought of another possibility.

How would Sam feel to know he almost had been a father? What if he condemned her for the choices she'd made, for not telling him sooner? Would the compassion in his gaze turn to resentment? Would he kiss her tenderly then, or would he turn away?

The moment passed, along with the last of her grogginess. She looked around. "What are you doing here, Sam? How did you get in?"

"Second question first." He motioned toward the sitting room with a tilt of his head. "I climbed up the balconies on the side of the building until I got to yours, then let myself in through the window."

"You *what?* This is the fifth floor."

"Yeah, I noticed. My quarters are on the third. Don't worry, nobody saw me."

"Why would you—"

"Which brings us to your first question," he said. He looked behind him, then reached for something on a small table, the table that used to be beside the wall. "I brought you breakfast, like we agreed."

"I never agreed to anything of the sort."

"Sure you did. Yesterday you refused my invitation to dinner and lunch, but I distinctly remember that you didn't turn me down for breakfast."

"Sam…"

"Yes, that's exactly what you said yesterday when I asked." He brought his arm forward. He was holding a rose. "Sorry if this is looking crushed. I had it in my pack. It was under the pastries. I don't know what they're called, but they look as if they're mostly butter and sugar. All the major food groups."

She must still be dreaming. This was unreal.

He leaned over to put the rose in her palm. "Don't worry, it doesn't have any thorns."

"But—"

"I'm not sure how much coffee's left." He smiled. "But from what I sampled, it's pretty good."

Heat flooded her cheeks as she remembered how he'd cleaned up the coffee that had splashed on her. That part had definitely been too real for a dream. Her body still tingled in the spots where he'd kissed her. With her free hand she grabbed the hem of her nightgown and tugged it over her knees. "Sam, you shouldn't be here."

"I'm glad I was. That was some nightmare you were having." He stroked his knuckle down her cheek, his smile softening. "How are you feeling?"

She clenched her jaw at the urge to lean into his caress. "Fine, thank you."

"No, you're not. You were crying."

"It was just a bad dream. They happen to everyone. Forget it."

Before she could voice a protest, he slipped one arm under her knees and the other behind her back and lifted her from the floor. He deposited her on the bed so that she was sitting up against the headboard, then sat on the edge of the mattress beside her hip. "It's nothing to be ashamed of, Kate. I know plenty of men who've been in combat and wake up sobbing."

She dropped her gaze to the rose she still held. "It's not a big deal. Where did you get the flower?"

"You're changing the subject."

"Yes."

"You're running again. You do that a lot, you know."

"I wouldn't need to if you weren't so pushy."

"Am I?"

"How can you ask me that after you broke into my quarters?"

He chuckled. "Point taken." He retrieved her pillow from the floor, fluffed it and put it behind her back. "I got the rose from a street vendor who was just setting up his cart across the square from the bakery where I got the pastry."

"What time is it, anyway?" She glanced at the clock beside the bed. "Sam, it's not even six. What bakery would be open at this hour?"

"A very accommodating one." He took the plate from the table and offered her a pastry.

The scent of cinnamon made her mouth water. So did the white icing that gleamed on the top of the flaky crust. Normally she had fruit and whole grain cereal for breakfast. She hadn't indulged in this kind of treat since…

Since the last time she'd awakened in Sam's embrace.

"This is ridiculous," she said. "You know perfectly well that I didn't agree to have breakfast with you, and I certainly didn't invite you here. Sam, you have to leave."

He broke off an edge of one pastry and held it to her mouth. "Come on, Kate. I know you want it."

"Sam, I—"

He popped the morsel between her lips and grinned. "There. Good, isn't it?"

Yes, it was. It was as warm and sweet and hard to resist as the man who gave it to her. She chewed slowly, not wanting to feel the pleasure but unable to stop. "You still should leave," she mumbled, knowing she had to protest the intimacy of the situation. "This is completely inappropriate."

"Ah, and this has to be the first occasion in history that Navy regulations have been bent."

"Sam, just because I kissed you on the boat—"

"And under a tree, and on the floor."

"—doesn't mean that we're going to repeat the past," she finished.

"I don't want to repeat the past."

"You don't? Then why are you here?"

"To make some new memories." He took the rose from her hand and stroked the flower along her arm. "I've carried you around with me for five years, Kate. You've haunted me. You've spoiled me for anyone else."

The petals were velvet against her skin, as softly seductive as Sam's words. She leaned away. "Your team calls you Casanova. That doesn't sound as if you've lacked feminine companionship."

"They chose the nickname out of irony. We call Reilly Tiny."

"Oh, right. Sure."

"It's true, Kate. I've compared every woman I've met to you and never found one who came close." He brushed the rose over the hollow at the base of her throat. "I never should have made you that promise. We shouldn't have made our goodbye so final. That was a mistake."

"But we had agreed it was for the best," she said, repeating what she'd told herself a thousand times. "We both had our careers to think about. Neither of us wanted anything more than what we had."

"There was another alternative, Kate. We could have stayed in touch. You could have answered my letters. We could have gotten together when we were on leave."

"For sex."

"For company. For fun. For sharing cinnamon pastries at dawn." He moved the rose downward, tracing a path between her breasts. "And I've never made a secret of the fact that I want you. We have a connection between us, Kate. The years didn't change that."

"But we're on a mission."

"What we do on our own time isn't going to interfere with our duty. If anything, it's going to allow us to concentrate better." He dropped the rose in her lap and leaned over her, bracing his hands on either side of her hips. "Look at me, Kate."

She hesitated, then lifted her gaze.

"I'm not involved with anyone," he said. "I haven't dated, I haven't been interested in another woman for longer than I can remember. But you haven't said anything about your love life. Are you currently involved with someone? Is that why you don't want to be with me?"

"I'm not involved with anyone, but that's got nothing to do with us."

"I think it does. Someone hurt you, didn't they? Someone made you bury the fun-loving woman you used to be under your career."

"People change, Sam. If the way I am now bothers you so much, nothing's stopping you from leaving."

"Bothers me?" he repeated, his voice low. "Kate, you fascinate me. Every time I look at you I want you more."

"Sam…"

"Can you honestly say you don't want me?"

It would be so easy if she could lie. She knew Sam was

honorable enough not to pursue her if she said she felt nothing for him.

But she couldn't lie about this. Not after the way she had kissed him. Not with his weight dipping the mattress at her side and his eyes gleaming golden as he held her gaze and her nightgown still damp from the spots he'd licked. She slowly shook her head. "No, I can't say that."

"So why not give in, Kate? What harm would there be in enjoying the special bond we have between us?"

What harm? It would mean disaster. It would mean ripping open all the old pain. She lifted her hand to her neck, reflexively feeling for her necklace, but it wasn't there. The chain was still broken. The butterfly was swaddled in cotton in the bottom of her jewelry box where she'd stored it after she and Sam had kissed on the boat.

That kiss hadn't been painful. Neither had any of the others. Sam's embrace had blunted the force of her nightmare this morning. She'd felt good, wanted, like a desirable woman.

Making love with Sam would be another way to escape, better than running, better than burying herself in her work—

Oh, God, after everything she had been through, was she really fool enough to consider having another affair with Sam Coburn?

As far as her body was concerned, there was no debate. There never had been. The physical pull she felt toward him was stronger than ever.

But it wasn't that simple. The past they shared was the source of their bond…and it was also what stood between them.

She dropped her gaze to the bruised rose in her lap before she finally replied. "There are things you don't know, Sam. Things about the past."

"Then tell me. Help me to understand why you keep pushing me away."

"I can't."

"Sure, you can." His hands closed over her shoulders. "What happened?"

"It doesn't matter now. It's over."

"No, it isn't. You woke up crying."

"Forget it."

"It's clear that you haven't forgotten it. Tell me, and you might be able to stop running."

The rose blurred as she blinked back a fresh wave of tears. Was he right? Did he hold the key to releasing her from the past?

Tell him. Once more the urge crept into her mind, and this time, it wouldn't go away. Her heart pounded. Why was she fighting this? What was she so afraid of? So what if Sam condemned her for what she'd concealed? If he turned away, if he rejected her, that would solve one problem, wouldn't it? She wanted him out of her life, didn't she?

Well, didn't she?

"Kate?"

She lifted her gaze to his. "I just want you to remember that I kept my promise, Sam."

"What promise?"

"Five years ago I promised to give you an easy goodbye."

"I know what we said. It was a mistake. We never should have—"

"Please, Sam. Just remember that I kept my word."

"All right."

"That's why I didn't tell you about the baby."

Chapter 11

It was like doing a night dive into forty-degree water. Sam felt the shock flow over him, freezing his lungs. He stared at Kate as he struggled for breath. "Baby?"

"It happened on our last night together," she said. "We weren't as careful as we should have been. We ran out of condoms and—"

"Baby?" His grip on her shoulders tightened. "You got pregnant? With my baby?"

"Yes."

He dropped his gaze to her stomach. "We made a child together?"

"I don't know how many other ways to say it, but—"

"A baby. Our baby." He released her shoulders and put his hand over her stomach. He splayed his fingers, imagining Kate's taut, firm body swelling with a life they had created. "We made a child. My God, Kate. I have a child?"

"Sam—"

"I'm a father?" The ice switched to fire. Something hot

and primal stirred inside him. It was too savage to be called joy. He felt dizzy. "A father."

"Sam, stop." She pushed his hand off her stomach. "Listen to me."

Kate's voice seemed to be coming from a great distance. He inhaled deeply, trying to clear his head.

"Sam, you're not a father. Our baby didn't.... I didn't—" Her voice broke.

"What?"

"I miscarried when I was six months along. I lost the baby."

His head was reeling. It was too much to take in all at once. He had just grasped the fact that they'd created a life. How could that life already be gone?

"I tried, Sam. I tried to get to the hospital but I was too late. They couldn't save him."

Him? They'd had a boy? A son? He felt a renewed spark of savage happiness before it was submerged beneath a wave of loss.

"I'm sorry," Kate whispered. Fresh tears flowed down her cheeks. "I'm sorry."

Her anguish penetrated the haze of his roiling emotions. Without hesitation he slipped his arms around her and drew her against his chest. "Ah, Kate. My Kate."

"He was too small. They said he didn't have a chance." Her words were muffled as she buried her face in the crook of his neck. "I tried."

"I'm sure you did."

"It happened so fast."

He felt his shirt grow damp from her tears, and his heart turned over. Kate never cried, but this was twice in one day… Something fell into place. "The nightmare you were having when I got here. This is what you were dreaming about."

"I always dream about it. I'm always too late."

He stroked her head, her back, trying to give comfort. A baby. They had conceived a child and it had died before it could live. He felt as if a part of him that he hadn't known he possessed had just been torn away. "Oh, Kate, I wish I'd been there for you."

"It wouldn't have made any difference."

"You shouldn't have gone through this alone. All that pain—"

"You couldn't have helped."

"We both made the baby."

"That didn't matter. I did what we'd agreed."

His hand stilled. *I kept my promise,* she'd said. "Kate, when we agreed to say goodbye, we hadn't known there was a baby. That would have changed everything."

She pulled away from him and slid to the other side of the bed. She got to her feet and shrugged on a silk robe. For a moment she stood in silence, bending her head as she concentrated on tying a knot in the belt of the robe. "There was no need for you to know about my miscarriage," she said finally. "I handled it by myself."

He stood up and rounded the bed, reaching for her hand. "No one should have to go through that on their own. I should have been there to take my share of your pain."

"I managed. It's over. I got on with my life."

Her words were clipped and matter-of-fact, but her cheeks still gleamed with tears. "No, you didn't," he said. "It still hurts, doesn't it?"

"I managed," she repeated. "I was doing fine until a week and a half ago. Finding the prince's baby and seeing you again stirred the memories up, that's all."

He passed his knuckle under each of her eyes to catch her tears. "No, you weren't doing fine, Kate. You don't smile. You don't play. You're still keeping the pain inside."

Her lips trembled. She stepped away from his touch and crossed her arms. "I deal with it, Sam."

"Why didn't you tell me?" he asked gently. "If I'd known you were pregnant…"

"You would have done what?" She took another step back and lifted her chin. "Would you have jeopardized your future with the SEALs before your first training mission so you could come running to my side? We'd already been through the reasons we wanted to say goodbye. You had put off your dreams for too long and you were finally going to have your freedom. My pregnancy wasn't your concern."

"My God, Kate. How can you say that? What kind of man do you think I am? I wouldn't have turned my back on you. I would have taken responsibility."

"And what would that have meant?"

He didn't even have to think about the answer. It came full blown into his mind. "We would have been married."

"Married?" She tightened her belt. "Our relationship was about sex, remember? Simple, no-strings sex."

"Well, yes, but—"

"And you still haven't changed your mind about that, have you? You came here this morning because you wanted more of the same. What was it you said? Getting together when we were on leave? Having fun? That's no way to raise a child."

"Kate, you're not being fair. A baby would have changed everything."

"Getting married only for the sake of a child leads to disaster. That's what my parents did, and I know firsthand it doesn't work. I would have raised my child alone and given him enough love for two parents instead of making everyone miserable by forcing an instant family on a man who hadn't planned to settle down."

Her words struck a chord in his memory. He thought

back to their conversation at the palace when the royal family had been celebrating baby Luke's homecoming. Kate had said the same thing then when they'd been talking about the prince and Jessica.

Only they hadn't really been talking about the prince and Jessica, had they?

Other snippets of memory started to click in his mind, small unexplained comments, odd reactions. Now that he knew the truth, he saw them from a whole new perspective.

"You weren't ever going to tell me," he said, realization slowly dawning. "If you hadn't lost the baby, you wouldn't have told me I was a father."

"It's what would have been best for everyone. I was fully prepared to give up my career in the Navy if I had to so I could provide my child a stable home."

He looked at the way she lifted her chin—damn, he was starting to hate that gesture. He could see her pain, but she didn't want his comfort. She didn't want anything from him. While he'd carried her in his heart for five years, she'd already judged and condemned him. Kate. His Kate.

Only she wasn't *his* Kate any longer, was she? Maybe she never had been. He must have deluded himself by idealizing her memory. The Kate he'd thought he'd known never would have…betrayed him like this.

Yes, betrayed. That's how he felt. Conceiving a child was the most intimate of acts, but she had dismissed his part in it.

"You would have raised our son by yourself," he said. "You would have kept me from my child."

"You weren't ready to settle down. You still aren't."

"That's not fair. You judged me without giving me a chance."

"I wasn't willing to gamble my baby's future."

"He was my baby, too. You had no right—"

"How dare you say that? I'm the one who would have

given up her dreams and turned her life upside-down for a child that wasn't planned. I'm the one who felt the butterfly kicks from a baby in my belly. I'm the one who left a trail of blood from the taxi to the operating room floor while you were off on an adventure in the Pacific somewhere, so don't you tell me about rights.''

Despite his growing resentment, he reached for her. ''Oh, Kate.''

She batted his hand away and strode past him to the small table where he'd laid out their breakfast. She snatched his backpack from the floor. ''I want you to leave now, Sam.''

''Kate…''

She threw the pack at him and pointed at the door. ''Get out.''

He caught the pack by one strap. ''Why are you angry at me for something I didn't have any say in?''

''You put the baby in me, Sam. It didn't get there by itself.''

''That's my point. I was his father. The choice of whether or not to tell me wasn't yours to make.''

''It was the right choice, damn it.''

''If you're so sure it was the right choice, Kate, then why do you still have nightmares?''

The flag in the center of the square snapped in a sudden gust. Kate glanced at the sky as she hurried toward the north building and the office that housed the command center. Clouds covered the sun, smothering its warmth, turning the morning to dull slate. The seagulls that rode the air currents over the base were more numerous than usual today. Their cries sounded like mocking laughter.

The bleak weather suited Kate's mood. So did the birds.

Whoever said that the truth would set you free? It didn't. It sucked you down into a tangle of questions that were better left buried. What on earth had she been expecting when she told Sam about the baby?

She'd hoped for understanding. She'd feared condemnation. She hadn't anticipated seeing his joy.

His reaction had been so swift, there was no doubt in her mind that it was real. His eyes had glowed with the news that he'd fathered a child. And his grief when he realized the child hadn't lived was as genuine as her own. Had she underestimated him? Had she misjudged him? What if she'd told him earlier? He'd said he would have married her. Could it have worked? Could he have grown to love her?

A gull screamed a series of grating jeers. Kate winced.

They were useless questions. Pointless thoughts. Love hadn't even been mentioned. And if the look on Sam's face when he'd left had been any indication, the topic of love wasn't likely to come up.

Why had she lost her temper with him? Was it really him she was angry with, or herself?

Or was she angry with the whole twisted situation? She'd spent a week and a half pushing him away. Now that she considered letting him get close to her again, she'd succeeded in driving him even further away.

But that's what she'd wanted in the first place, wasn't it?

Yes. No. Damn.

She reached the entrance to the north building and grasped the handle of the door, only to have it wrenched out of her hand as it was pushed open. She sidestepped quickly, barely avoiding a collision with the man who was coming out.

He caught her arms to steady her. "Sorry. I—" He paused. "Hello, Kate."

Of course, the first person she saw would have to be him. Give the seagulls something else to laugh at. She looked at the place where he touched her, fighting a sudden urge to fall into his embrace.

But she and Sam were no longer in her bedroom. They were in public, in full view of every building that ringed the square and every sailor who crossed it. "Sam."

"I wasn't sure you were coming in today."

"Why?"

"You were upset when I left you."

"I got over it."

"Kate…"

"We still have a mission to complete, Sam."

He dropped his hands and stepped back.

Oh, God, she hadn't meant to say it that way. But doing her duty was how she coped. It's what had forced her to get out of bed and get dressed on those dark days after the miscarriage and it was what filled her life now.

She moved her gaze to Sam's face. His expression was shuttered. He didn't look like the same man who had brought breakfast and a rose to her quarters and who had greeted her with kisses mere hours ago. There was a distance between them. It was brittle and wary. It made her feel as if something precious had been broken.

She had hurt him, she realized. She'd carried her secret for so long by herself and she'd been so wrapped up in her own pain, she hadn't considered the pain he would feel when he learned the truth. "Sam…"

"You're right. We do have a mission to complete." He moved aside to give room to a pair of enlisted men who emerged from the building before he continued. "We got a call from the base hospital a few minutes ago."

"The hospital?"

"Petty Officer Thurlow was brought in this morning. That's where I'm heading. Excuse me," he said, starting off in that direction.

It took a moment for Kate to switch mental gears. She

hurried to catch up to Sam. "Thurlow?" she asked when she reached his side. "He's captaining a fishing boat in Sector C, right?"

"Yes."

"What happened? Was there an accident?"

"It appears he was mugged. He was found in an alley. His watch and his money were gone."

"How bad is he?"

"He has a head wound and hasn't regained consciousness. The medics figure he has a concussion."

"The crime rate in Montebello is low. Muggings aren't common occurrences."

"So I've heard."

"Do you think there could be more to it?"

"That's what I hope to find out."

They walked the rest of the way to the base hospital in silence. It wasn't an easy silence, but Kate didn't attempt to break it. She rubbed her arms. She wasn't sure whether the wind that curled around the buildings was getting colder or whether the coolness came from the man who strode beside her.

Thurlow was in a curtained cubicle in the emergency ward. A white bandage circled his head and an IV bag dripped fluid into his arm. The doctor on duty reiterated what Sam had told Kate, then moved to his next patient, leaving them alone with the young officer.

Sam stepped to Thurlow's side and laid his hand on his arm. "Petty Officer Thurlow," he said. "Tom, can you hear me?"

There was no response. Not even the flicker of an eyelid.

Sam leaned closer. "It's Lieutenant Coburn, Tom. I need you to tell me what happened."

"He might be out for hours," Kate said.

"Or he could wake up in the next minute."

"Sure, but—"

"I prefer not to assume the worst, Kate." He shot her a look from under his brows. "It's always better to give people a fair chance."

She knew by the hard line of his jaw that he wasn't only talking about Petty Officer Thurlow. And she sensed the rift between her and Sam gape wider.

But she couldn't think of anything to say in reply. She could understand his bitterness. He'd only had a few hours to come to terms with something she'd been trying to resolve for five years. A few quick words weren't going to fix this.

The curtain at the foot of the bed moved aside. The blond policewoman who had been handling the weather data for the fleet burst into the cubicle. "Tommy. Oh, my God, I—" She pulled up short when she saw Sam and Kate. "Oh. I just heard and… I hadn't known anyone else was here."

"Hello, Sergeant Winters," Kate said.

She glanced at Sam, her cheeks flushing, before she returned Kate's greeting. "How is he?"

"According to the doctor, he's holding his own."

"I heard he was mugged," Winters said. "I can't believe it. He was fine when we left the Flying Jib."

"You saw him last night?" Sam asked.

The sergeant nodded. She flicked Sam another quick glance but seemed unwilling to meet his gaze. Kate was momentarily puzzled—Shannon Winters hadn't been very subtle about her interest in Sam. Until now, she'd barely been able to keep her eyes off him.

"What time did he leave?" Kate asked.

"It was after midnight," she replied. "Maybe around one. I'm not sure of the time. I had…" She cleared her throat. "I had a little too much wine."

"It happens," Sam said.

Winters clutched the rail at the side of the bed. "It's

embarrassing. Sometimes I do things…I wouldn't normally do.''

"I understand," Sam said.

Winters gave him a tight smile. "Thanks."

"No problem. Where did you and Thurlow go when you left the Jib?"

Kate looked from Winters to Sam. She had the feeling there was a subtext to this conversation that she was missing.

"Tom wanted to show me his boat," Winters said. "I, uh, left about an hour later. He was still there. He was asleep."

"He was found in an alley near the harbor." Sam turned his attention to the motionless form on the bed. "I'm wondering whether there was a connection."

"Do you think someone mugged him for the boat, not his money?" Kate asked.

"Possibly."

"That fishing boat he had been assigned to wouldn't normally interest a thief," Kate said. "Unless…"

"Unless the thief was desperate for transportation," Sam finished.

"Ursula Chambers?"

"Possibly."

"Where's the boat now?" Kate asked. "What about the rest of the crew?"

"Good questions. We'd better find out. Sergeant Winters?"

She started. "Yes, Lieutenant Coburn?"

"Stay with Thurlow. Let us know the instant he regains consciousness and can answer questions," he ordered. He held the curtain aside and looked at Kate. "We'd better get back to the command center. We can check things out faster from there."

The moment they entered the command center, Kate

sensed the tension in the air. It took only eight minutes to confirm that the *Penelope,* the fishing boat Thurlow had been using, was not in its berth at the harbor. The two recruits who had completed the crew had no idea of its whereabouts.

With each piece of news, a buzz began to grow. There was an edge to people's movements and a hint of sharpness in their voices. It had been eleven days since the hunt for Ursula Chambers had begun. The wait had worn on everyone's nerves. Even if this proved to be a false alarm, at least something was finally happening.

"Thurlow and the *Penelope* were assigned to the grid in Sector C," Kate said after checking her master list. "Whoever has the boat now would be able to hear everything that's said over the open frequency on the radio. Sergeant Chelios?"

The policeman at the communications console looked up quickly. "Yes, ma'am?"

"Instruct the personnel in Sector C to switch to their alternate frequency immediately."

"Right away, ma'am."

"Then get the description of the *Penelope* out to everyone on patrol," Sam ordered. "Contact the naval vessels offshore and alert them to the situation. In the meantime, we have to carry on with the regular search and maintain cover until we can confirm whether or not Chambers is on that fishing boat."

"Yes, sir."

Kate frowned at the list on her clipboard. "Without Thurlow's boat, we'll be short one vessel in his area of the search grid. We need to plug the gap."

"We should have every available vessel on the water, anyway," Sam said. "The more pairs of eyes we have looking, the better our chances. I'm taking out the sloop."

Kate looked up quickly. "The weather is unsettled. The sailing conditions could become difficult."

"It's the same weather the rest of the fleet is facing. And the sloop has a full keel. She can handle rough seas."

"Yes, I know, but—"

"I wouldn't ask my men to do anything I wasn't willing to do myself." He paused. "And I'm not asking anything of you, Lieutenant Mulvaney."

"What do you mean?"

"I can manage the boat solo."

He didn't want her with him, she realized. Until now he'd taken full advantage of their mission to make sure they spent as much time as possible together. His persistence had annoyed her and upset her, but it had been better than this…distance.

"We're still partners, Lieutenant Coburn," she said recklessly, tossing her clipboard aside. "I'm coming with you."

Sam strained to hold the wheel steady as he squinted at the western horizon. Over the course of the last few hours, the weather had deteriorated more quickly than he'd anticipated. Heavy, steel-bellied clouds hung low over the water while their tops reached to block the sun. The sea was a shifting carpet of gray, pushed into restless swells by the strengthening wind. Spray shot from the bow as the sloop sliced through the waves.

Kate emerged from the cabin, fastening the toggles on the yellow slicker she'd donned. She held another one out to Sam. "I found these in the locker under the bunk. It looks as if we might need them."

He mumbled his thanks and shrugged on the raincoat. He wouldn't mistake her gesture for concern or caring. She had given him the raincoat so he would be able to continue the mission. That's what she would claim if he asked her, anyway.

It had been a frustrating day. Even though he and Kate were completely alone, neither one of them had broached any subject that wasn't related to the mission. Yet the things that were left unsaid crackled in the air between them.

He had trusted her. He had believed that they had honesty between them. Even though he tried to tell himself it was all in the past, he couldn't seem to suppress his resentment. He was only human. She had decided to keep the existence of his child a secret from him. She had decided he was unworthy. How was he supposed to shrug that off?

"Did you get through to the command center on the radio?" he asked.

"Yes. There's a major system approaching Montebello from the west. This weather is just the leading edge."

Sam wiped a film of spray from his face. "The fleet has a standing order to return to port if conditions deteriorate to the point of becoming dangerous. It's the call of each acting captain. Anything else?"

"Yes. Sergeant Winters reported from the hospital. Thurlow regained consciousness."

"How is he? Does he remember what happened?"

"Apparently he's got a major headache, but he should recover. He's hazy about the details of the attack. There were two people, a man and a woman. He surprised them as they were coming on board the *Penelope*."

"So they were after the boat."

"That's how it appears. I think they took his money and dumped him away from the pier to throw the police off track."

"Did he give a description?"

"The man was bearded, the woman was a tall brunette."

"Brunette?"

"Chambers could have dyed her hair. The rest of the physical description matches."

"Did he identify the photograph?"

"It was too dark for him to make out features, and it all happened quickly, but I think it was Chambers," Kate said. "Thurlow was taken off guard because it was the woman who hit him. She used an oar."

Sam adjusted his weight to compensate for the pitch of the deck as the boat rode another swell. Ursula Chambers had cracked the skull of the king's nephew with a marble statue. She had killed her own sister. A woman like that wouldn't hesitate to smash an oar into the head of a groggy, unarmed man.

"If it was Chambers," Sam said, "then it means she not only has a boat but she has an ally."

"That's not good news."

"No. But this weather could be too much for that boat to handle unless the crew knew what they were doing."

"Possibly." Kate studied the clouds, her hair whipping around her face in the strengthening wind. "What do we know about Chambers's sailing experience?"

"Nothing. She and her sister grew up on a ranch in Colorado, but Ursula lived on the east coast for several years. She could be anything from an amateur to an expert. If she's hooked up with someone who knows these waters, they wouldn't be scared off by this weather."

"Then why hasn't anyone spotted them yet?"

"They might be staying close to shore, waiting for the weather to improve."

"Or maybe they've already slipped past us and reached Tamir."

"I have faith in our people," Sam said immediately. "If Chambers and the *Penelope* had made a run for it, she would have been caught."

"Not necessarily." She retrieved the life jacket she'd

discarded in order to put on the slicker. "Not if one of our crews got distracted."

"Still ready to assume the worst about everyone, I see."

"Sam, this isn't about us."

He gritted his teeth. "Right. It's about our duty. That's all that matters to you. It's the only reason we're together. How could I forget?"

A thread of lightning flashed on the horizon. Kate let the life jacket dangle from her hand as she turned to face him. "All right, Sam. This has gone on long enough I can understand that you're still upset about what I told you this morning, so if you've got something more to say to me, just say it."

Something more to say? Where should he start? There were so many conflicting emotions inside him he wasn't even close to sorting them out. "I think it's the other way around, Kate."

"What do you mean?"

"You have more to say. You haven't told me everything."

She flinched. Whether it was from what he said or from the thunder that rumbled over the noise of the wind, he couldn't tell. "I don't know what you're talking about."

"You can call me an insensitive jerk if you want, but I know there has to be more to what happened than you've told me. Losing a baby is tragic, but it isn't that uncommon. Many women go through the heartache of a miscarriage but they eventually put it behind them. You haven't."

"Yes, I have. It's just the circumstances that stirred it all up."

"No, it's more. You claim you didn't tell me because it was wrong to get married for the sake of a child, and you didn't want us to end up miserable like your parents."

"That's right."

"So how much of your decision was because of me, and how much was because of you?"

The rigging creaked as the head sail snapped and billowed in the wind. Kate watched him, her eyes narrowed. "What do you mean?"

"You said I wasn't ready to settle down, and at the time that might have been true. But neither were you, Kate."

"No, you're wrong. I was willing to raise the baby—"

"To sacrifice your career for the baby. That's what you said. To turn your life upside-down. To give up your dreams."

"Yes, that's right."

"Are you sure? I wasn't there, so I was an easy target to focus your blame on. You've spent five years convincing yourself you made the choice because I wasn't suitable husband or father material, but if that's true, why does it still haunt you?"

She started to turn away.

"Don't you think it's time to stop running, Kate?" He raised his voice over the noise of the wind. "Isn't it about time you were honest?"

She caught the railing, her knuckles white. She wouldn't meet his gaze.

Sam braced his weight against the wheel so he could keep it steady. "I told you I've seen men who came back from combat with nightmares. Do you know what most of those nightmares were about? They were about failure. They were about guilt. What do you feel guilty about, Kate?"

Lightning cracked between the clouds, flickering over her stark expression. Sam told himself to stop, but they'd come this far, why not get it all out in the open? "Do you blame yourself for losing the baby?"

"Of course, I blame myself," she shouted. "I should have tried harder to get to the hospital. I shouldn't have walked so far alone, I should have gotten more rest, I should have been more careful.''

''Would that really have made a difference?''

''The doctor said it wouldn't have, but—''

''You weren't to blame. I know you. You would have done everything humanly possible to save that child.''

''And I did.''

''But you still feel guilty.''

''Yes!''

''Do you feel guilty because you think things might have gone differently if you'd given me a chance?''

''It was the right choice. The only choice. You weren't—''

''Is that what you feel guilty about, Kate? Or do you have nightmares because you're terrified that somewhere deep down inside you were relieved you lost the baby?''

Thunder crashed. There was a sudden lull in the wind. Sam's statement hung in the air between them like the sound of a slap.

He had gone too far. His anger had deflated the instant he'd uttered the words. He wanted to take them back. He wanted to beg her to forgive him for the cruel accusation. ''Kate…''

''You bastard.'' She released her grip on the railing and curled her hands into fists. ''You bast—''

Her curse ended on a shriek as the boat pitched nose first into a wave. Kate lost her footing on the slick deck and disappeared over the side.

Chapter 12

Kate didn't know which way was up. Everything was gray. The water pressed in on her from all sides, making her weightless and disoriented. She had to clamp her jaw shut against the compulsion to inhale as her lungs screamed for air.

It had happened so fast. She hadn't had a chance to take a breath before she'd gone overboard. All her attention had been focused on Sam...and on what he'd said.

Relieved. Relieved.

It was horrible. It was unthinkable. She'd *wanted* that child. She'd felt him move. She'd yearned to hold him in her arms....

But she'd also yearned for freedom and a career that would take her far away from the snare of a family and a soulless house in the suburbs.

She wriggled out of the heavy slicker and kicked, propelling herself toward what she thought was the surface. The gray mass around her remained the same. Her heart

contracted as it vainly tried to pump oxygen to her muscles.
She changed direction and kicked again but she couldn't
escape the water or her thoughts.

Sam had to be wrong. She couldn't have been relieved.
She couldn't have been thankful that she wouldn't have to
turn her life upside-down or give up her dreams. The guilt
she ran from was because of her choice, that's all.

If she'd told Sam about her pregnancy, she knew he
would have taken care of her. That's the way he was. He
would have swooped in like a knight on a white charger.
He would have made sure that she had no need to exert
herself. She would have been coddled and protected, and
she might not have been too late. Sam might have gotten
her to the hospital sooner. She might have been a mother
now.

That's where the guilt came from. That's what she ran
from.

But there was nowhere to run now.

Spots flickered in front of her. Her toes and fingertips
tingled with a creeping numbness. Her chest spasmed with
the need to inhale. She was drowning.

She was terrified.

*You're terrified that somewhere deep down inside you
were relieved....*

No!

You were relieved....

No, it was Sam's fault. If he hadn't been so adamant
about having his freedom, if he hadn't craved adventure, if
he'd loved her, then her choice would have been different.
She would have told him about the pregnancy, and the baby
might have lived. It was because of Sam, not her.

Relieved you lost the baby...

The thought wouldn't go away. It taunted just out of
reach like the bursts of light on the edge of her vision.

For one cowardly moment she wondered what would

happen if she stopped struggling and let herself drift. It would be so much simpler if she let the water take her. That would be the ultimate escape, wouldn't it? Then she'd never have to face the truth.

Since she'd walked out of the hospital she'd only been half-alive, anyway. Sam was right. She didn't smile, she didn't play. She'd buried her passion so that she wasn't the woman she'd been before. She'd been punishing herself.

When would it be enough?

She could die here. Then the struggle would be over.

But if she lived, she would never be the same. Sam had seen to that. She would have to face the rest of the truth. She would really have to *live*.

Light flickered again. She fought to turn her head toward it and felt a rumble of thunder envelope her body.

Thunder. Light. The realization of what she was seeing finally blossomed in her oxygen-starved brain. It was lightning. With the last dregs of her strength, she propelled herself toward it.

"Kate!" Sam's voice was hoarse from shouting. His throat stung from the spray he'd swallowed. He shouted again. "Kate, where are you!"

The sloop shuddered as it took a wave broadside. Sam checked his heading, then wiped the water drops from the lenses of the binoculars and raised them to his eyes.

He was surrounded by a writhing mass of gray swells and white foam. With each second that crept by, the sky grew darker. The storm was about to break. Sam could feel it in the stiffening wind and the charged air. Once the rain started, the visibility would be reduced to nil. He'd have no hope of spotting Kate.

The panic that had been hovering since he'd seen Kate go overboard was tough to control. But he knew he had to. He needed to keep a clear head. With the iron discipline that he'd learned on countless missions where one wrong move could mean disaster, he struggled to focus his thoughts.

It had happened so quickly. One instant she had been there, cursing him, the next she was gone. He'd lunged for the rail, but she'd been nowhere in sight. The forward momentum of the boat had already left the place where she'd gone into the water far behind, beyond reach. Every instinct inside him had urged him to jump overboard and swim after her, but without the boat, without notifying anyone where they were, neither of them would have had much chance of survival.

Kate was an expert swimmer and an intelligent woman. She would know he would be back for her, wouldn't she?

He'd used up precious minutes to swing the boat around and reverse course. That was seventeen minutes ago. He should have spotted her by now, but the waves had remained empty. He'd furled the mainsail and started the auxiliary motor to better control his position, but still each sweep of his binoculars found nothing, each shout was unanswered.

And as seventeen minutes became twenty and then twenty-five and the daylight faded, Sam felt the hovering panic inch its way to despair.

"Kate! Answer me!"

Nothing, only a roll of thunder.

"Go ahead and call me a bastard," he shouted. "You're right. I am a bastard."

The motor chugged. The boat shuddered through another wave.

"Kate, I'm sorry!"

The wind snatched the words away.

He wished it could have taken away those other words, the last ones he'd spoken to her.

Remorse was a cold lump in his stomach. She hadn't

deserved his anger. When had everything become so complicated? Things used to be so simple, as simple as a relationship could be between a man and a woman.

At least, that's what he'd always told himself.

Yet had their relationship ever been that simple? Was Kate the only one who had been running all these years? Sam knew he could have tried harder to contact her after she had returned his letters. Had he been using their promise as an excuse to cover up his fear? Was that why he had lashed out at her?

He had to find her. Even if she never forgave him, even if she hated him for the rest of her life, it wouldn't matter, as long as she was alive.

No, that wasn't right. It did matter. He didn't want her to hate him. He wanted another chance. He'd already thrown one chance away because he hadn't had the courage to recognize it. If he found her—

Not if. When. He *would* find her. He *would* hold her. The alternative was unthinkable.

"Kate!"

Was that a flash of movement on the crest of a wave? Holding the wheel steady with one hand, he swept the area with his binoculars, waiting for the boat to ride up the next swell.

There! Something pale lifted from the water. A hand, an arm.

"Kate!"

The reply was faint, so faint it might have been his imagination, but Sam didn't hesitate. He cut the engine, spared only enough time to strip off his slicker and his shoes and fasten an extra length of rope to his safety line, then dove into the water. In spite of the rest of his clothes weighing him down and the waves tossing him everywhere but straight ahead, he covered the distance in what would have been world record time if anyone had been there to witness it.

She was pale and weak but she was swimming toward him when he reached her. That seemed right somehow. His strong, independent Kate wouldn't wait for anyone to rescue her.

Sam didn't have words for how he felt. Instead, he caught her hand and pressed it hard to his mouth.

She was alive. She would be fine. Thank God, thank God.

A wave broke over them Kate coughed and drew her hand away to stay afloat. "Sam, where's the boat?"

He nodded behind them. "I've got a line. Hang on, I'll pull you with me."

Rain started falling as they hauled themselves on board. Sam looked at Kate's red-rimmed eyes and wet cheeks and knew that more than the weather and the sea were responsible.

But there was no time for the soft words or apologies that pushed to get past the lump in his throat. Lightning snaked overhead, and the deck vibrated with a blast of thunder. "Get below and dry off!" he shouted. "I'll take us back to port."

"No!"

"Kate—"

"Chambers could be out here."

"We won't be able to spot her in this."

"We have to try."

He didn't waste his breath arguing. He threw out the sea anchors to give them some stability, then tossed Kate over his shoulder and carried her down the companionway to the cabin. He set her on her feet beside the bunk and turned to fasten the hatch closed.

She swayed, her legs unsteady. In the dim light that came from the fixture in the cabin ceiling, the water that streamed from her sodden clothes glistened like silver. "Have you radioed our position?" she demanded.

He didn't know where they were, where they stood, where they'd go from here. After what he'd said, he didn't know how to ask.

But she wasn't talking about them, she was still talking about the mission. That's what a good naval officer would do. He didn't resent it, he understood and respected it. That's what he would have done if their circumstances had been reversed. "Yes," he replied. "Ten minutes ago."

"What's the condition of the fleet?"

"More than half the small vessels were already on their way back to Montebello when I requested assistance to search for you. The two that were still in this sector will be on their way here." He yanked off his dripping shirt and moved to the radio. With a few curt words he informed the other boats that Kate was safely on board, then abruptly terminated the transmission and moved to stand in front of her. "Were there any extra clothes in the locker where you found the raincoats?"

"A few T-shirts. Some jogging pants. Sam, we have to make sure the fleet moves into position as soon as the storm—"

"We will." He lifted his hands to the front of her blouse.

"Sam, what are you doing?"

"There's nothing we can do about Chambers right now. The first priority is to get you into something dry." He struggled to push her buttons through the wet fabric, but between the rocking of the boat and the adrenaline that still sped through his veins he couldn't manage the task. He inhaled, trying to steady his shaking hands…and his senses filled with the scent of the sea and of Kate.

His Kate.

And he knew in that instant that no matter what she did,

what she told him, where she went or who she became, she would forever be his.

He started to tremble.

"Sam?"

The control he'd clutched while he'd searched for her was finally crumbling. He felt it drop away, piece by piece. The panic he'd thought he'd suppressed surged over him. His hands fisted in her blouse front. He couldn't breathe.

She caught his wrists. "Sam..."

He pressed his forehead to hers. "I'm sorry for leaving you, Kate. God, I'm sorry."

"You had to. You must have been doing thirty knots and couldn't reverse—"

"No." He rolled his head in a quick negative. Drops of water from their hair trickled down his temples. "I don't mean now. I mean then. Five years ago. I hadn't known. And I'm sorry for what I said before...before you fell...." He couldn't go on. He swallowed.

Her fingers tightened, her nails pressing into his wrists. "It's over, Sam."

No, it can't be over, he thought. *Please, don't let it be over.*

He brushed his lips across her cheek. He tasted cold rain and hot tears. His heart swelled. He pressed a line of kisses along her jaw to her chin. Her stubborn, wonderful chin.

He didn't hate the way she lifted her chin, he loved it. He loved her strength. Another woman might have collapsed after the ordeal she'd just been through, but not his Kate.

He could have lost her.

Everything else faded to insignificance, leaving that one thought. He kissed her mouth.

Her lips were cool. He tilted his head and continued to kiss her until they started to warm.

She released his wrists and caught his head between her

hands, parting her lips. At the feel of her tongue probing his the last piece of his control shattered. He tightened his fists on her blouse and ripped it apart.

Thunder roared overhead. Waves crashed against the hull. The storm didn't check Sam's need, it intensified it. The desire he felt was as primitive as the elements. He knew that what lay between him and Kate wasn't this simple, but their physical bond was how it had all begun. They could deal with the rest later.

Kate's breath caught at the feel of Sam's hands on her breasts. Her skin was slick and cool, his palms were warm. He rubbed his thumbs across her nipples in short, hard, demanding strokes, then clamped his hands at her sides and lifted her to his mouth.

The rush of pleasure made Kate dizzy. She had been near exhaustion mere moments ago, but now her body sparked with renewed energy. She was alive. And she was through running away from life. Never again would she hide from her passion. She arched her back and flattened her palms against the low ceiling of the cabin, pressing her breast more firmly into Sam's kiss.

His chest rumbled with approval. He circled her nipple with his tongue, his cheeks flexing as he drew on her. She hooked her legs around his waist and urged him on with sharp, wordless sounds.

The cabin rocked as the boat rode a wave. Sam staggered, his back crashing into a bulkhead. He slid to the floor with her on his lap, her legs still wrapped around him. She tunneled her fingers into his hair and caught his lower lip between her teeth.

She felt as if she couldn't get close enough. Every one of her senses was reeling with delight as she tasted, touched and smelled. It was the same as it used to be, this rush of desire. And yet it was different. Better. Necessary.

She stroked his back and felt the ripple of hard muscle

under his damp skin. She spread her fingers possessively, rediscovering the ridges and dips she'd once known so well. And once again, she felt as if she were coming home.

Sam slipped his hand between them and rubbed his knuckles against the juncture of her thighs.

Kate cried out at the intimate contact. It was right. It was as natural as following the lightning for her first gasp of air.

Their wet clothes were hell to remove. Sam wasn't gentle as he peeled her pants and underwear down her legs and tossed her on the bunk. Neither was she when she lowered his zipper and reached for him. She bit his shoulder to muffle her scream of impatience as Sam groped in the pocket of his discarded jeans for a condom, but then he was inside her at last.

And despite the pitching boat, the rumbling thunder and the drumming rain, Kate felt as if the world had just righted itself.

Sam dug his fingertips into her buttocks, straining to get closer with each thrust. It was quick and savage and exactly the way Kate wanted it. She was alive. And she intended to live. She raked her nails down Sam's back and angled her hips to pull him deeper.

They climaxed suddenly, their damp bodies trembling as wave after wave sped through them. She heard him say her name. She felt him shudder.

Then thunder exploded directly overhead. Something heavy crashed onto the top of the cabin, and the ceiling light snicked out.

Kate jerked and lifted her head, her heart pounding.

Sam's weight left her immediately as he rolled to his side.

She thrust out her hand, groping for him in the darkness. She caught his arm. "Sam?" Her voice was rough. "What—"

"Lightning. We must have been hit. Looks like the electrical system's out."

She fought to get her brain functioning. "Oh, my God."

"Stay put. I'll check the damage."

"Sam—"

Somehow he found her mouth. He kissed her hard, his tongue plunging inside in an echo of the act they'd shared moments before.

She moaned, her body responding mindlessly. She dropped her hand to his thigh.

He broke the kiss, dragging his lips down her throat to nuzzle her breasts. With a muttered curse, he pulled up one edge of the blanket she was lying on and tucked it around her. "Stay put," he repeated.

"There's a flashlight...."

The bunk creaked. "Where?"

"In the locker beside the stairs." She gathered the blanket around her with one hand and swung her feet to the floor. "I'll get it—"

The boat rocked violently, throwing her forward. She collided with Sam.

He caught her around the waist and jerked her against him. He was still naked.

Kate opened her mouth over his collarbone, molding her body to his, absorbing his heat and the musky tang of his skin for a breathless, giddy moment.

But there was no time for more. The boat listed sharply to starboard, and water poured over her feet.

Chapter 13

The main mast was down, sheared off two feet above the boom. It trailed over the starboard side like a broken wing, held by the shrouds and what was left of the storm jib. Sam saw immediately that its drag in the water was making the boat heel on its side, allowing the sea to wash over the deck. Only the counterweight of the full lead keel was keeping them from capsizing.

"Can we pull it back on board?"

Kate was standing directly behind him, yet he barely heard her voice over the noise of the wind. He turned his head. "There's no point," he shouted. "We don't have the means to repair it ourselves. We'll have to cut it loose."

Lightning flickered, illuminating her rain-streaked face. "Okay. I'll get some cutters," she yelled.

They scrambled over the pitching deck, using their life-lines and each other as they grappled for handholds. When Sam crawled onto the boom to cut through the rigging, Kate was right behind him, wrapping her arms around his legs to steady him so he could use both hands as he worked.

He hadn't wanted her to come topside. He'd wanted her to stay safe and warm in the cabin. But he hadn't been surprised when she'd refused to be ordered. She'd retrieved the flashlight, pulled on her wet clothes without complaint alongside him and followed him up the ladder.

Was this the same woman who had fallen overboard and could have drowned? And who had left teeth marks in his shoulder ten minutes ago?

Yes, by God. And she was one hell of a woman, wasn't she?

"Hang on!" Sam shouted as he cut through the last strand of wire.

The mast fell away. Freed from the weight, the boat rolled sharply to the other side. They both clung to the boom until the boat righted itself.

But their problems were far from over. The lightning had knocked out the radio. The electric pump wasn't working. The water in the cabin was ankle deep, and they had to use a hand pump and buckets to bail it out.

For the rest of the night, they spoke little, saving their strength for their struggle with the sea. Sam lost track of time. It wasn't until Kate pointed to the twinkle of stars that he realized the storm was finally blowing itself out. Exhausted, they sealed the hatch behind them and discarded their wet clothes. With no energy left for modesty or anything else they wrapped themselves in dry blankets.

Kate was asleep before she reached the bunk. Her knees buckled, and she would have fallen face first onto the mattress if Sam hadn't seen her going over. He scooped her up and laid her on her side, then stretched out behind her and drew her back to his chest.

The bunk was narrow, but that suited him fine. He pressed his lips to her damp hair. Every muscle in his body ached. His brain was fuzzy with fatigue. He craved sleep, but he didn't want to waste one minute of his time with Kate. He'd wasted too much time already.

"You're not getting away again, Lieutenant Mulvaney," he whispered. "You're mine, you hear me?"

Her chest rose and fell with the slow, steady breathing of deep sleep.

He draped his arm over hers and twined their fingers together. There was more he wanted to say. He was sure of it. But first he'd close his eyes just for a minute....

Sometime before dawn, Sam came awake with a start. Something was wrong. He was instantly alert, his senses searching for what had disturbed him. The boat rocked and dipped as it rode the swells, but the wind had dropped. The storm hadn't returned.

The sound came again. It was a low moan that made the hair on his arms rise. It came from Kate.

Sam lifted up on his elbow to look at her. In the starlight that streamed through the portholes he saw that her eyes were still closed. She was dreaming.

No, she was having a nightmare. Probably the same nightmare she'd had yesterday morning...and for the past five years.

Sam felt as if someone had punched him in the heart. He wanted to help her, but he knew that his actions, however unknowing, had been the root cause of her pain. The words he'd shouted in anger the day before had only made it worse.

They'd made love yesterday without any words spoken. They'd been swept away by passion and an adrenaline high. He'd known then that their relationship wasn't as simple as sex. No, it wasn't simple at all.

He'd hoped they might have had more time together before the complications had come crashing back on top of them.

''Oh, Kate,'' he murmured, stroking her hair back from her forehead. ''Kate, I'm sorry.''

It started out the same as it always did. Kate was running, trying to find the baby. Her lungs were bursting, she couldn't get enough air, but she kept going. She wouldn't give up. She couldn't.

She drew her knees to her chest, curling into a protective ball, but the pain came anyway. It gnawed at her belly and shot down to her toes.

The baby. She was losing the baby.

''No.'' She groaned, splaying her fingers and reaching to stop the inevitable. ''No, please, no.''

Kate, I'm sorry.

She strained forward, Sam's words weaving themselves into the fabric of the nightmare. Sorry. She was sorry she couldn't move faster. Sorry she wasn't able to try harder. The baby. He wasn't here. She had to find him.

The hospital corridor stretched in a gleaming tunnel. The pain was tinging everything red. The doctor's voice was weary. ''I'm sorry. We did everything we could.''

She moved her head back and forth. *No!* This time she wasn't giving up. She wasn't running away. She was going to see this through.

''He's gone.'' The doctor was turning away. ''He was too small. I'm sorry.''

Kate pushed through the pain. No. She wasn't finished. Didn't they understand? *She was through running, damn it. From everything.*

The red haze faded to white as the pain slowly ebbed. Kate breathed hard, her throat tight. The dream was changing. For the first time in five years, it was different. Hope unfurled in her chest. She reached out her other hand.

The baby. Maybe this time she'd find the baby. She had to save him....

Something warm touched her face. A whisper of air on her cheek. She whirled.

There was no baby. No doctor, no hospital. No pain.

Only a butterfly.

Sunlight gleamed from wings of gold lace. The butterfly was so beautiful it took Kate's breath away. It fluttered a heartbeat beyond her grasp. She stretched out her arms and hurried after it, wanting to catch it....

But then her steps slowed. Something that delicate wasn't meant to be captured, was it? It would be selfish to force it to stay with her. Those lacy gold wings weren't made for the earth. It shouldn't be chained. It was meant to be free.

Kate dropped her arms.

The butterfly hovered for an endless, dreamy moment as if...as if it were saying goodbye. Then it spread its wings and spiraled into the sky.

She watched it soar. It danced on the breeze, playing in the clouds, rejoicing in the freedom to finally go where souls have always gone.

And softly, painlessly, a piece of Kate's heart broke away and went with it.

She woke up sobbing.

Sam was leaning over her, his fingers in her hair, his breath on her cheek.

But she couldn't see him. Her vision was blurred by tears.

"Oh, Kate." He stroked her shoulder, his fingers trembling. "Kate, I'm so sorry. Don't cry."

The tears came faster. She swallowed hard, she closed her eyes, but she couldn't stop crying. It was as if a dam had burst...or as if...

As if a wound that had been festering for years had finally been lanced.

Sam pulled her into his arms. "Kate, I was wrong. So

wrong. I was angry and hurt, but that's no excuse. I never should have said those things about your miscarriage or your nightmares. I'm sorry.''

She felt the warmth of Sam's body draw her out of the dream. She gradually became aware of her surroundings. With wakefulness came the memory of the last twenty-four hours. The storm. The sex. Falling overboard....and the accusation Sam had hurled at her that had sent her there.

She pressed her face to his neck as another surge of tears washed over her. "No, Sam. I'm glad you did."

"I wasn't being fair. I couldn't possibly understand what you went through."

"Maybe not, but you were right."

"I was cruel."

"I needed it."

"Kate—"

"I had to...let go, Sam." Her words mixed with sobs. "I had to let him go."

He stroked her back, not saying anything more, just holding her while she cried. And she needed to cry. She'd believed she'd sucked up the pain and gotten on with her life, but she hadn't. She'd been fooling herself.

Everything she'd realized during those desperate moments underwater came back to her. She hadn't had the chance to think it through until now. She should have thought it all through years ago, but she'd been too busy blaming Sam and running away.

As cruel as his words had been, he was right. A part of her was relieved when she'd lost the baby. Deep in her subconscious she must have known she wasn't ready to have a child. She would have loved her baby, but she was afraid of loving anyone.

That was the real reason she hadn't contacted Sam. That was why she hadn't let go of her pain. The guilt that had haunted her had been buried too deeply to heal, but now, because of Sam's honesty, it had been exposed and was finally draining away.

And so she wept for what might have been. She grieved for the tiny life she and Sam had created that magical, star-filled night in the Keys. With each tear she shed, she let go of more guilt and more pain. When the tears ran out, she remained where she was, safe in Sam's embrace as the boat rocked gently in the breaking dawn.

His heartbeat was strong and steady beneath her ear. His arms were secure around her back. His chin rubbed the top of her head, his early-morning beard stubble catching her hair. He smoothed her hair with his palm, then wiped away the last of her tears.

Kate turned her head to look out the porthole over the bunk. A new day was about to begin. For the first time in much too long, she felt she could greet it without looking back. She lifted one hand to her throat, rubbing the place where the familiar necklace had been. It hadn't weighed more than an ounce or two. Why, then, did she suddenly feel so much lighter without it?

"Kate?" Sam's voice reached out to her as warmly as his arms.

She returned her head to his shoulder. Oh, how she loved this man.

Yes. She loved him. That's why she had resisted him for so long. That was the final piece of truth she had to face, but it was the easiest part. She was hopelessly in love with Sam Coburn. She probably had been from the moment they'd met. That's why the sex had always been so good. She was letting her body express what her heart and her mind had been too afraid to admit. They weren't just having sex, they were making love.

She splayed her hand, feeling his chest rise and fall with his breathing. Even now, with her body bruised and aching from the battle with the storm, she couldn't ignore the tingles that chased over her skin wherever he touched her. The passion that had exploded last night had been inevitable.

Facing the truth was a good start, but there were still issues she and Sam needed to resolve. They had both made mistakes. They had hurt each other. She wanted another chance to repair their relationship, but would she get one?

The boat tilted lazily as it rode up the side of a swell. Kate used the motion to slide her leg across Sam's thighs and roll on top of him. She pressed her lips over his heart.

"Kate?"

She slid lower, raking her fingernails along his hips, tracing the sharp contours of his bones, following the lean bulge of his muscles. Her lips brushed a ridge of puckered skin beside his navel. It was one of the scars he'd acquired while he'd been gone. He'd healed. Her emotional scars would heal, too. The process was already beginning.

"Kate, I hope you're awake," Sam said.

"Mmm?"

"Because if you're not, I'm not feeling particularly noble."

"Oh, I'm awake, Sam." She rubbed her cheek along the silky line of hair that arrowed downward from his navel. "And I know exactly what I'm doing."

"You do, huh?"

She could hear a smile in his voice, and her lips curved. "Uh-huh. Whatever else we've messed up, we always got this part right."

He stretched. It was a long, lazy, masculine stretch as he straightened his legs and tensed his muscles. His hips lifted from the mattress, carrying her upward before he exhaled slowly on a gravelly moan. "Yeah. We did always get this part right."

She closed her eyes and inhaled, savoring the scent of

Sam's skin. She didn't fight the memories that flooded her. There was no longer any need.

Sam curled forward and caught her under her arms. He pulled her up his body until their faces were level, then pressed his mouth to hers.

It was a slow kiss, a tender kiss. The passion was there in the tremor of his hands as he held her close, but he was taking his time, as if he, too, wanted to savor. He kissed her thoroughly, using his lips and his tongue and his teeth until she had to pull back simply to take a breath.

He moved to her ear and leisurely repeated the process, then worked his way downward. He took the time that neither of them had wanted to spare during their frenzied lovemaking the night before.

They were already naked. There was no need to struggle with the nuisance of clothing. As if of their own accord, their bodies moved together.

Kate gasped as she felt Sam fill her. It was more than sex. It was life. She hooked her leg over his and clasped his buttocks, no longer wanting to go slow.

But Sam wouldn't be rushed. He caught her hands and drew them over her head. With their fingers laced against the rail at the head of the bunk, he settled himself more comfortably on top of her.

"Sam..."

"We're getting there, Kate." He kissed the side of her neck and rotated his hips. "Trust me, it will be worth the wait."

Kate shuddered in pleasure as his teeth grazed her earlobe. That was something else she loved about Sam. He never lied.

Dawn was already breaking when Kate awoke again. She couldn't have been asleep for long—her body still tingled from the attention Sam had lavished on her. She smiled and reached for him, only to grasp an empty blanket.

She raised herself on her elbow and glanced around the cabin. The clothes she'd worn the night before were gone, as were Sam's. Weak daylight streamed through the open hatch, but the companionway steps were missing.

Sam was squatting in front of the hole where the steps had been. An open toolbox lay beside him. A pair of gray jogging pants drooped low on his hips, and he wore nothing from the waist up. As she watched, he picked up a screwdriver and leaned forward, his head disappearing into the opening.

The light from the hatch fell over his shoulders and back, highlighting the shift of muscle and sinew as he moved. Kate swallowed a yawn and decided to indulge herself, propping her head on her hand as she observed the play of light on his body.

He was like a living sculpture, a study of the perfect male form. She knew now that it was love that made sex with Sam so satisfying, but she readily admitted that his magnificent body sure enhanced the experience. He twisted to reach into the opening under the steps, and the jogging pants he wore inched perilously lower.

Kate moistened her lips, tempted to give those pants a tug and end the suspense. But before she could throw back the blanket and act on her impulse, she heard a metallic clank. An engine sputtered, made a few halfhearted turns, then subsided to silence.

Sam muttered an oath and went to work with the screwdriver.

Kate sighed and rubbed her eyes. Of course. Sam had removed the stairs so he could access the auxiliary engine that was mounted aft of the cabin. Getting it operational would be his priority. He wouldn't have the time to come back to bed.

It would be so much simpler if he did, though. If only they could stay in bed forever. Then they wouldn't have to think about their mission...or about what would happen when the mission was over.

They'd only begun to resolve their past. One emotional night together didn't make a present, and neither of them had spoken about the future. Had anything really changed? He still craved freedom and adventure. They still hadn't made any promises. Would loving him make that much difference?

One step at a time, Kate told herself. She combed her hair with her fingers and rolled from the bunk. She donned an oversize T-shirt she found in the locker that held the spare clothes and went to offer Sam help.

The gleam in his eyes when he saw her bare legs warmed her better than any clothes would have. "Good morning, Kate," he said, without rising from his crouch over the engine. "How are you feeling?"

"Fine, thanks."

His gaze rose from her legs to her breasts. "You're sure?"

"Uh-huh."

"About what happened..."

"Sam, you don't need to apologize. I wanted it as much as you did."

He lifted his eyebrows. "Kate, I have plenty I'm sorry for, but I wasn't going to apologize about the sex."

"Oh."

"Like you said, we always did get that part right." He slipped his arm behind her knees and pulled her closer. He pressed his face to her legs.

Kate put her hands on his shoulders for balance, her knees oddly weak. "How's the engine?"

He turned his head, nosing the hem of her T-shirt upward. "Still working on it."

"Do you know where we are?"

"About twenty miles west of Tamir." He flicked his tongue over the skin at the top of her thigh. "I have to get the engine going to give us some maneuvering power and to charge the batteries so we can use the electronics. Kate, I love the way you taste in the morning."

"Sam…"

"I'm hoping that once we have some power, we might get the radio working again."

"Right. That's a…" She rubbed the ridge of his shoulders with her thumbs. "Good idea."

"Yeah." He rose to his knees and slid his hands up the backs of her thighs. "We need to contact the fleet."

"Mmm. See how they weathered the storm."

"We might need to adjust the search grid if more vessels are out of commission."

"Mmm."

He cupped her bottom and squeezed lightly. "I have another idea."

"What?"

"We could forget about the engine and just keep drifting."

"Drifting?"

"Forget the fleet, forget the mission. They can manage without us."

She'd already considered the idea and had rejected it. "Sam…"

"We could go back to bed and let the current carry us for a while. Who would know?" He laid his forehead against her stomach. "We have so much lost time to make up for."

At this moment, with Sam's arms around her legs and his breath on her skin, there was nothing she wanted more. Oh, yes. To drift where the sea took them. Just her and the man she loved. No obligations, no complications. It was so tempting.

His fingertips dug into her buttocks. "What would you say, Kate? If I asked you?"

She put her hands on his head, tunneling her fingers through his sun-streaked hair. She looked at the tensed muscles along his back, the shadowed dip at the base of his spine, and she was so close, so very, very close to giving him the answer they both knew was wrong....

"Kate?"

"I'd say nothing, Sam."

"Nothing?"

"Because I know you wouldn't ask me."

"Kate..."

She tipped his head so she could see his face. "You're a naval officer, Sam. So am I. We wouldn't be able to respect ourselves if we forgot that. As much as I'd like to make love with you for the rest of the day, we have to face reality sometime."

He looked at her, his golden brown gaze snapping. He surged to his feet and caught her arms. "Damn it, Kate!"

"I'm not using our duty to avoid what's going on between us this time, Sam. You helped me to see that running away doesn't solve anything."

"That may be, but life isn't only about duty. We let ourselves make that mistake five years ago. Hell, we both used it for an excuse. When this mission ends..." He paused. He whipped his head toward the open hatch.

She heard it then. Over the noise of her pulse and the sound of waves lapping against the hull came the distant throb of an engine.

Sam tightened his grip on her arms for a moment, then released her. He grabbed the sides of the companionway, vaulted over the hole where the steps had been and thudded to the deck.

Kate braced her hand on the galley counter as she tried to catch her breath. *When this mission ends…* What had he been about to say? When this mission ends, they would go their separate ways? They would get together sometimes on leave? They would have to talk?

Her questions would have to wait. She twitched her T-shirt into place to cover her thighs, then followed him above deck.

The breeze was cool. The storm had signaled a change in the weather. Kate shivered at her first clear sight of their ravaged boat. Only a ragged stump of the wooden mast remained. Tangled rigging littered the deck, and the brass fittings were dulled by a film of dried salt. Her pants and the blouse that Sam had ripped the night before—no, she couldn't think about that now—were spread out among the debris to dry, along with his shirt and jeans. He was standing at the bow, a pair of binoculars lifted to his eyes.

Kate followed his gaze and saw a boat approaching slowly from the west. It was riding low in the water, wallowing as it struggled with each wave.

Sam lowered the binoculars and turned to Kate. ''It looks like the *Penelope*.''

She took the binoculars from him and studied the vessel. It was a dark blue fishing boat, the same size and design as the one Petty Officer Thurlow had been using. ''You're right. It does look like the *Penelope*.''

''Yeah. Things just keep getting better. We've got no radio, we're dead in the water and Chambers is heading straight for us.''

Chapter 14

"Oh, for pity's sake." Ursula propped her hands on her hips and scowled. "How can you have anything left to throw up?"

Edwardo Scarpa wiped his mouth on his sleeve and lifted his head from the railing. Beneath his beard, his face was the color of a blanched olive. "We should have gone back to port when I told you. The storm—"

"You should have told me you got seasick."

He glared. "Would that have made any difference?"

Of course not, Ursula thought. She wrinkled her nose at his futile attempts to clean himself up. Once she got home, she'd have to remind herself never to date a man with a beard. "We couldn't go back to the place where we took your cousin's boat," she said. "That would have been stupid."

"You didn't have to hit that sailor. We could have waited for him to leave."

The argument was getting stale. He'd been complaining

about her actions ever since they left Montebello. But they'd gotten the boat, hadn't they? If she'd left things up to him, she'd still be stuck in that hillside hovel.

How much more of this whining would she be able to take? She'd put up with Scarpa until now because he'd been useful to her. Despite his disgusting seasickness, he knew how to handle his cousin's boat. He'd done a pretty good job steering it through the storm, even though it had been a rough ride. But she'd been watching how he worked the wheel and those levers that controlled the engine. She was certain she'd be able to get the rest of the way to Tamir on her own.

Ursula climbed down the stairs from the flying bridge and went across the deck to where Scarpa sagged against the railing. "How far are we from Tamir?" she asked.

"I'm not sure."

She breathed slowly through her nose to hold on to her patience. "Take a guess."

"The storm knocked us off course. I had to head into the wind."

"But to get to Tamir all we have to do is head east, right?"

"As long as we don't run out of fuel."

That was yet another old argument. He'd wanted to delay their departure from Montebello in order to take on more fuel, but she'd insisted on getting away immediately. "Well, are we pointed in the right direction now?"

"I have to check our heading."

"Why don't you show me how to do that, Edwardo?" she said, forcing a smile. If she knew where to point the boat, she was sure she wouldn't need him anymore. "That way you could go and rest for a while."

A wave slapped into the side, sending the boat into another pitching roll. Scarpa shuddered, his cheeks puffing with his effort to hold back his nausea. When the wave passed, he stumbled toward the bridge. "Rest would be good," he muttered. "All you need to remember with the compass is to…" He grabbed the edge of the cabin doorway, his words trailing off.

Ursula wanted to scream with impatience. "Remember to do what, Edwardo?"

"Someone's out there."

"What?"

He pointed into the rising sun. "There's a boat."

She lifted her hand to shield her eyes and looked for herself. It took her a moment to pick out the white hull amid the rolling swells. "It's only some old sailboat. It's nothing to worry about. Police don't go around in sailboats."

"There might have been a bulletin. They might report us. You have to get out of sight."

"I'm not going in the cabin. Thanks to you that place reeks."

"Then go on the flying bridge and stay low so that they can't see you."

"All right, all right. Quit worrying." She squinted, trying to get a better look at the boat. It was missing its mast. "I don't see anyone. Maybe they got washed overboard."

Scarpa paused. "It does look as if they were hit pretty hard by the storm."

Ursula was struck by a sudden idea. "Sailboats sometimes have engines, right?"

"One that size would."

"Then that means they'd have fuel, right?"

He turned to face her. "What are you thinking?"

"We need fuel. They have fuel. It's obvious, isn't it?"

"Even if they had diesel instead of gasoline, we can't take it. That would be piracy."

Ursula laughed. "Edwardo, you're already an accessory to murder. It's a little late to get squeamish on me now."

"But—"

"Just get us close to that boat and leave the thinking to me."

He returned his gaze to the sailboat that bobbed on the waves, then groaned and doubled over.

Ursula hurriedly stepped out of range.

Kate took the ammunition clip out of the pistol, checked to make sure it contained its full complement of bullets, then shoved it back in place. Considering the swells the boat rode, she wouldn't be able to fire the weapon with much accuracy unless she was directly in front of her target. Nevertheless, it was better than nothing. She tucked the gun into the damp waistband of her pants at the small of her back and flipped her T-shirt down to cover it.

"How much time do you figure we have?" Sam called.

Kate leaned over the galley counter to peer out the port-hole. The dark blue fishing boat was plowing through the swells. There was no doubt anymore that it was the *Penelope*. She'd thought she'd seen two figures moving around the deck at first, but now she only saw one. "Three minutes, maybe more," she replied. "They seem to be having problems making headway."

There was a metal-on-metal scraping sound. Something clanged dully from the engine compartment.

Kate moved to reposition the flashlight Sam had wedged in the opening under the steps. "Is there anything I can do to help?"

Without looking he thrust his hand behind him. "Give me a cup of water. Fresh water."

She filled a cup and put it in his hand. Instead of drinking it, he poured it over the battery.

"I need to clean the leads and dry them off," he said in explanation. "It looks as if seawater got into the battery box last night and shorted the connection. That's why the battery drained.''

''Is there any power left in the battery at all?''

''I'm hoping there's enough to give the engine one more try.''

''Good.''

He fumbled behind him for a rag. ''Once the engine's going and we have time to recharge, we'll be able to fire up the radio and call in the fleet.''

''But if the electronics were damaged by the lightning and it's not the battery that's the problem...''

''Then we're on our own.'' He backed out of the opening and wiped his hands on the rag. He was still bare from the waist up, but he'd exchanged the loose jogging pants he'd worn earlier for his damp jeans. ''Okay. Here goes.''

The engine turned over sluggishly. Kate held her breath and leaned forward, as if she could will it to work, but it went silent.

''Damn,'' Sam muttered. ''It needs more time to dry off.''

Kate went to the porthole. ''She's still heading directly for us.''

''That's good. We're in no shape to chase her.''

''I'd think Chambers would try to avoid contact with another vessel. Why wouldn't she have changed course?''

''Good question. We're almost within hailing distance. How do you want to play it?''

''Maintain our cover as vacationing tourists. Stall for time until we can start the engine and try the radio.''

''Sounds like a plan.'' He stood up and grabbed the top of the companionway, his arms bent as he prepared to haul himself out of the cabin. He paused, then looked at her over his shoulder. ''Kate?''

''Yes?''

"I don't suppose it would do any good if I ordered you to stay belowdecks."

"Why? Do you think I won't be able to do my job?"

"There isn't another officer I'd rather have at my back at a time like this. It's the woman I want to keep safe."

How could she have chaffed at his protectiveness in the past? She understood his urge to keep her safe—she wanted to do the same for him. "You'd better not try and order me, Coburn. We never did decide who's captaining this sloop, so you don't outrank me."

"Kate…"

"Besides, we're still partners, remember?"

He continued to regard her. He wasn't smiling. "I'll keep that in mind."

She followed Sam onto the deck. The *Penelope* was close enough for her to see a figure standing on the flying bridge above the fishing boat's cabin. It was a bearded man. He was a stranger to her, and yet… "Sam, he looks familiar."

"Thurlow said the man who took the boat with Chambers had a beard."

"I think I've seen this man before, but I can't place him."

"Whoever he is, he looks sick," Sam muttered.

The man lifted a hand in greeting.

Sam waved back. "Ahoy!" he shouted.

"Do you need assistance?" the man yelled.

Kate pressed close to Sam's side. "This has to be a ploy," she said quickly. "Chambers wouldn't want to help anyone."

"Yeah." He slid his arm around her. "What do you want to do?"

"Let's play along, keep stalling."

"Right." He cupped one hand around his mouth. "We're all right except we lost our mast," he called.

"I saw that." The man slowed the boat as he brought it closer. He reversed the engine, then held it steady twenty yards off the port bow. "Is your engine working?"

"The engine's fine," Sam replied.

"Good, good." He paused. He glanced down for a moment, then coughed and called, "What about fuel? Do you have enough?"

"Sure."

"Diesel?"

Why would it matter what kind of fuel they carried? Kate wondered. Unless… "Sam, that's what they're after," she said quietly.

He tightened his arm around her to indicate he'd heard. "Yes, diesel," he called.

The man glanced down again before he spoke, as if he were looking for advice. "Can you spare us a few gallons so we can make it to port? I'll pay whatever you ask."

Had he realized he'd said *us?* Kate wondered. Or didn't he care whether they knew there was someone else on board? "She's there with him," Kate whispered. "She has to be."

"Looks like you need a pump, too," Sam called.

"Yes."

"The sea's too rough to come alongside. I don't want to risk a collision. I'll lower the dinghy."

The man started to nod when his shoulders heaved suddenly as the boat rolled over the top of a swell. He spun, clamping his hand to his mouth.

"Poor bastard's seasick," Sam said, dipping his head toward Kate. "He wouldn't be hard to overpower."

"What are you thinking?"

"This is perfect. If I could get on that boat, I could apprehend Chambers."

"It's too dangerous," she said immediately. "Chambers will be watching the dinghy and be ready for you."

"Who says I'll be using the dinghy?"

Kate studied him. His jaw was set. His eyes gleamed with anticipation. It was the same expression she'd seen when he'd jumped from the helicopter and when he'd dived in the cavern.

Damn him, she thought. She even loved his recklessness.

"I think Chambers has to be concealed on the bridge," Sam continued. "Looks like her friend has been taking orders from her."

"That's what I thought, but—"

"As long as you keep them distracted, I can take them off guard. Tell him I'm finding an extra pump or filling fuel cans."

"Sam—"

"We don't know whether the fleet got back in place after the storm, Kate. There might be no one else in the vicinity to catch up to Chambers and her friend."

"If they're low on fuel—"

"They could still disappear. We can't let her get past us."

She knew that. She had to put her worry aside and have faith in Sam. "For God's sake, be careful. You know what that woman is capable of."

"No problem. She doesn't know what I'm capable of."

"Take the gun. I've got it behind my back."

"No, you keep it."

"Sam—"

"You can give me cover fire if I need it."

"But—"

"Wish me luck, partner." He gave her a swift kiss and slipped to the other side of the cabin.

Sam steeled himself to ignore the shock of cold as he lowered himself into the water. He heard Kate call to the man on the *Penelope,* something about having to locate a spare fuel can, and he smiled tightly in satisfaction. He'd meant what he'd said—she was a good officer to have at his back. But every protective instinct in him wished her post was a bit farther away.

Flattening his palms against the hull, he rode the swells with the boat as he moved toward the stern. He breathed deeply to saturate his blood with oxygen. Even though Kate would do her best to distract attention, Sam intended to cover the distance between the two boats underwater. He checked the position of the sun relative to the boats to fix his bearings, then pushed off from the hull and submerged.

The silence was startling, as it always was on a dive. He kicked downward to propel himself beneath the rolling surface, and the pressure of the sea turned him weightless. He'd done countless dives on countless missions, so he didn't doubt his ability. Only this mission was different because it wasn't his team who depended on him, it was Kate.

She'd been correct in her reasoning that Chambers and her accomplice needed fuel. But Sam was sure Chambers wouldn't want to leave witnesses. That's why Sam wanted Kate to keep the gun. Chambers had killed the king's nephew and her own sister. She had nothing to lose.

Simply because Sam hadn't seen Chambers yet didn't mean that she wasn't there. He'd been studying the body language of her accomplice, and it wasn't only seasickness that was making the man sweat. He was scared.

Which should make what Sam had to do that much easier. He saw the dark shape materialize in the distance and swam toward it. By the time the hull of the fishing boat loomed overhead his lungs were aching for air, but he continued to the far side of the boat, taking care to keep clear of the propeller. Although the sound of the idling engine and the waves would mask any splashing, he took care to surface quietly. He resisted the urge to gasp. Instead, he filled his lungs in slow, steady inhalations, keeping as close to the hull as possible.

Sam heard voices overhead, a man's and a woman's, confirming his assumption that the bearded man wasn't alone. They were speaking low so the sound wouldn't carry across the water. Sam had to strain to make out what they were saying.

"That's disgusting, Edwardo. Can't you throw up somewhere else? I have to sit on this floor."

"I need to keep the boat steady but I want to stay where I can see that sloop. I don't trust them."

"You're being paranoid. Didn't you take a good look at them? They're just a pair of dumb tourists."

"Then where's the man?"

"That beach boy's filling the gas cans, just like his girlfriend said. They want to help."

"He could be using the radio and—"

"Once we get their gas we'll be long gone. They're not going to be telling anybody anything."

"What do you mean? I didn't agree—"

"Like I said, leave the thinking to me." The boat rocked on a wave. "Edwardo, watch out! These are my last pair of shoes."

There was a retching sound. Sam felt a twinge of sympathy for the man's discomfort, but then he heard the sound of heavy footsteps on the deck and he wiped all other thoughts out of his mind. The man called Edwardo must have descended from the flying bridge. This was Sam's chance.

He craned his neck, assessing potential handholds and judging the distance to the gunwale. He kicked hard to propel himself as far as possible out of the water, caught the edge of a scupper with his fingertips and hoisted himself over the side of the boat.

He came down practically on top of Edwardo. The element of surprise was definitely in Sam's favor. The man had no time for more than a strangled curse before Sam administered a swift knuckle jab to his solar plexus.

Edwardo crumpled to the deck unconscious. Sam patted him down to check for weapons, all the while watching for any sign of movement from the bridge where he deduced Chambers was hiding. He moved to the base of the steps and flattened himself against the cabin, only then sparing a quick glance across the water.

The gap between the two boats was widening. Kate was at the stern, her attention apparently focused on unlashing the dinghy, but he knew she'd seen what had happened. He could tell by the stiff set of her shoulders and the way she was keeping her right hand free near her side.

"Edwardo?" a voice whispered. "Where are you? The boat's drifting. You have to get back up here."

Sam settled his weight on the balls of his feet, his gaze riveted to the top of the stairs.

"Edwardo?" The voice spoke again, growing nearer. The crown of a dark head appeared above him. "What... oh, get up, you idiot. You're not that sick."

Chambers was some piece of work, Sam thought. The sooner she was in custody, the better. He leaped up the stairs to the bridge, hoping surprise would work as well with her as it did with her accomplice.

It did. The woman screamed and scrambled backward.

Sam had seen Ursula Chambers's photo. He'd read every detail about her background and her actions that he could get his hands on. He thought he'd known what to expect. But the woman who was crouching on the floor beside the wheel was like a poor artist's caricature of someone once considered beautiful.

The hair that had been blond, her flowing, shoulder-length, trademark locks, was now a dull black. It hung in limp tangles to her chin. The features that had looked so striking in her photograph were pinched with fatigue and impatience. Dark, puffy circles marred the skin beneath her eyes, and her full lips were colorless and pressed thin.

All these details Sam registered in an instant. Yet Chambers's loss of beauty couldn't be attributed to her ragged appearance. Her looks had been a shell. It was the character of the woman inside the shell that now shone through.

And within the blue gaze that was directed at him, Sam glimpsed pure evil.

"Ursula Chambers," he said. "As an officer in the United States Navy under King Marcus's command, I'm placing you under arrest."

There was a flicker of defiance on her face. "Who are you? How did you get here? What—"

"I'm placing you under arrest," he repeated.

She didn't move. Defiance changed instantly to calculation. From her crouch she studied him, her gaze traveling up and down his body in a perusal that made Sam's flesh crawl. "There's some mistake," she said. "I'm not—"

"Ma'am, I'm wet, I'm tired and I'm not in the mood for games. Please stand up and move away from the wheel."

She tossed her hair with a flick of her head and held out her hand toward him. "I hurt my ankle in the storm. I can't stand up."

He looked down. She wore skintight black pants that ended at the base of her calves. Her feet were squeezed into narrow open-back shoes. There was no sign of discoloration or swelling on her ankles, so she was probably lying. He crossed his arms. "Then slide away from the wheel."

She looked down. There was a puddle of bile near her feet, likely the result of her friend's last bout of nausea. She lifted her shoulders and shuddered. It appeared she was deliberately making her breasts jiggle under her sweater. "Please. I can't. Couldn't you help me?"

It would be so much simpler if he could knock Chambers out, Sam thought, but he'd never yet struck a woman. He would have to get something to tie her up with. He glanced around.

In the next instant, the boat surged forward. Sam staggered to regain his balance, whipping his gaze to Chambers.

She was on her feet, one hand on the throttle lever, the other holding a speargun.

He lunged at Chambers, but his foot came down on something slippery. Pain exploded in his chest, sending Sam tumbling backward down the steps to the deck.

Chapter 15

It was a nightmare. Not a dream produced by her guilt and memories but a real, living nightmare. As if in slow motion, Kate watched Sam arch backward through the air and fall to the deck. A gleaming metal shaft projected obscenely from his chest.

She wanted to scream and cover her eyes. She wanted to tell herself it wasn't really happening. But it was. Ursula Chambers had just shot Sam. And Kate was the only one who could help him. She whipped the pistol from her waistband and sighted on the black-haired female who stood on the *Penelope*'s bridge, but the boat was pitching too badly. If Kate fired and missed, she might hit Sam.

She raced for the cockpit. Willing her fingers to stop trembling, she hit the starter button for the engine. "Oh, please. Please start."

There was a slow cranking noise, then nothing.

"No," she shouted. "No!"

At Kate's cry, Chambers looked toward her. She was fumbling for something out of sight on the bridge. A moment later, she straightened with another thin metal shaft in her hand.

Kate had thought she'd known what fear was. Less than a day ago, she had faced drowning. But that was nothing compared to the terror she knew now. Sam was hurt. He wasn't moving. And he was at the mercy of a murderer with a speargun.

She pushed the starter again. "Come on, come on," she said. "Start, you piece of sh—"

This time the engine caught. It coughed and sputtered twice before it settled into a steady chug. Kate opened the throttle, spun the wheel and pointed the bow straight at the other boat.

The wind gusted, sending ripples of spray into the hull. Chambers tossed her hair from her eyes and fumbled to fit the second spear into the gun.

Kate rocked on her feet, urging the sloop forward, but the auxiliary engine wasn't meant for speed. The twenty yards that had separated the boats stretched like twenty miles.

"Please," she murmured, her throat tight, her body shaking. "Please, don't let me be too late."

It's too late. He's gone.

She fisted her hands on the wheel and rocked faster, refusing to give in to the nightmare. No. She wasn't going to lose him.

Chambers finally managed to load the speargun. She walked to the top of the steps and pointed the weapon at Sam's motionless body.

Two yards to go. "Sam!" Kate screamed. She cut the engine and ran to the bow as two yards became two feet. "Sam, watch out!"

Chambers squeezed the trigger at the same moment the sloop rammed the fishing boat. The low-speed impact didn't cause more damage than a splintered gunwale, but it was enough to throw Chambers sideways, sending the spear whistling into the sea.

Before the sloop could recoil and drift backward, Kate climbed onto the railing and jumped to the deck of the *Penelope*. She scrambled to Sam's side, her heart freezing at the sight of the blood that pooled beneath him. No. Oh, God, no.

Chambers grabbed another spear from a compartment on the bridge and climbed to the deck. "You made me miss, you bitch," she said, pointing the speargun at Kate. "It's your fault that—"

Kate whirled and kicked the speargun out of Chambers's hand, sending it spinning end over end past the gunwale.

"Ow! Don't—"

Kate wasn't listening. Fear was giving her strength she hadn't known she had. Her next kick caught Chambers square on the jaw.

The woman screamed as she flew backward and hit the cabin wall. She slumped to the deck, landing on top of the inert form of her bearded accomplice.

Kate lifted her pistol and aimed at Chambers. "Put your hands on your head and don't move."

Chambers slid off her companion and got to her knees, cradling her jaw in her hands. She whimpered. "You hit me in the face. My *face*. My God. How could you?"

Kate moved the gun to the side and fired a warning shot into the cabin wall. "I said don't move!"

From between black strands of hair that had fallen over her eyes, Chambers glared at her. Slowly she lifted her hands to her head and laced her fingers together.

Kate observed that the man didn't move. He hadn't even grunted when Chambers had fallen on him. Nevertheless, Kate kept the gun pointed in their direction as she dropped to her knees beside Sam. Battling to stay focused, she extended her arm and laid her fingertips against the side of Sam's neck.

There was a pulse. She could breathe again. There was a pulse.

Blood seeped through the fabric of her pants where she knelt. She swallowed hard and took her gaze off Chambers long enough to glance at the shaft that protruded from Sam's chest. It had gone in under his ribs. She couldn't tell if it had hit any vital organs. She wouldn't be able to help him if it had. Pulling the spearhead out could double the damage it had done on the way in. All she could do was to make a compress to slow down the bleeding and get him to a hospital as quickly as possible.

Using her free hand and her teeth, she grabbed the hem of her T-shirt and ripped off a foot-wide swath, then rolled the fabric into a cylindrical bandage to fit around the spear…

Oh, God. This was *Sam,* not some first aid training exercise. The man she loved. And his blood was flowing over her hand. What if she couldn't save him? How could she live with herself if she failed him, too?

No. She couldn't think like that. She ripped another strip from the bottom of her shirt and fixed the compress in place. "Sam Coburn, don't you dare die on me now," she whispered. "I love you, do you hear me? I love you."

His skin was clammy. He still didn't move.

Kate got to her feet. She spotted a storage box that was fixed to the deck near the cabin. She needed rope or duct tape, something to immobilize the two prisoners so she could leave them long enough to use the radio. "Don't move," she said, keeping the gun trained on Chambers as she hurried toward the box.

"This is all just a misunderstanding," Chambers began.

"Tell it to the king. He calls it something else. You killed his nephew."

"That wasn't my fault."

"And your sister." Kate undid the hasp and threw back

the lid of the box. "You killed your own sister so you could use her child."

"Jessica? I never killed Jessica."

"We know she didn't die in an accident or childbirth."

"Well, I didn't kill her. Who told you that?"

Kate glanced through the contents of the box. Flares, life jackets and several coils of rope. She grabbed the rope and moved toward Chambers. "It doesn't matter."

"It was Gretchen, wasn't it?" Chambers persisted. "That idiot. She's trying to blame it on me when she's the one who did Jessica."

Did Jessica? Kate wanted to shudder at the callousness of the woman. "Tell it to the king. And to Prince Lucas. Hold out your hands."

"Of course. Whatever you say." She shifted her gaze and took her hands from her head. "Edwardo, now!"

Kate forgot for an instant that Chambers was an actress—the shout had been so convincing. Assuming the bearded man must have regained consciousness, she firmed her grip on her pistol and stepped back, prepared to defend herself.

But the man was still out cold. Chambers used Kate's momentary distraction to lunge across the deck to Sam. Quick as a striking snake, she wrapped her fingers around the shaft of the spear that still stuck out of his chest.

"No, don't!" Kate cried. "Don't touch that!"

"I won't hurt him if you put down your gun and slide it toward me."

Kate knew that the moment Chambers got her hands on the gun, she would use it on all of them. Yet if Kate delayed, with one twist of her hand Chambers could rupture something vital in Sam's chest, and he would bleed to death before her eyes.

No. She wasn't going to lose him. No matter what.

With a cry that came from somewhere darker than her

nightmares, Kate brought her gun around and took aim at Chambers's heart.

Another cry mingled with her own, a deeper one. Before Kate could pull the trigger, Sam reached up and clamped his hand around Chambers's wrist. He squeezed, his blood-smeared forearm cording in a burst of strength. Chambers screeched in pain and released the spear.

Sam didn't let go. Despite being flat on his back, despite being gravely injured, he flexed his arm and yanked her downward. Her forehead smashed into the deck.

Kate was already running forward, her gun trained on Chambers. But Chambers wasn't moving. Sam had knocked her out cold.

"Oh, Sam! Sam!"

He turned his head. One corner of his mouth lifted in a weak smile. "Sorry," he rasped.

"Lie still. I'll call for help as soon as I deal with her." She tucked her gun into her waistband and dragged Chambers aside. She retrieved the rope she'd found, pulled Chambers's limp arms behind her back and bound her hands.

"Sorry," he repeated. "Never…hurt…a woman before."

"For this one, I'm glad you made an exception." Kate had extra rope. She wrapped it around Chambers's feet for good measure and pulled it taut, trussing her like a calf.

"Had to hit her, Kate. She would…have killed you…if she got…the gun."

It wasn't his welfare but hers that had concerned him, Kate thought. She blinked back a rush of tears. She couldn't give in to her emotions now. She had to get Sam to a hospital. "I know, Sam. But you just saved her life."

He frowned. "Don't…understand."

Kate dropped down at Sam's side. She checked the compress, then laid her shaking fingers over his heart. "I would have shot her because she would have killed you."

His eyelids drooped. He blinked, fighting to hold onto consciousness. He lifted his hand to her cheek. "You're one…hell of a woman, Kate."

"I love you, Sam."

His hand fell to his side as his eyes drifted shut. He didn't reply.

The island of Montebello appeared in the west, gleaming like a jewel in the noon sun. Freshly washed by the rain, the stone buildings around the harbor of San Sebastian formed a beacon of white as the helicopter neared the shore. Kate glanced at the waves that blurred past beneath them and felt the lump in her throat grow.

From the time she'd used the *Penelope*'s radio to call for help, everything had seemed to happen in fast-forward. The search grid she and Sam had set up for the mission had worked, after all—even before she had completed her transmission, a sleek cabin cruiser full of Navy personnel had been bearing down on them with a Coast Guard cutter close behind.

The mission was a success. The Montebellan police chief, Admiral Howe and the royal family had been notified that Chambers and her accomplice were in custody and were on their way back to face Montebellan justice.

As a co-commander of the operation, Kate should have accompanied the suspects on the trip to shore. It was her responsibility to see this through to the end and ensure they were handed to the police.

But there was no way she was leaving Sam's side until he was out of danger. To the surprise of her colleagues, who were accustomed to her rigid devotion to her duty, she put the first man to arrive in charge of wrapping up so she could board the helicopter with the medics.

She shifted her gaze from the window to the man on the stretcher beside her. She brought Sam's hand to her lips and brushed a kiss across each of his knuckles. He hadn't regained consciousness. It worried her, but it was a mercy to him—the agony he must be enduring from his injury was unimaginable. How could anyone in those circumstances have had the strength to do what he'd done?

The lump in her throat was getting too big to swallow past. Yes, love hurt, but she'd never run from it again.

In another one of those spurts of fast-forward, the naval base appeared below. The helicopter swooped toward the landing pad on the roof of the base hospital. Medical personnel were gathered, waiting, their green gowns fluttering in the rotor backwash. Kate had to relinquish her post at Sam's side to let the doctors do their job. She held herself together and jogged behind the gurney as he was wheeled directly to surgery, but when the doors closed behind him, she felt her legs give way.

Before she could hit the floor, someone caught her elbow. "Hang on," a deep voice said. "I'll call a doctor."

"No, I'm okay. Thanks." She took a few quick breaths and lifted her head.

At her first sight of the tall, dark-haired man who held her arm, she started in surprise. "Your Highness!"

Prince Lucas lifted his eyebrows, evidently as startled as she was. "Lieutenant Mulvaney?"

Kate straightened. She was aware how little like an officer she must look in her bloodstained pants and ripped T-shirt. She looked even worse than the first time she'd met the Montebellan royalty, but right now she didn't care. "Sam's in there. Lieutenant Coburn, I mean. I have to make sure the doctors know I'm here so they'll tell me—"

"They will, Lieutenant Mulvaney," Prince Lucas said. He firmed his grip on her elbow and steered her away from the operating room doors toward a grouping of chairs. "When I heard what happened I came down to see how Lieutenant Coburn is. The doctors know where I am."

She wavered on her feet and gazed at the closed doors before finally sinking into a chair. "Ursula Chambers did this, Your Highness. She's a snake, she's not a woman. She's—''

"She's in custody, thanks to the two of you. I won't forget that. My country and I owe you a debt we'll never be able to repay.''

"We were doing our duty, Your Highness.''

"You did more than that. And please, call me Lucas. This is no time to worry about protocol.''

Kate raked her fingers through her salt-stiffened hair. "You might as well call me Kate, then. I'm not behaving much like an officer.''

"No, Kate." His blue eyes softened as he studied her. "You're behaving like someone in love.''

That's all it took. A kind look, an understanding word, and the tears she'd managed to hold back finally flowed. After the way she had wept this morning, she was amazed she had any left. "Does it show that badly?''

He took a neatly folded square of linen from the pocket of his sport coat and handed it to her. "Let's just say I'm familiar with the symptoms.''

Even through her tears Kate recognized the Sebastiani family crest on the handkerchief. She should be aghast at her unprofessional behavior, but she blew her nose on it anyway. "Sam's not going to die. He can't. He's too strong. He's too stubborn. He won't stop fighting.''

"That's right. You have to have faith.''

"He doesn't even know how I feel," she said. "It took me too long to realize I loved him.''

"That's what happened to me. Jessica never knew, either.''

Kate wiped her eyes and looked at him. Behind his chiseled features she glimpsed a flicker of suppressed pain. "I'm sorry, Your Highness. Lucas. I didn't mean to remind you—''

"It was my own fault, Kate. I left her because of duty. I thought there would be time. I hadn't known…life is so fragile.'' He leaned over, bracing his forearms on his thighs as he laced his fingers together. ''Things would have been different if it hadn't been for her sister's twisted schemes.''

''Ursula Chambers denies she killed Jessica. She said Gretchen Hanson did.''

''Hanson? Do you mean that woman who abandoned my son?''

''Yes, that's what Chambers told me on the boat.''

''What else did she say?''

''I'm sorry. That's all I heard. I wasn't able to question her further. She was still unconscious when I came back on the helicopter with Sam.''

A flash of resolution chased the pain from Lucas's features. ''We'll have plenty of time to deal with everyone involved later. Believe me, I intend to see that justice is done.''

''We all are.'' She glanced once more at the closed doors. ''It's the least we can do for the people we love.''

It was a long, slow climb back to consciousness. Sam noticed the sounds first. The beeping of electronic equipment, the steady *whoosh-click* of a respirator. The murmur of voices and the squeak of shoes. Then came the smell of antiseptic and boiled cotton. And then, of course, the pain.

Sam rode the wave of red agony until he was on top of it, then pushed it into a corner of his mind. He knew this drill. He'd been here before. What was it this time? Another gunshot? A saber wound? Shrapnel? What about the mission? Where was his team?

''Lieutenant Coburn?'' It was a stranger's voice, but Sam recognized the tone of brisk concern. It was the same on every base around the world. Had to be a medic.

Sam concentrated on opening his eyes, but his lids were too heavy. He must have been anesthetized—whatever had happened, it must have been bad.

Something warm brushed his forehead. Mixed with the hospital smells came the scent of…gardenias.

Kate. She was here. He tried once more to open his eyes. This time, he saw a sliver of light.

"Go and get some rest, Lieutenant Mulvaney." It was the medic's voice. It was receding as if he were turning away. "The surgery was a success, in large part because the internal lacerations from the barbed spearhead were limited by the way you immobilized the object so promptly." There was the scratch of a pen on paper. A door opened. "You won't be able to talk to him until tomorrow. Aside from his concussion, the drugs in his system would knock out a horse."

The door closed. There was a long silence, but Sam knew he wasn't alone. The touch came again. Sam turned his head toward the caress. He parted his lips and said Kate's name. But it didn't come out that way. It sounded like the creaking of a rusty hinge.

Frustrated, he gathered his strength and willed his eyes to open.

Kate was leaning over him. Her eyes were red. He lifted his hand to touch her cheek. "Okay?" he asked.

She seized his hand and pressed his fingers to her mouth. Her lips quivered. "Yes, Sam. You're going to be fine."

"Not me. You." He felt a tear drop onto his thumb. "Are you okay? You're crying."

She made a noise that was half laugh, half sob. "Oh, Sam. I'm all right now. Everything's going to be all right now."

"The mission?"

"It's over. It was a complete success."

"Over?"

"I'll tell you about it later."

"Not over," he tried to say. The rusty hinge noise was back. He could feel himself fading. But this was important. He had to tell her something. "Please. Don't say it's over."

* * *

The prison-issue coveralls were no protection against the cold that seeped through the stone walls. What kind of backward place was this, anyway? She was an American citizen. She had rights, didn't she?

Ursula rubbed her arms, wincing at the tenderness in her wrist. That lawyer and the consulate guy they'd sent to talk to her yesterday had been idiots. She'd told them to sue someone for police brutality or Navy brutality or whatever they wanted to call it—she'd even agreed to let the lawyer take a percentage of the settlement—but they kept pointing out that she had committed murder, attempted murder, kidnapping and assault and resisted arrest.

She never got a break. That was the story of her life. She was surrounded by fools. It was all Scarpa's fault that she'd been caught. And now her face, her perfect face, it was…it was… Oh, God. How bad was it?

With trembling fingers, she lifted her hand and tenderly touched her jaw. There was no mirror in here. No one had listened to her pleas for one, so she hadn't been able to see the extent of the damage, but she'd felt it.

Her fair skin and beautiful bone structure had been the few gifts her father hadn't been able to take back. But she could no longer trace the clean line that had defined her face so strikingly because her jaw was too swollen. Gingerly she moved her fingers to her forehead. The lump there was going down, but she could feel that her skin was rough with unsightly scabs where she had struck the deck.

Oh, it was simply too upsetting to think about. She sank to the bunk, shocked to feel real tears well in her eyes. She could produce attractive little tears on cue when she needed to play a role, but she never actually wept because it was unflattering. It would make her eyes puffy and her nose red. She hadn't cried for her sister or for Desmond, but she couldn't help crying for herself.

There was a shuffle of footsteps outside her cell. "Chambers, you have visitors."

Ursula shook her head. "No, I can't see anyone right now. I can't."

"You don't have a choice, ma'am."

Was there no end to what she had to endure? She dipped her head, using the cuff of her sleeve to pat her eyes dry. She fluffed her hair, swallowing another sob as some strands caught on her ragged fingernails. She needed a deep conditioning and a trim as well as a manicure, but she was a great actress, she would overcome this adversity. She'd show them. She'd show them all.

Keys jangled. The door creaked open. Ursula crossed her legs in a pose she knew would show her slim thighs to advantage, even in these shapeless orange prison clothes. She pulled a lock of hair forward to hide her scraped forehead, then angled her head so that her hand could mask her jaw. She could still be beautiful if she tried.

Four people stood in front of her. She recognized the lawyer and the cop named Sergeant Winters who had tried to question her when she'd arrived yesterday, and she mentally dismissed them as unimportant. Her gaze went to the tall, dark-haired man who leaned against the bars of the door. She recognized him instantly. This was the ranch hand with amnesia who'd turned out to be Jessica's prince. Lucas Sebastiani. He was even more handsome than she remembered. Reflexively she braced one arm on the bunk behind her so she could push out her bust.

Lucas stared at her with an expression of revulsion.

It must be because of the scrape on her forehead, she thought, trying to smooth more hair over it. That would repulse anyone. Her gaze moved to the fourth person in the group. It was a tall, red-haired woman in a Navy uniform....

"You!" Ursula said. "You're the bitch who knocked off my aim and kicked—"

"Ms. Chambers, please," the lawyer said. "You're not

helping your case by outbursts like this. I strongly advise you to cooperate.''

''That's good advice,'' the redhead said. ''After what you've done to the people we care about, none of us here have much patience left.''

''What do you mean, after what I've done?'' Ursula exclaimed. ''I had no choice. It wasn't my fault. I only wanted what was rightfully mine.''

Lucas continued to regard her as if she were a specimen in a zoo.

Ursula wished the prison guards had allowed her some makeup. She moistened her lips and moved them into a pouting smile. ''Give me a chance to explain. Then you'll see.''

Finally, she was going to get the chance to tell her side. And so she started at the beginning, with her father who had unjustly willed everything to Jessica. She told about how her sister had given a mysterious drifter a job as a ranch hand, only to be heartbroken when the drifter left and she discovered she was pregnant. Ursula saw how Prince Lucas clenched his jaw at this part of her story, but she ignored him. She had center stage now. She wasn't going to give it up.

It would have been so easy if Jessica had left her beloved ranch and traveled to Montebello the way Ursula had urged her to when they realized the drifter was actually a prince. They would have been set for life once the king had learned Jessica was carrying the royal heir. But no, her softhearted sister refused to use her child to tie her to a man who had never made promises or spoken of love.

Ursula saw the Navy woman flinch at that part of the story, and she felt a burst of energy, knowing she had everyone's attention. She must be giving the performance of her life. She explained how Desmond had come looking for his half cousin the prince and had ended up joining forces with Ursula. They had planned to bring the prince's baby to Montebello after Jessica's death so the royal heir could assume his rightful place. Gretchen Hanson had already been on her way here with the brat, but it had all gone horribly wrong when Desmond had betrayed Ursula with another woman. He'd made her kill him. Just like Jessica's refusal to profit from her child had brought about her own death. They could see now that none of it was her fault—

"I can't listen to any more of this," Lucas said, turning away. "Anyone can see that she's insane."

Ursula clawed more hair across her forehead and smoothed her orange coveralls suggestively over her breasts. "Wait. I'm not finished."

Her lawyer shook his head and filed out with the policewoman. "I'm sorry, Ms. Chambers. I'll find someone else to take your case."

Only the red-haired Navy woman remained. She stared at Ursula, her gaze pinning her to the bunk.

"What are you looking at?" Ursula snarled.

The woman smiled and held something out to her. "Here. I heard you were asking for this."

"What?"

"You wanted to know what I was looking at. I think it's a fitting punishment to let you see for yourself."

Ursula focused on the object. It was a mirror.

The prison door clanged shut to the echoes of Ursula's scream.

Chapter 16

Kate turned the jeep toward the base and pressed down on the accelerator. The wind was brisk, yet she welcomed the cool rush on her face. She needed to smell fresh air. She needed to see sunshine. After the dank evil she had encountered in the jail cells under the police station, she had a pressing need to cleanse the taint from her lungs.

Ursula Chambers would spend the rest of her life behind bars. The only question that remained was where. Both the Montebellan police and the FBI wanted a piece of her.

Similarly, Gretchen Hanson wouldn't be breathing freely anytime soon, either. She admitted she'd lied about who had killed Jessica, but now she claimed her simpleminded brother who helped around Jessica's ranch had committed the deed.

The final prisoner Kate had interviewed had been Edwardo Scarpa, a palace guard. She understood why he had seemed familiar—she must have seen him when she'd visited the palace. He was falling all over himself to cooperate with the police, hoping for leniency, but it was unlikely he'd get it. He'd betrayed the trust placed in him by the king. Montebellans dealt swiftly with treason.

Kate tilted her face to the wind, feeling her spirit revive with each turn of the road. If she could have flown, she would have. She couldn't get back to the base fast enough. After what she'd seen and heard today, she wanted only to be with the man she loved.

Sam had been asleep when she'd left the hospital this morning. The doctors had said that rest was what he needed most. It would be days before he'd be able to get out of bed. He'd lost a substantial amount of blood, and he'd received a serious concussion when he'd fallen to the deck, but astonishingly, the wound in his side was already showing signs of healing.

But that was her Sam, wasn't it? One in a million. If he'd heard the doctor's cautious prognosis, he'd probably laugh and say something about SEALs being tough.

Kate smiled, remembering how Sam had defied another one of the doctor's predictions and had managed to steal a few moments of lucidity the night before. The crazy, wonderful, stubborn man had just undergone emergency surgery, but he'd only been worried about *her*.

Oh, how she loved him. If he wanted to be crazy and stubborn, that was fine with her. She loved him for who he was. She didn't want him any other way.

Kate chaffed with impatience as she had to pause for the checkpoint at the gate. As soon as she was on the base, she drove straight to the hospital. She screeched to a stop in the parking area and headed for the entrance.

Sam wasn't in the room where she'd left him. Kate wasn't concerned at first—she assumed he'd been moved. But when she inquired at the nurses' station, she was informed he'd left almost an hour ago.

"Left?" Kate repeated, incredulous. "How could he have been discharged already?"

"Lieutenant Coburn discharged himself," the nurse said.

"But he's just had surgery."

"I'm aware of that, ma'am. You don't need to shout."

Kate glanced around. "Do you know where he went?"

"Sorry." The phone on the desk rang. "Excuse me."

It shouldn't surprise her that Sam would have wanted to leave. He wasn't a man who liked to wait around. He'd come to Montebello in the first place because he was supposed to be recuperating from a gunshot wound, but instead he'd taken on a new mission.

Was that what had happened? She thought back to what she'd told him the night before. She'd said the mission was over. That had seemed important to him. He'd seemed to want to tell her something before he'd slipped back into sleep. Was that what he'd wanted to say?

She hurried across the base to the command center she and Sam had set up twelve days ago, but Sam wasn't there, either. The room was oddly silent. Much of the equipment they had requisitioned had already been removed. Most of the personnel had resumed their regular duties. Is that what Sam had done? Had he joined Reilly and the other men on his SEAL team?

She tried his quarters next. She pounded on his door until a bleary-eyed bald man opened the door of the room across the hall to find out what she wanted. Yawning, he told her he'd run into Sam in the corridor twenty minutes ago. Sam had been carrying a bag. He hadn't said where he was going.

Kate slumped against the wall. After everything she and Sam had been through, had he really left without a word?

She didn't want to believe it. Yet that's what they'd both insisted on the last time. Did he still think she wanted an easy goodbye?

She should have told him she loved him sooner. She should have *realized* she loved him sooner.

But would it have made any difference? His thirst for adventure and his need for freedom were part of him. She loved him as he was, she reminded herself. They hadn't spoken of a future. Was that because there hadn't been time—or because they didn't have one?

She pushed away from the wall and raked her fingers through her hair. What could she do? Wait until the next time they ran into each other on duty or got together on leave?

No. She wanted to see him *now*. This minute, this second. She didn't want to end up haunted by regrets, like Lucas. He'd lost his chance with Jessica. She wouldn't lose her chance with Sam.

She lifted her chin and headed for the stairs. She would call Lucas from her quarters. The prince of Montebello said he was in her debt. He could repay her by having his father pull some strings with Admiral Howe and have the base commander delay whatever plane Sam was intending to leave on. One way or another, she wasn't going to make anything easy about *this* goodbye.

She threw open the door to her quarters…and stopped.

The sitting room drapes were closed, but the room glowed with light. Dozens of candles flickered from every surface, filling the air with the heady aroma of gardenias.

Kate swung the door closed behind her, her pulse pounding from more than her run up the stairs. She couldn't catch her breath. "Sam?"

He stood in the doorway of her bedroom. He held his body stiffly, his arm trembling as he leaned his weight on a cane.

She swayed forward. "Sam."

He extended his free hand.

The room was small. She crossed it in a heartbeat.

She wanted to barrel into his arms and bury her face in his chest and hold him until her ribs ached, but then she looked at the bulge under his shirt where the dressing would be and she stopped a breath away. "Sam…"

He grabbed the back of her neck and pulled her head to his shoulder. His lips tickled her ear. "Hello, Kate."

She turned her face to his neck, filling her lungs with the scent of him. "I looked for you. I thought you had gone."

"Where would I have gone?"

"Anywhere. Everywhere." She kissed his throat, his chin, the side of his jaw. "I thought you'd rejoined your team."

"You're my team, Kate. We're still partners, remember?"

"But the mission's over. Ursula Chambers is in custody and she's going to pay for every evil thing she's done." Her breath hitched. "Sam, you shouldn't be on your feet. You should have stayed in the hospital."

"I had to see you."

"And I had to see you. I had to touch you, but—" She put her hand lightly on his chest. "It must hurt."

"Minor detail."

"I thought you'd left, but you've been here all along. Why the candles?"

"I like the smell."

"And how—"

"Shh. We'll talk later," he said, tipping her face to his. In the candlelight his golden-brown eyes gleamed as brightly as a promise. "First, we kiss."

"Sam, I—"

He didn't kiss like a man who could have died the day before. Then again, maybe he did. He kissed her as if he wanted to pour a lifetime of passion into a moment. His cane clattered to the floor as he cupped her face in his hands, holding her steady even as his knees began to buckle. He leaned his shoulder against the door frame and kept kissing her until the world faded, leaving only the two of them and their need for each other.

Somehow they managed to make it to the bed. She helped Sam peel off his clothes along the way, moving carefully—oh, so carefully—yet with an eagerness that made them both smile. Sam eased down on his back, his glorious body naked except for the thick gauze pad that was taped under his ribs. In the flickering candlelight he looked like a warrior, a wounded warrior who had finally come home.

Kate stripped and then stretched out beside him. He lifted his arm, pulling her to his side with a strength that no longer surprised her. He was amazing, this man she loved. He caressed her tenderly, keeping his body still even as he made her writhe.

It was as if the time that had sped past the day before now slowed. Kate made love to him gently, always mindful of his injury. She tried to tell herself he needed closeness more than he needed sex. But each time her gaze strayed to his bandage, she thought of how she could have lost him, and the urge for completion became overwhelming.

She felt no awkwardness as she climbed over him. Nothing was awkward when it came to love. He shuddered. She sighed.

The candle beside the bed burned itself out as she watched him fall asleep in her arms.

Night had fallen by the time Sam awoke. He knew instantly where he was. He didn't have even a split second of disorientation. He could tell by the scent and by the bone-deep satisfaction he felt.

But the afterglow of good, healthy sex wasn't all he felt. A persistent throbbing in his side reminded him of the doctor's advice. Bed rest. Well, he was in a bed, wasn't he?

Sam turned his head. Kate was lying beside him, her cheek propped on her hand. She had put on a silk robe, but he could tell by the cleavage he glimpsed at her neckline that she hadn't put on anything else.

Incredibly, despite the haze of exhaustion that dulled his senses, he felt himself stir. He couldn't get enough of her. He smiled and ran his fingertip along the edge of her robe. "Hey."

She smiled back. "Hey, yourself. How are you feeling?"

"Better by the second. Want me to show you?"

She leaned over and kissed him. But before he could do anything more, she pulled back. "Sam, before I came home and found you here, I thought you'd left."

"Yeah, you mentioned that a few times."

"And while I was looking for you, I realized something."

"What?"

"I'm not as good a person as I thought I was."

He slipped his hand into her robe and rubbed his thumb over the curve of her breast. "Kate, if you were any better you'd kill me."

"Sam, I'm serious."

"So am I."

She pulled his hand out of her robe and sat up. "Please, Sam. We already know we get this part right. I'm trying to figure out the rest."

He tucked his hand under his head and watched her. "Do you have any idea how beautiful you are right after we make love?"

She pushed her hair off her forehead shakily. "You're pretty appealing yourself."

"Your cheeks are flushed, and your eyes have this dreamy glow. Your whole body is soft and relaxed and—"

"Sam, please. I'm trying to tell you something."

"Okay. What?"

"I have to break our promise."

"Our promise? What do you mean?"

"No more easy goodbyes. It will mean compromises and probably a few changes in our careers. I know it's not going to be easy, and we'll have a lot to work on, so maybe loving you has made me selfish, but—"

"Wait a second. Did you just say that you love me?"

She knelt on the mattress at his side and placed her hands on his shoulders. "Love was the last thing that I thought I wanted. It doesn't fit into the plans we made for our lives, but it happened anyway, and these past two weeks have shown me that it's too precious a gift to squander." She moved her hands to his cheeks, cradling his face as she leaned over to kiss him, then she sat back on her heels and smiled. "I love you, Sam. You make me complete. When I'm with you, I'm home."

If it hadn't been for the pain in his side, he might have thought that he was dreaming. He hadn't believed it would be this easy. He'd been fully prepared for a long, difficult campaign. That's why he'd dragged himself out of the hospital when any sane man would have stayed put, and that's why he'd broken into these quarters to set the scene with candles. Yet while he'd been busy laying plans to breach the barricades around Kate's heart, she'd opened the gates and invited him in.

But what else could he expect from this stubborn, independent, passionate, maddening woman?

He covered her hands with his and turned his head to press a kiss to each of her palms. "Me, too."

"Sam?"

He tugged her downward until she stretched out beside him. "I love you, Kate Mulvaney."

Her smile widened. "Say it again."

"I love you. I love everything about you."

"And I love you, Sam Coburn. And I'll try to understand when you go off on your adventures but—"

"Kate, loving you is all the adventure I need. Next time I travel, I want to do it with you. How would you feel about a honeymoon in Fiji?"

"A…honeymoon?"

"After you marry me, of course."

"After what?"

This wasn't how he'd planned to propose. He'd rehearsed the words so carefully over the past two days, but he couldn't remember any of the arguments he'd memorized. Instead, he gathered her hands in his and pressed them to his heart. "You mentioned compromise, and this is a big one. I know how you feel about marriage, Kate, but not all of them turn out like your parents'. We'll be building from a solid base. Love." He tightened his grip on her hands. "I used to believe that love made a person vulnerable, but I was wrong. It's the other way around. Love gives you strength."

Her eyes brimmed. "I've seen that, Sam. Love can hurt, but it also heals."

"I want to spend the rest of my life with you, Kate. We're a team, you and I. Together we can do anything."

"Yes."

"Yes?"

"I'll marry you."

He cupped the back of her head and brought his lips to hers. "Well, what do you know?" he murmured. "Looks like we finally got this part right, too."

She laughed. "Yes, it looks like we did."

"But just in case, we'd better practice some more."

The throne room was decorated with sunshine. That's how it seemed to Kate. The splendor that adorned the rest of the palace paled in comparison to the wonder of this chamber.

"I have to hand it to these Sebastianis," Sam said, leaning his weight on his cane as he glanced around. "They sure know how to create an effect."

"It's as if they captured the essence of the Mediterranean." Kate craned her neck and tried not to stare. It was an enormous room, large enough to have appeared cavernous, but the natural light that streamed through the long windows on every wall gave it the warmth of a sun-washed hillside.

Not that the room was simple. Wealth was evident everywhere, from the gilded pillars to the gleaming marble floor. In the spaces between the windows there were intricate mosaics that told the story of Montebellan history. Color and light collided in a joyful celebration.

On the other hand, any place would appear joyful to Kate. She was in love. And her husband-to-be was looking so handsome in his dress blues that he took her breath away.

Sam turned his head and winked at her. "Have I mentioned how beautiful you look today, Lieutenant Mulvaney?"

"Do you want an exact number, Lieutenant Coburn, or will a round figure do?"

He chuckled. "Think anyone will miss us if we skip out early and go back to your quarters?"

She rolled her eyes. "Sam, we can't do that. We're the guests of honor."

A heavyset man with a face like a bulldog approached them.

Sam took one hand off his cane to salute. "Admiral Howe."

The admiral's perpetual frown mellowed into what was likely his version of a smile. "Lieutenant Coburn. I'm pleased to see you on your feet already. I trust your recovery is progressing well?''

''Yes, thank you, sir.''

''And I'd like to congratulate both of you.''

Kate and Sam exchanged a smile. ''Thank you, sir,'' Sam said. ''We haven't set a date yet. I'm waiting to hear from the base commander at Coronado about a teaching position with the SEALs there.''

''That's why I've put in the request for a transfer back to the States, Admiral Howe,'' Kate added. ''We thought we'd see more of each other if—''

''What are you talking about, Lieutenant?'' the admiral interrupted, looking from one to the other. ''What date? What transfer?''

''We're getting married, sir. I thought that's what you meant.''

''I'm talking about this ceremony, Lieutenant.''

''Ah.''

''It's the first time the Montebellan Silver Star is being awarded to foreigners,'' Howe said. ''That's quite an honor.''

''Indeed it is, Admiral,'' Sam said.

''We're very grateful to King Marcus,'' Kate added.

Howe nodded, studying them from beneath his heavy brows. ''And congratulations about the other thing, too.''

''Thank you, sir,'' they replied in unison.

He shook his head and moved into the gathering crowd.

''You know what he's thinking, don't you?'' Sam murmured.

Kate laughed. ''If the Navy had wanted you to have a spouse…''

''…they would have issued you with one,'' Sam finished.

The level of conversation in the room rose to a hum as dignitaries continued to arrive. Navy personnel mingled with people in the black and gold dress uniforms of the

Montebellan police and civilians in formal clothes. The ceremony was ostensibly to honor Sam and Kate, but it was also an occasion to bring closure to what had been a difficult time for the Sebastiani family. Many lives had changed forever since Prince Lucas had gone missing almost two years ago.

There was a flurry of conversation near the entrance. Kate and Sam turned toward the noise. A group of people moved into the throne room. They were dressed formally like the other civilians, yet their bearing set them apart. Kate recognized several members of the royal family whom she had met during her previous visit to the palace.

Prince Lucas separated himself from the group and moved to greet Kate and Sam. "Congratulations to both of you."

"Thank you, Your Highness," Sam said. "It's a great honor."

"I'll say. That's an exceptional woman you're marrying, Lieutenant."

Kate smothered a laugh. "We're very honored to be receiving the Silver Star as well, Lucas."

His smile didn't quite reach his eyes. "I'm in complete agreement with my father on this. You both deserve to be honored for your service to my country."

There was a sudden wail from the center of the royal group. To Kate's astonishment, she saw the petite, dark-haired Princess Anna hurry forward with a baby on her shoulder. "I'm sorry, Lucas," Anna said. "You were right, we should have left him with his nurse."

Lucas scooped the baby from his sister's arms. The child immediately quieted, looking at his father with solemn blue eyes. "No, he's part of this family, Anna," Lucas said. He turned to Kate and Sam. "It's never too early for him to learn the responsibilities that will come with the crown. But rest assured I'll see that my son doesn't disrupt the ceremony.''

Kate looked at the child. She felt Sam's hand on the small of her back, a private offer of support. He was the only one who realized this might be difficult for her.

Yet it wasn't difficult, Kate thought. When she looked at Lucas's baby, she no longer felt the sorrow and the guilt that had haunted her. She saw an innocent new life. She smiled and held out her hands. "May I?"

Lucas hesitated only briefly before he passed the child to her. "He's gained almost two pounds since you found him. The doctors say he's doing extremely well."

As the baby settled warmly in her arms, Kate felt a twinge deep inside. She knew what it was. It was her heart expanding. She was already healing. She looked at Sam.

The love in his gaze was more dazzling than the sunlight that danced around him. An image flashed into Kate's mind, of a little girl with sun-streaked hair and golden-brown eyes.

Someday, she thought. There would be many more magic nights ahead. With love and faith, anything was possible.

Kate was brought back to the present when the baby tugged at one of the brass buttons on her uniform jacket, then squirmed sideways to put it in his mouth.

"Isn't that just like a man," Anna said, laughing. "They always pick the worst time to decide to mess us up. Here, I'll take him. Now that he's seen his daddy hasn't disappeared, he should be fine."

Kate handed the baby to his aunt. It was clear the entire family doted on him. She hoped that would help to compensate for the tragedy that surrounded his birth.

Sam polished her button with the edge of his cuff and caught her gaze. *I love you,* he mouthed.

She straightened the knot of his tie and smiled.

"Good afternoon, Lieutenant Mulvaney, Lieutenant Coburn."

They turned as one to greet the king and queen of Montebello. The royal couple were resplendent in finery that fitted their position. They were gracious monarchs, putting their guests at ease despite the grandeur of their surroundings.

"I believe that congratulations are in order," King Marcus said.

Rather than making the wrong assumption about what the congratulations were for this time, Kate and Sam simply thanked him.

"And I'm happy to see you looking so well, Lieutenant Coburn," the king said. "According to my son, the injuries you received while apprehending the fugitive were rather serious."

"Yes, Your Highness. I'm still recovering." Sam shifted both hands to his cane and leaned heavily on it. "Actually, my doctor recommends bed rest."

"Well, then, we'd better get this ceremony under way. We wouldn't want to keep you on your feet any longer than necessary." King Marcus signaled to the liveried footmen at the entrance and motioned to his family to take their places.

Kate put her hand on Sam's elbow and glanced at him in concern. "I hadn't realized you were getting tired. Maybe we should sit down...." Her words trailed off when she saw the glint in his eye. He wasn't tired at all. He had a much different reason for going back to bed. "Sam..."

"Yes?"

"Behave."

A fanfare trumpeted through the chamber. King Marcus offered his arm to his wife. She placed her gloved hand delicately on the crook of his elbow and proceeded to the dais at his side. They ascended the steps to a pair of magnificently carved thrones, then turned to face the gathering.

Before King Marcus could speak, there was a sudden commotion at the doors. A pair of dark-suited men struggled briefly with the palace guards. Kate couldn't hear what they were saying, but evidently it was enough to convince the guards to let them pass. They hurried toward the dais. The king met them at the bottom step and dipped his head to listen as they spoke.

A hum of speculation spread through the crowd. Tension grew as the conversation at the dais continued. "What do you think is going on?" Kate asked Sam.

Sam spoke into her ear. "I don't know, but those two have cop written all over them."

She agreed. And by the way the color was draining from the king's face, whatever news they had brought was important.

The two dark-suited men exited as quickly as they had come. King Marcus stepped off the dais and motioned Sam and Kate forward. "I regret we'll have to postpone the ceremony," he said. "Something urgent has come up."

"Father?" Lucas strode to join them. "What's happening?"

"Yes, Marcus," Queen Gwendolyn said, holding her gown aside with one hand as she hurried down the steps. "Who were those men? What did they say?"

"Those were special detectives who have been working with the FBI in the United States," the king said. "They have been following up on the statements we obtained from Ursula Chambers and Gretchen Hanson."

"Those horrid women," the queen murmured. "Is there no end to their evil?"

"As a matter of fact, in this instance, there is." King Marcus turned to Lucas. "Gretchen Hanson claimed that her brother murdered Jessica Chambers, so the FBI in Colorado have been questioning Gerald Hanson. For two days now he has denied his guilt, but an hour ago, he finally confessed.''

''So he admits he murdered her,'' Lucas said hollowly. ''It's over.''

''No, son. Gerald Hanson confessed to something else entirely. He's a simple man. Some might call him mentally challenged. His older sister ordered him to kill Jessica the night Luke was born, but he couldn't do it. Jessica had been kind to him, and in his way, he believed he was in love with her. He didn't kill her.''

Kate pressed closer to Sam's good side, needing to feel his warmth. The room had gone completely silent.

''Because Gerald Hanson was afraid to disobey his sister, he told everyone that Jessica was dead.'' King Marcus's voice grew hoarse. He cleared his throat. ''But instead of killing her, he hid her in a cellar underneath one of the outbuildings on her ranch. He has the mind of a child. He thought he could make her love him and they'd run away together to live happily ever after, just like in his storybooks.'' The king grasped his son's shoulders as if to help brace him for a blow. ''Lucas, the FBI just arrived at the building where Jessica was being kept.''

Lucas didn't say anything. He didn't ask anything. He stood completely motionless and looked at his father as if he could will him to say what he wanted to hear.

The king smiled. ''Jessica's alive, son.''

Lucas trembled. He took a step back. ''Alive? She's *alive?*''

''Yes, and she's fine.''

''Jess is alive.'' Lucas pressed the heels of his hands to his temples and spun around. ''Oh, God! *Jess is alive!*''

''The jet could be ready to go within the hour, Lucas,'' the king said, clapping him on the back. ''I thought that under the circumstances you'd want to—''

Kate hadn't known an aristocrat could sprint like that. Lucas was a man transformed. His smile not only reached his eyes, it transfused every line of his body. As the rest of the royal family broke out in excited conversation, she turned to Sam. "Isn't that wonderful?"

He nodded. His eyes were suspiciously moist. "Yeah. Seeing that sure beats getting a medal, doesn't it?"

"You're right. Who needs a medal?" She put her hand over his heart. "I already have everything I could possibly want."

"I love you, Kate."

"And I love you, Sam." She smiled and turned away, then crooked her finger at him to follow. "But I think we're still going to need some more practice."

* * * * *

Coming in December
from Silhouette Intimate Moments!
The exciting conclusion to
ROMANCING THE CROWN
THE PRINCE'S WEDDING
By Justine Davis
Turn the page for a sneak preview....

Chapter 1

At least it didn't show.

If nothing else, Lucas Sebastiani was certain of that. All those years of training, virtually from the cradle, on how to put on a public face were paying off now in a way he'd never expected. No one would be able to guess at his agitated state of mind.

But never before had it been such an effort to maintain that practiced facade—a fact he was very aware of and not particularly happy about.

"We'll be landing in Colorado in approximately one hour, Your Highness."

Lucas nodded without looking at the attendant in the Montebellan uniform. Not because he was fascinated by the view out the small jet's window, but because he didn't want to see the speculation he was sure would be in the woman's eyes. She would never say anything—anyone who worked for the Sebastianis was too well trained for that—but Lucas suspected they were all wondering how he was feeling as they headed toward the scene of his own personal disaster, the place where his last flight had ended so abruptly and painfully.

How did they think he felt? That crash had done more than rattle his brain, temporarily wiping out his memory. It had changed his life—and he himself—forever.

Restlessly, Lucas stood up. Normally when he felt like this he would head for the cockpit and take over the controls for a while. Flying his beloved new Redstone Hawk V was usually just the thing to settle his nerves. Something about flying the responsive craft made all his problems fade in significance, although it set Roark, the Sebastianis' chief pilot, on edge not to be at the controls himself.

But instead of heading for the cockpit, he found himself moving the other way, toward the stateroom at the back of the plane's cabin. Once he'd been pleased with the richly appointed fixtures and lush furnishings of the powerful little jet. Now he barely noticed any of the many amenities. The sleek plane was merely the quickest and easiest way to carry out this all-important mission.

Once, he thought wryly, *you were the walking personification of a stereotype, the guy the term "playboy prince" was coined for. And now?*

He wasn't sure who he was now.

He stepped through the door of the stateroom, and immediately some of his tension eased. That carefree, sometimes heedless man had died in that plane crash in the mountains ahead of them. The man who stood here now had been reborn, given a fresh start, and he was determined to make the most of it.

The reason for his determination lay sleeping peacefully in a small portable crib. As Lucas approached, the older woman who sat vigilantly beside his baby son's bed rose to her feet and inclined her head respectfully.

"Your Highness."

"How is he?"

"He is sleeping quietly, Your Highness."

"Thank you, Eliya. I'll watch him for a while."

The nurse nodded, reached into the small crib to adjust the blanket, gave the baby a last gentle pat, then gathered up the length of silk she'd been embroidering and quietly exited the stateroom.

Lucas sat down in the chair she'd vacated and stared down at the tiny being, this miracle who was part of him, and part of history. The next prince of the kingdom of Montebello, heir to the more-than-a-century-old island throne that had been held by his family since its inception in 1880.

Luke Marcus Augustus Sebastiani. Such a big name for such a little boy.

Of course, when he'd come to them he'd been only Luke. But once his identity had been confirmed beyond a doubt, he'd been renamed after his father, grandfather and illustrious ancestor in an official royal ceremony designating him as Lucas's—and Montebello's—heir.

Now, at three months old, he was blissfully ignorant of the fact that he was aboard a royal Montebellan jet, winging his way toward a reunion with the mother he'd never known. The mother he'd been stolen away from on the very day he'd come into the world.

Lucas shrugged his shoulders rather fiercely, as if the sudden action could somehow shed the memories of the confused emotions he'd felt when he'd first gotten word of Jessica's death. And his state of confusion had only gotten worse when he'd pressed for details and his cousin Drew had reluctantly told him that the man who'd supposedly been the caretaker at Jessie's ranch had also said she'd died giving birth to a stillborn child. He'd later learned the man, Gerald, had kidnapped Jessie after the baby had been stolen from her by her own sister.

The thought that Jessie had been pregnant when he'd left her had been a hammer blow. First had come wonder, that they had created new life out of their love. Then had come more confusion—why hadn't she told him? Judging by the timing, she had to have known.

Of course, he had had to admit with much reluctance, he hadn't exactly stayed around long enough to give her time to work up to it.

When his memory had suddenly returned, he'd left her for her own good, he'd thought, knowing what chaos would descend on her beloved ranch if he stayed and was discovered there. He'd spent many a long night since torturing himself with guilt, especially after the report of her death— if he'd stayed, would she still be alive?

And the knowledge that his child, a baby whose existence he hadn't been aware of, had also died had made the hollow ache inside him almost unbearable. He'd told himself he couldn't possibly feel so bad over a baby he hadn't even known about, who hadn't even lived to draw a breath.

But he had. And there it was.

He'd thrown himself into a passion of work, until even his father had suggested he slow down. He'd ridden on his favorite horse over the island of Montebello from one end to the other, until rumors about the mental state of their returned prince began to circulate among the people.

And then the miracle had happened. Out of the morass of evil hatched by Jessica's sister had come a tiny, precious bit of goodness. Gerald had lied, and his son was alive.

There had been the formality of paternity testing, but Lucas hadn't needed any DNA report to prove what he'd known the moment he looked at the child. His mother had gasped aloud when she'd first seen the boy, and then tears had come to her lovely blue eyes as she looked upon the very image of her own firstborn child.

Lucas stared at his sleeping son. He saw a chin and

cheekbones familiar from photographs of his own baby-hood, the dark hair, knew that when the baby's eyes were open they were the same dark blue as his own. But the beautiful, trusting smile that made Lucas's chest tighten painfully, was a gift from his mother.

From Jessica.

Jessie.

A shiver rippled through him. She'd been his touchstone, his center in a world spun out of control, the only anchor in the storm that had swamped his life. She'd quite literally saved his life and his sanity. She'd given him peace, a reason to go on, and hot, sweet love in the darkness.

And he'd walked out on her, in the middle of a Colorado winter night.

"I didn't know about you," he whispered to his sleeping son. "I didn't know."

And what would you have done if you had?

He didn't answer the self-directed question. He didn't have an answer. Because the man who had walked out that night was not the man who sat here with this child now. Just as the man who had fallen in love with Jessie wasn't that man. The man who had fallen in love had been Joe, a simple ranch hand who led a simple life, knowing nothing of his own past yet finding beauty and a sort of peace in the present, in the arms of the loving woman who had captivated him with her courage, her strength, her gentle caring, her beauty.

The woman he'd been mourning since word had come she'd been murdered in the plot to cash in on the existence of the child sleeping here peacefully. The woman who had haunted his days and filled his nights.

The woman he'd thought dead and buried until just a few days ago.

His pilot's instincts told him when the plane's slow descent began. In his mind he could picture the rough terrain at the foot of the Rocky Mountains, that backbone of America.

"We will be at the hotel within fifteen minutes, Your Highness."

Lucas suddenly tuned in to the aide's words, realizing he should have been paying more attention.

"Your suite is prepared, and—"

"No."

Gallini blinked. "Your Highness?"

"We'll go to the hospital first."

"But the security hasn't been finalized—"

Lucas shook his head. "The hospital. This has waited too long already."

An image of Jessie as he'd last seen her, asleep in her huge old brass bed, coalesced with all-too-perfect clarity in his mind. A shaft of winter moonlight turning her long, blond hair to silver as it lay, still tousled from his eager fingers, across both her pillow and his. Her soft lips, slightly parted, curved into a slight smile even in sleep, and if the sheet had slipped one more inch down the soft swell of her breast, one of the lovely pink nipples he'd caressed and sucked and rubbed until she cried out in pleasure would have drawn him irresistibly back to her.

She'd had the look of a woman who'd been well loved, and leaving her had been the hardest thing he'd ever done in his life. Only the fact that he'd known it was the best thing he could do for her had gotten him through it.

Now he was about to see her again, for the first time since that night. And he didn't know what to expect from her.

Or from himself.

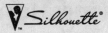

$ Saving Money $ Has Never Been This Easy!

Just fill out and send in this form from any October, November and December 2002 books and we will send you a coupon booklet worth a total savings of $20.00 off future purchases of Harlequin and Silhouette books in 2003.

Yes! It's that easy!

I accept your incredible offer!
Please send me a coupon booklet:

Name (PLEASE PRINT)

Address   Apt. #

City   State/Prov.   Zip/Postal Code

In a typical month, how many
Harlequin and Silhouette novels do you read?

❑ 0-2   ❑ 3+

097KJKDNC7   097KJKDNDP

Please send this form to:
In the U.S.: Harlequin Books, P.O. Box 9071, Buffalo, NY 14269-9071
In Canada: Harlequin Books, P.O. Box 609, Fort Erie, Ontario L2A 5X3

Allow 4-6 weeks for delivery. Limit one coupon booklet per household. Must be postmarked no later than January 15, 2003.

HARLEQUIN®
Makes any time special®

Silhouette®
Where love comes alive™

© 2002 Harlequin Enterprises Limited   PHQ402

If you enjoyed what you just read,
then we've got an offer you can't resist!

Take 2 bestselling love stories FREE!
Plus get a FREE surprise gift!

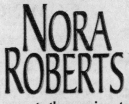

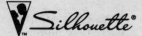
Silhouette®

COMING NEXT MONTH